Mark heard
her soft sigh

The sound tore through him. It wasn't supposed to be like this. He didn't know how to deal with her. The town's texture was different simply because Kim was in it. "Kim, are you all right?"

Kim looked up at Mark. "I was thinking. Where do you stand?"

Mark backed up until he was leaning against a brick wall. "I'm not going to give you legal advice, Kim. But if you believe in something, you should fight for it. Life isn't worth much if we don't have passion for it."

Mark's words were undoing her. Kim could handle a cool, logical attorney discussing facts and dismissing emotion. But the attorney was gone now. Only the man remained.

ABOUT THE AUTHOR

Vella Munn's idea for using a reconstructed town as the setting of her ninth Harlequin American Romance was inspired by the author's love of living among the treasures of the past in the historic town of Jacksonville, Oregon. Though the town of Camp Oro and its inhabitants are totally imaginary, *Memory Lane* offers an intriguing glimpse into the special pleasures and predicaments involved in living in such a town.

Books by Vella Munn

HARLEQUIN AMERICAN ROMANCE

HARLEQUIN INTRIGUE

Don't miss any of our special offers Write to us at the following address for information on our newest releases

Harlequin Reader Service
901 Fuhrmann Blvd., P.O. Box 1397, Buffalo, NY 14240
Canadian address: P.O. Box 603,
Fort Erie, Ont. L2A 5X3

MEMORY LANE

VELLA MUNN

Harlequin Books

TORONTO • NEW YORK • LONDON
AMSTERDAM • PARIS • SYDNEY • HAMBURG
STOCKHOLM • ATHENS • TOKYO • MILAN

To Judee—
my sister and my friend

Published February 1990

First printing December 1989

ISBN 0-373-16332-0

Prologue

Kim Revis had just stepped into her office when the phone rang. Her mind had been on two things: lunch and cleaning off her desk, in that order. The hollowed sound of a long-distance call instantly drew her thoughts in a new direction.

"Ms. Revis? This is Stephan Jarvis. I assume your boss mentioned I would be getting in touch with you."

Although the director of the Golden Gate Museum technically wasn't Kim's boss, Kim didn't bother to correct the man. Stephan Jarvis? The name sounded familiar, but it wasn't until she connected it with the fact that this was a long-distance call that the pieces fell into place. "Carlton said someone from the museum in Camp Oro had been trying to reach me. This doesn't have anything to do with my grandmother does it?"

"Your grandmother? Oh, Margaret Revis. Only indirectly in that the museum owes Mrs. Revis a debt we'll never be able to repay. Actually, from what Carlton told me, I'd be contacting you even if you weren't related to Mrs. Revis."

Kim stifled a smile. Her grandmother hated being called Mrs. Revis. "What has Carlton been saying about me?"

"That you know more about museum security systems than anyone else he has on staff. As much as anyone on the West Coast, in fact."

Kim whistled, but so softly that she didn't think the sound would carry over the phone to California's mother lode country. "I try to keep abreast of the latest developments."

"That's what I'm calling about, Ms. Revis. I'm chairman of the board for the Comstock Museum. We need you here."

"In Camp Oro? I'm afraid I don't understand."

"I didn't mention the specifics to Carlton because, well, I suppose it's no more complicated than pride."

"Pride?"

"Ms. Revis, I must be frank. We have a diamond in the rough with the Comstock Museum. Through the efforts of volunteers and staff members, we've acquired a collection that could rival some of the largest metropolitan museums. However, security has not kept pace with the collection. We've come to regret that." Stephan cleared his throat. "Actually, regret is understating the problem." His voice seemed to catch on the last word.

"And you want me to recommend a security system?"

"We'd like to hire you to come here as soon as possible, assess the situation and oversee the installation. If I may be frank, there's no one locally with the necessary expertise. No one we can trust."

"Trust?"

"I really don't want to say more than that over the phone. Ms. Revis, we need help. Your help."

This time Kim didn't attempt to hide her whistle. "That's a tall order, Mr. Jarvis. I don't see how I can—"

"How you can take the time? I already talked to your boss about that. I'm sorry if I was out of line, but I had to do something." The man rushed his words. "Time is of— If you're willing, he would agree to a leave of absence while we have you on retainer. I understand this isn't the first time you've entered into that kind of arrangement."

"No." Kim was intrigued by the sense of urgency in the man's voice. But her interest went beyond that. Several weeks ago she had promised her grandmother that she'd get the family home ready to sell. Until this moment she hadn't known how she was going to accomplish that. But—was it possible for her to combine consultant work with the promise she'd made to the woman who was more mother than grandmother? She'd have to try. "It sounds as if you've already started the wheels in motion."

"I had to, Ms. Revis. What I didn't tell Carlton is that we simply cannot continue to function without an effective security system. It's either make some major changes, or close the doors."

"You've had some losses," Kim guessed.

"Serious losses."

Kim tapped short nails on her scarred, durable desk. She felt charged, charged and challenged. "Do you have any idea how it's happening?"

"Not really. Ms. Revis, I'm a volunteer. So are the other board members. And Camp Oro has only two police officers. So far they haven't been able to come up with much. Their recommendation is for us to update our security as soon as possible. Is there anything to prevent you from coming?"

"If you've talked to Carlton and gotten his approval, then we should be able to work something out. Give me a few days to wind things up here. I'll call you later in the week." She paused and then said what had to be said. "Mr. Jarvis? If there has been a series of thefts, we may uncover things no one connected with the museum wants to think about."

The somber tone from the other end of the line matched hers. "You don't have to spell it out, Ms. Revis. I feel as if my back's against a wall. There's been so much blaming and suspicion. No one trusts anyone these days."

Chapter One

Kim Revis took a deep, exploratory breath. There was no scent of disinfectant, nothing to give Cobblestone Manor the air of a nursing home. After a moment, Kim walked over to the middle-aged woman at the reception desk. "I'm here to see Margaret Revis," Kim explained. "I'm not sure which apartment is hers."

The woman flattened her lips. "Do you have an appointment? Mrs. Revis usually rests in the afternoon."

"She's my grandmother," Kim offered.

An amazing transformation turned stern disapproval into something much more human. "Oh. You must be Kimberly. Margaret talks about you all the time. She's so proud of you. You don't know how delighted we are to have her living here. I don't know how Camp Oro is going to be the same without her, but of course she can't stay in her home alone anymore. She's a delightful woman. So committed. So interested in everything that goes on. And, thanks to her friends, she still gets over to Camp Oro every few days."

Kim held up a hand in an effort to restrain the woman's enthusiasm. "My father and I think it's wonderful that the county named that walkway after her. As I understand, she had a great deal to do with the area being left in its natural state." Kim shook her head, tousling shoulder-length auburn hair that was overdue for a trim. "I'll never be able to accomplish half what she has. Could you please tell me how to get to her apartment?"

"I'll do better than that, my dear. Much better. If you'll follow me—"

The animated woman led Kim down a long corridor that started at the rear of the dayroom. As they walked, Kim took note of the plush carpet under her feet, the fresh paint and healthy plants. When Kim was growing up, the manor had been an empty house on a barren hill, overlooking the town of Grass Valley. Now, obviously, it was where the county's well-to-do settled when they no longer could or wanted to live in their own homes.

Before the woman could reach for the brass knocker, Kim stopped her. She needed a moment to prepare to face the changes in the woman who became her mother when her own mother died. "Tell me. How is she doing?"

"Oh, marvelous!" the woman enthused. "Of course it's harder for her to get around now, but she still goes to all her committee meetings. We try to make sure your grandmother paces herself. But it hasn't been easy."

"I don't imagine it has," Kim said, and knocked.

Five weeks had changed Margaret Revis, but the changes were all for the better. Gone was the hospital gown and too-pale complexion. Margaret had recently had her hair done and her flowing lounging gown was a bold splash of blue and green. But the smile, free of pain, was what made Kim's trip from San Francisco worth every mile.

"You're right on time, my dear." Margaret smiled as she wrapped her arms around Kim and pulled her inside. Once Kim was in her arms, Margaret's smile faded. For a moment she gnawed on her lower lip, fighting her emotions. Then she took a deep breath, held her granddaughter tightly and put the smile back into place.

"My goodness. All those bones are still there aren't they?" Margaret said. "Thank you so much for bringing her here, Sandra." It wasn't until Margaret closed the door that she let out the full-bodied laugh reserved for family members and intimate friends. No matter what fears might attack Margaret Revis, she wouldn't let her granddaughter see them. "That Sandra. She wants to know everything that's going on. Of course, so does everyone here. No one has anything to do except gossip."

"Grandmother!" Kim admonished. She turned her grandmother toward the light coming in from a sparkling picture window. "You'll have everyone here involved in your projects inside of a month. Good. You've gotten your color back. You looked so washed-out in the hospital that it scared me."

"I was not washed-out," Margaret contradicted. "White isn't my color and I will *never* go to a hospital again if they won't let me have my makeup. Let's sit down dear. That darn hip still gives me trouble." Margaret slid gracefully into an easy chair. "The doctor said I should still be using the walker. A walker! That'll be the day. My exact words to him were, 'I am not going to let my granddaughter tell me she's taller than me.'"

Kim quickly picked up the threads of the long-running argument. "But I am. I'm five-six. You've never made that, even on a day with low humidity."

"Who's five-six? How someone who can't drive a car without a booster seat worked her way up the ladder of success is beyond me."

"I was raised by a cutthroat businesswoman who taught me that nothing is impossible. Be honest, please. The doctor thinks you're coming along all right?"

Kim settled herself onto a corner of the couch while her grandmother gave her a blow-by-blow account of her last visit with the doctor. Despite the immaculate condition of the apartment and her grandmother's improved health, Kim was vaguely disturbed. It wasn't until she'd been in the apartment for at least five minutes that she realized what was bothering her.

Margaret Revis belonged in her own home with its lovingly cared for antiques, pictures of relatives both living and dead gracing the walls, her rose garden outside her bedroom window. "Don't they let you have your own belongings?" Kim asked. "Where is your Victorian furniture? What about your collection of button boxes? You still have those don't you?"

Margaret stilled Kim's concern with a shrug of her own slender shoulders. "The button boxes are in my bedroom at home. And the old jewelry is, too. At least most of it is," she said quietly. "I hope I can trust you not to wear it in the backyard now."

"I'll try to resist the temptation. What about your furniture?" The idea of her grandmother's beloved mahogany desk sitting uncared for in the Camp Oro home saddened her. "What's going to happen to it?"

"You are a worrier aren't you," Margaret chided gently. "I'll be getting rid of this plastic stuff—" she snorted disdainfully at the bland furniture, "as soon as Mark finds someone who can bring it here without breaking it."

"Mark? I thought I was—"

"You're going to take care of the house," Margaret interrupted. "That's enough. I'm delighted with the way everything has turned out. Having you come here—" For an instant, the smile faltered. "Mark Stockton is my lawyer. And my friend. I told him not to bother about the furniture, but he insisted. And when Mark makes up his mind that he's going to do something, the rest of us would be well-advised to stay out of his way."

Kim was uneasy about trusting her grandmother's belongings to this Mark Stockton person. But Margaret Revis had lived in Camp Oro for most of her eighty years. She'd only moved to Grass Valley because Camp Oro didn't have the facilities for a woman with her physical limitations. Margaret hadn't been supporting herself in San Francisco the way Kim had. And, Kim believed, her grandmother trusted everyone. "Does this Mark person have a key to the house?"

"Of course. You're not going to lecture me about that are you?" Margaret admonished. "You don't know how glad I am to have you out of the city. They must not have any good food there. Look how thin you are. Not only that, you've become so suspicious—"

Not suspicious, Kim amended silently. Wiser. More aware. "Just because a man is a lawyer doesn't mean you can trust him with the family jewelry."

Margaret laughed her hearty laugh. "You know I don't care about that sort of thing. The jewelry has sentimental value, but I couldn't care less about what it could be pawned for. You'd like Mark. He's such a hardworking young man."

"How young?"

"Young. About your age." Amusement glittered behind Margaret's glasses. "Barely old enough to have a driver's license."

Kim knew it would be impossible to get her point across now that her grandmother was in a teasing mood. Margaret Revis delighted in pretending that Kim still needed someone to hold her hand when she crossed the street. "I see a broken hip hasn't changed your disposition. I'm still your little girl, aren't I?"

To her surprise, Margaret turned serious. "You're a long way from being a little girl. You've turned into the beautiful woman I knew you would. Still a little on the thin side, but everyone's obsessed with being skinny now aren't they?"

Kim poked at her rib cage. "I can't help the way I turned out. I think I run off the fat. This job—"

"Are you happy?"

"Do I look sad?" Kim asked. "I'm not. I just wish you didn't have to be here." They'd always been honest with each other. Today wouldn't be any different. "You belong in Camp Oro. Grandmother, the town wouldn't be a living replica of the gold rush era if it wasn't for you."

"Don't make me into a saint, Kimberly." Although Margaret spoke with a teasing tone, her hazel eyes didn't reflect that message. "And don't try to change the subject. I was asking about you, not me."

"I'm doing fine."

"Are you?"

Kim knew where the conversation was heading. Still, she had to make an effort. "I'm excited about what I'll be doing here. I like the idea of working with a small staff, and it certainly sounds as if the Comstock Museum needs help. Do you know the board chairman? I'd like to think I'm capable of providing the assistance they need."

"That isn't what I'm talking about. I have no doubt that you're going to show the staff what they have to do if they want people to stop robbing them blind, although they're such opinionated hardheads that if it was me, I'd can the bunch of them and start over. How they've kept this out of the news is beyond me. Stephan isn't bad, but he and the rest of the board haven't gotten as involved as they should. Listen to me! I promised myself I wasn't going to pass on any gossip. I'm talking about your personal life, my dear." Margaret was looking openly at Kim's left hand.

"One thing at a time. If you'll look at my game plan, you'll see that I've set next year aside for getting married. I had to find a way to support myself first." Kim stopped herself. It wasn't right to make light of affairs of the heart around her grandmother.

Margaret Revis had loved and lost two husbands. She'd been little more than a child herself the first time she fell in love. A month after she turned seventeen, she'd walked down the aisle on the arm of Jeromiah Jacobs, the owner of a logging operation who was fifteen years her senior. Despite the age difference, the marriage had worked. Margaret gave birth to their first child the week she turned eighteen. Two more children had come along in rapid succession. Margaret had cared for three babies, made a warm home for her husband and enjoyed the benefits of being married to one of the area's most successful men.

It must have been rough after Kim's grandfather was killed when their youngest was only a few months old. But a year and a half later, she'd married another wonderful man. Dow Revis had given Jeromiah's children a home and his name.

"Don't worry about me, grandmother. I have a full life, friends. I date. I'd date more if I had the time."

"But I do worry about you, honey." Margaret winced as she changed position. "Sometimes I think it's my fault."

"Your fault?" Despite having spent the past six hours in a car, Kim wasn't so tired that she didn't pick up on the concern in her grandmother's voice. "Just because you raised me, doesn't mean you have to run out and snag me a husband."

"You don't need my help in that department, young lady. Unless today's men are all blind, they're going to notice what a lovely woman you are." When Kim tried to protest, Margaret went on. "But, honey, sometimes I think I made a mistake by going on so about what a wonderful marriage Dow and I had."

"And you and Grandfather, too," Kim prompted. "His death was such a tragedy."

"Some of that's an old woman's memories," Margaret said softly, slowly. "Your grandfather was killed such a long time ago— Dow and I had our share of disagreements."

"Dad always said Dow was everything a real father could be. Still—" Kim paused. "It would have been easier for you if Jeromiah hadn't been killed."

Margaret rose to her feet and slowly walked to the sliding glass door. She stood with her back to Kim, staring at the hummingbirds darting around the feeder hanging from the nearest tree. The birds weren't enough; they couldn't distract Margaret from her thoughts. Or give her escape from her fears.

"That's history, Kim," Margaret said so softly that Kim could barely catch the words. "I don't want to be an old woman living in the past. Spinning fantasies—" She turned around, a bright if artificial smile on her lips. "I'm one old woman who's going to live in the present."

"Are you sure this move is right for you? You don't regret leaving home?"

"Home." Margaret whispered the word. "It's four walls, Kim. An old place full of memories. I don't believe in wallowing in the past." She sat down before continuing. "I am content. What I had was precious. The house is alive with the memories Dow gave me, but I don't need possessions to remember what we had."

Kim wrapped her arms around her grandmother's shoulders, fighting tears. This woman had lived an incredible life. She'd been loved by two very special men. She'd had the strength to pull herself together after a devastating loss and had gone on to raise three healthy, well-adjusted children. "What a beautiful sentiment," Kim whispered. "You had a good marriage. Two of them. I just wish Grandfather—"

Margaret interrupted. "Don't you worry about me. I want you to find someone of your own to love."

"I'd like that," Kim admitted as she cradled her grandmother's head against her shoulder. "It just hasn't happened yet. There aren't many men like Grandfather or Dow out there these days. Strong, good men may be a dying breed."

MARGARET REVIS waited until Kim had been gone for the better part of an hour. In that time, the older woman watched the shadows stretch up to the glass door and enter the room.

She'd done wrong by Kim. In her love for a motherless child, and her own need to pass on what Dow had given her,

Margaret had given Kim a warm, solid background. She'd spun wonderful stories about a man who loved a woman enough to allow that woman to grow in ways most women of her generation weren't able to. Margaret didn't regret letting Kim know that.

But she had gone too far. She shouldn't have told Kim as much as she had about the never-ending wonder of being married. And she shouldn't have lied.

It was dark now. But when Margaret got to her feet, it wasn't to chase away the shadows. She reached for the phone, dialed a number, but after listening to it ring twice, hung up. Shaking her head, her lower lip once again caught between her teeth, Margaret made her way to the glass door. She could no longer see the hummingbirds. There was nothing to distract her from the past.

And from her lies.

The second time she picked up the phone she completed her call. The sound of Mark Stockton's deep, competent voice calmed her a little.

Chapter Two

Kim's mind was going in three directions at once as she got into her car and started down the private drive that would take her from her grandmother's house to one of Camp Oro's narrow streets. She was on her way to her first meeting with the staff members of the Comstock Museum and determined to be as prepared as possible given what little she knew. Although Kim had served as a consultant before, this was the first time the request for her services had been prompted by desperation and embarrassment. According to Stephan, the losses, although each relatively minor, added up to thousands of dollars.

It was obvious that the museum should have had an effective security system installed long ago, but the Comstock Museum wasn't unique in its failure to do so. Many museum personnel shied away from anything that would make their structure look like a fortress. Unless Kim was mistaken, even with the thefts, she would have her work cut out for her convincing the employees that an open-door policy wasn't going to work.

Maybe she should have talked to the local police first, Kim was thinking as she reached Rich Gulch Street and prepared to turn. She jerked to a stop in front of a gaping hole where the street had been as recently as last night.

A group of elementary school students was standing off to one side, jostling each other for a better view of the large, dark pit. A city work truck was parked nearby, but the two men leaning against the truck seemed more intent on responding to questions than doing anything. A trio of men Kim had seen lounging outside the Camp Oro Tavern Saturday night were closest to the cracked and buckled pavement.

Kim jumped out of her car. This made absolutely no sense whatsoever. As she shut her door, she heard one of the men ask the other two if they were sure the TV station had been called.

"I told you," the one with the least amount of hair snapped. "They said they were on their way. Bringing cameras. You want I should draw you a map?"

The one who'd asked the question took the put-down in stride. "I told 'em. Told 'em it was going to happen again."

"You didn't tell anyone anything. And even if you did, no one would listen to you. Would you look at that thing! That's the biggest damn cave-in we've ever had."

Kim stifled the impulse to order the men to stop arguing with each other and answer the thousand and one questions running through her mind. If their chortles and joking attempts to shove each other into the pit were any indication of their mood, they wouldn't give her a straight story, even if they knew anything.

This was incredible! She was going to be late for her first day of work because a street had caved in and she couldn't get her car out of the driveway. Last night there'd been pavement with a dividing line painted down the middle. Now there was absolutely nothing. A section of Rich Gulch Street some twenty feet in diameter had fallen out of sight.

When a couple of well-dressed women joined the growing crowd, Kim left her car and came close enough so she could catch what they were saying. "Do you think the mayor knows?'' one asked the other. "Knowing that man, it's going to take him a year to decide what to do."

The other woman laughed her agreement. "I served on the budget committee last spring. I know the town doesn't have the money to deal with this."

You can't just leave it! Kim stewed, but she wasn't going to waste time attempting to point that out to the women. Someone must be in charge. She could ask the women if there was a public-works foreman or how she could reach the mayor. That's what she'd do. She'd present her case to the mayor and insist he do something.

Kim started around the hole, angling toward the women, but stopped before she reached them. Was the hole getting larger? Now that she was within a few feet of it, she could see asphalt lying in huge chunks at the bottom of the pit. She estimated the depth at somewhere between ten and fifteen feet. It was so dark down there that it was hard to be certain.

Kim took another step before the strength left her legs. Fascinated, and fearful, she gave up the battle. Kim still sensed the presence of others, but their voices couldn't reach her. She was communicating with the cold, dark pit. She was being pulled emotionally as well as physically toward it.

Kim inched as close as she dared and dropped to a squatting position. This was a hole in the ground. A freak of nature in the middle of civilization. Something easily explained.

Something capable of reaching out and pulling her into it.

"You better get back, lady. The rest of it might go."

That made sense. Kim realized she should have known better than to stand on the cracked and tilting asphalt that ringed the hole. There might be solid earth beneath the asphalt and there might be nothing. She got to her feet, feeling a heaviness in her legs as she tried to step back.

Closer. Come just a little closer.

Thoroughly frightened now, Kim scrambled backward. Sweat broke out on her neck and shoulders, making a lie of her desperate attempt to deny what she'd heard or thought she'd heard. No one else was staring, white-lipped, into the hole.

She was the only one who had heard the eerie invitation.

Kim was relieved to see the TV camera pull up and start hauling equipment out of their vehicle. The sight of the professionally made-up woman and her blandly handsome companion gave the surroundings a reality that had been missing before. This was a newsworthy event. Something that would be logically explained during the evening news. Certainly not something to keep her awake at night.

"Does anyone know how many times this has happened before?" the TV woman was asking. "Wasn't the last cave-in over by the post office?"

"Last winter," the bald man from the tavern volunteered. "Just after Christmas."

"It was not near Christmas," he was contradicted by his companion. "It wasn't even Thanksgiving yet."

"Whadda you know? It was, too, Christmas. Cold as you know what, with so much fog that it was a couple of days before anyone noticed the parking lot had caved in."

"Says who? You make up more stories than my cat has kittens. The one by the post office wasn't near as big as this. If you ask me, they oughtta make it into a swimming pool."

Kim watched as the TV woman tried to extricate herself from the discussion between men who obviously believed themselves experts on cave-ins. The TV man was interested in finding out how to get in touch with the mayor. From what Kim gathered, being the mayor of Camp Oro was a volunteer position, and the man was probably at work and just now hearing about the cave-in. "He'll turn it over to Mark anyway," one of the two well-dressed women said. "That's what they pay him for."

"Forget Mark," her companion laughed. "You and I have to get to work."

"Forget Mark?" the first woman uttered as the other one pulled her away. "That's a lot easier said than done."

Kim was trying to remember where she'd heard the name Mark when the TV woman called out a hearty hello and signaled with expansive gestures that she wanted someone to join her. Kim glanced in the direction the woman was looking. The man making his way through the crowd was notable for two reasons: he was the only one moving with a sense of purpose and he was—was magnetic the right word?

"Did you just get here?" the TV woman asked. Kim watched as the hard professional veneer fell away. In its place emerged an eyelash batting flirt with one hip casually jutting in the newcomer's direction.

"I got a call a little while ago, but I had a client with me. It didn't take you people much time to get here."

"You know how it is, Mark." The TV woman switched her weight to her other hip. "Slow news day. If nothing else comes up by five o'clock, this'll be the feature."

"I was afraid of that." The man frowned. "Let me talk to the public-works crew and the mayor, and then we'll get you your story."

The woman glanced at her watch. "I'm supposed to see some woman who's heading a renters' protest group in an hour. Let me get it on film, Mark. We'll take some shots of you measuring the hole or something. You can fill me in on what's going to happen later."

"Don't rush me, Nora. I don't want to be misquoted the way I was the last time."

Kim felt like an eavesdropper but she couldn't wander away. A size forty-four long jacket, she decided. Slate hair made for a woman to run her fingers through. A chest—Kim blew out her breath.

"All right," the object of her not-too-civilized thoughts was saying. "Get your camera set up. We're going to have to get barriers around this before someone falls in it."

"Where's the cops?" a man standing near Mark asked. "What do we pay taxes for if there's no cop around when we need one?"

Mark turned quickly. Kim got her first clear look at his eyes, deep and smoke green as the swimming hole she'd known as a child. Like the river water, and like the cave-in, Mark's eyes demanded respect. "There's no cop on duty this morning because you, and others like you, decided the town didn't need full-time police protection, Howard. If you had your way, we wouldn't have a public-works crew, either."

"Hey," Howard spluttered. "You can't talk to me like that."

Mark's broad shoulders were more than a match for the other man's expanded belly. "Why not. I don't have time to listen to you shoot off your mouth."

Stunned, Kim took a backward step. She expected a man who dressed and looked like someone who could command respect simply by existing to speak in carefully modulated tones and sweep away any opposition with professional logic. Instead Mark was meeting the other man on his ground. And winning the argument.

Howard was still spluttering, but no one was paying any attention to him. Instead the crowd's attention was being diverted as the men from the public-works crew presented their case to Mark.

The workmen understood the need to put some kind of barrier around the cave-in but were in disagreement as to the effectiveness of what was in their truck. Mark suggested that they use signs proclaiming No Trespassing By Order Of Camp Oro Police Department and the workmen went into action. With the TV crew recording the event, one of the workmen started placing flashing portable signs around the hole. The other jumped into the truck and took off.

She'd gotten too close to the hole. Without having to turn and look at it, Kim sensed its drawing power. Half hoping no one was making note of what she was doing, half not caring, Kim put another ten feet between her and the darkness. Only then did she glance at her watch. She'd been here the better part of a half hour now. She was already late getting to the Comstock Museum. And she was going to be even later if she didn't do more than stand and listen.

Kim edged forward. She stopped with her arm inches from Mark's. He smelled of wool and the same spicy aftershave her father used. His presence separated her from the hold the cave-in had on her. "Excuse me. I need to talk to you." Her words were directed at the man's chest.

"What?"

"I need to talk to you," Kim repeated. "About my car."

"In a minute. I've got my hands full right now."

"I'm sure you do. However, I have a problem." He did look busy. She tried to sound reasonable. "I can't get my car onto the street. It's totally useless." She pointed at her trapped car to emphasize her point.

For the first time Kim felt the man was paying attention to her. He looked, looked again and then spoke. "Oh, brother. One more thing. All right. Look, I've got to do this TV thing first. Hang on a bit, will you?"

Kim couldn't decide whether that was an order or a request. Either way she had little choice but to stand back and watch the camera zero in on Mark. He was asked to get as close to the hole as possible so it would show up in the background. Kim expected him to straighten his tie or make some other concession for the camera, but he only waited with the patience of a man who'd been interviewed before.

"From what I understand," Mark was saying, "the cave-in was first noticed by some high-school students waiting for their bus. By the time they found someone to take a look at it, this whole section—'' Mark pointed ''—had broken off and dropped into the tunnel.''

''This isn't the first time this has happened in Camp Oro,'' the TV woman prompted as the blandly handsome man aimed the camera at her. ''Would you please explain.''

Kim didn't listen to Mark's response. Living in San Francisco had led her to believe that men either had their hair styled by professionals at such establishments as The Country Squire or had it attacked during the annual sheep shearing. Mark had a head of thick black hair a stylist would kill to get his hands on, and yet she was willing to bet he went to a barber where he could read back issues of fishing magazines. His suit was nothing outstanding. It fit magnificently because Mark had the physique to make anything look good, but she'd be surprised if he'd done more than snag it off a rack during his lunch hour.

He was clean shaven. As he tilted his head to one side, Kim caught a glimpse of a thin white line along his jawbone and called up the image of a boy fighting for honor or reputation on some dimly remembered playground. His hands were too big and square to fit the stereotype of a politician. She'd like to see him in jeans; jeans were, to her way of thinking, the ultimate in masculine attire.

The thought startled Kim. She'd never been a voyeur. Usually she had an excuse for not joining the other single women she knew for a night on the town. What interested Kim Revis was the inner man, not the outer package. At least that's what had always interested her before.

''Can you give us any predictions about when the street will be repaired?'' the TV woman asked.

Mark shrugged and gave a noncommittal answer. He was saying something about having to meet with the city council, and Kim was forced to acknowledge and admire his quick, logical mind.

The TV woman was trying to get Mark to commit himself to something, but he obviously wasn't going to be backed into whatever it was. With a last glance at the camera, he stepped away from where he'd been asked to stand. "Later, Nora. I thought you had another interview."

"I can reschedule." Nora was standing closer to Mark than necessary.

"I can't."

Kim silently applauded Mark's ability to turn down the woman's invitation without calling attention to what he was doing. Still it made approaching him an unsettling business. Everyone, it seemed, wanted a piece of the man. They expected him to take charge. But, maybe that wasn't the role he wanted to assume.

"Do you remember me?" Kim asked as she eased herself in front of Mark. "The woman without the car."

Mark could have turned his attention to her car, but he was looking down at her. The look lasted a long time. "I'm sorry about that."

"So am I." She should have worn heels instead of the flats she figured she'd need if she was going to spend the day touring the museum. Yet, more than height was tipping the balance in his favor. "It kind of puts me in a bind."

"Agreed. Unless you can hire a crane to hoist your car onto the main road, you're in a jam. Serious jam." The green eyes caught Kim and pulled her into them.

Thrown off balance, Kim seized the first thing to pop into her mind. "What do you mean, *I'm* in a jam? This hole—" She pointed without taking her eyes off Mark. "This hole is your responsibility."

"Mine?" he threw back at her. "Where did you get that idea?"

"I— You're telling everyone what to do. You're the one who just interviewed."

"It isn't my cave-in. Just like it isn't my town, although there're a lot of people who'd like to dump it in my lap this morning. Look. Why don't I have the mayor get in touch with you after we've hashed out a few things. I'm going to be late getting back to my office as it is.''

Mark's brusque dismissal was more than Kim could handle this morning. Facing a new job, spending the weekend alone in the house that had once held a three-generation family, the strange, uneasy mood that had overtaken her as she tried to look into the hole, had gotten the best of her. ''At least you can get to work,'' she whispered. She blinked twice, appalled by her tears.

It was the moisture glinting in the woman's large, deep-set hazel eyes that made the first impact. Mark had been aware, in a distracted way, that she was almost too slender. It gave her an intriguing frailty, but after having Nora thrust her hips at him, Mark wasn't in the mood to be confronted by another woman. Having this woman march up to him and threaten to sue the city because her car was stuck was not what he wanted to hear.

But the lady with the eyes wasn't screaming lawsuit. She was looking at him as if her morning was ten times worse than his. ''Where are you heading?'' he asked. ''Maybe I can give you a lift. It's—'' He didn't get any further.

''Mark. The phone's been ringing off the wall. I'm sorry I couldn't get here any earlier.''

Mark acknowledged the slightly built man with the bushy mustache who was Camp Oro's mayor. ''It's been a circus.'' Mark explained about the warning signs, then went on, ''I've already heard from Harden Langford and some women from the community pride group. I wasn't even out of my car when Harden snagged me. They want to see the cave-in left the way it is. Turn it into a tourist attraction. You know how Harden is when he digs in.'' Mark glanced over at the stranded woman.

''A tourist attraction? Interesting thought,'' Josh Bertrum acknowledged. ''Well, it looks as if you have things pretty well in hand.''

"There's one more problem. This woman isn't going to be able to use her car until we get the hole filled up."

Kim stuck out her hand, waiting for the mayor to acknowledge it. "I'm Kim Revis. I've been staying at my grandmother's house." She gestured up the driveway.

Kim. Margaret had said her granddaughter was an attractive young woman. Mark had chalked that up to grandmother talk, but now he knew Margaret hadn't exaggerated. "Help me, Mark," Margaret had begged him. "I should have never started—it's too late. If she ever finds out—" He had agreed to help, but suddenly the words were much more than an old woman's fear. They represented the loving bond between a dear friend and her granddaughter. Like it or not, he was now part of that bond. "Everyone knows Margaret, Ms. Revis," Mark supplied. "In fact I'm her attorney."

Mark. Mark Stockton. If she hadn't been upset, first by the cave-in and then by her reaction to the man, Kim would have put the pieces together sooner. "Grandmother mentioned you," she said, smiling a little. "She said you were going to arrange to have her furniture delivered to her."

Mark frowned. "That's going to be a major problem now, isn't it? If we can't get your car out of there, we're never going to get a moving van up to the house. In fact— Josh, we'd better make sure nothing heavy gets near the cave-in. Until we know how much is undermined, we've got to block off the whole street. Otherwise some fool is going to try to squeeze around. Ms. Revis, at the moment, the best I can offer you is a lift to wherever you're going." He turned toward the mayor. "What's your pleasure, your honor?"

"Don't do this to me, Mark. I'm not going to order the expenditure of who knows how many thousands of dollars without taking it to the council first. And I suppose Harden and the community pride people are going to demand to be heard. I'm sorry, Ms. Revis." The mayor smiled tentatively. "As you can see, not much that happens in this town is easily resolved."

"What do you mean?" Kim hadn't been able to get a reading on the mayor from his handshake, only that she was certain she knew him, or had once known him. "Can't you throw some dirt or gravel or something in the hole and pave over it?"

"I'm afraid not," Mark answered for the mayor. "Thanks to the efforts of your grandmother and others who feel the same about Camp Oro, this town's claim to fame is its history. This—" he jabbed a finger at the hole "—is history."

"I'm aware of the work my grandmother has done," Kim pointed out in an effort to hurry the conversation. Carrying on a rational discussion with Mark Stockton was taking more effort than it should. It'd be much easier on her nervous system if she could escape those fascinating eyes and the take-charge physique.

"I'm certain you are. However, what you may not be aware of is that we operate on a limited budget, as do all small towns. The budget is managed by an unpaid mayor and volunteer city council. People here can and do approach the governing body whenever they have a complaint or suggestion."

"What does this have to do with me?"

"Several members of the community pride group are looking at the commercial value of this particular hole in the ground."

"That's ridiculous. A hole doesn't have a commercial value."

"Mark?" the mayor spoke up. "I'll leave you to explain this to Kim. You do remember me, don't you, Kim? I'm Josh Bertrum. We went to school together. I was a few years ahead of you. If you went to any of the football games, I was the one sitting closest to the water bucket."

"Josh Bertrum. Of course. Didn't you live just outside the city limits? You rode a bike to school, didn't you?"

"You remember." Josh smiled. "I thought it was beneath my dignity to ride the bus or have my mother drop me off. One of these days, if you have time, you can tell me what you're doing back here and I'll tell you why I never left. Mark? I need to talk to Charles."

Neither Mark nor Kim spoke as they watched the mayor walk over to where the city police car had just pulled up. Seeing Josh Bertrum erased a lot of years. Yes, she would like to talk to Josh, to have him fill in some of the blanks about the people who'd made up her childhood world. But that would have to come later.

Mark interrupted her thoughts. "Your grandmother told me you've contracted to work with the museum. Something to do with their security system."

Kim nodded her head. She knew the necessity of keeping a low profile but certainly she could be open with the city attorney. "I haven't seen what they have yet, but it sounds as if there's a need for a major overhaul. Unfortunately, thanks to that—" She indicated the hole, the still-mocking hole. "I'm already late for my first meeting."

"I'll give you a lift, Ms. Revis. If I stay here, I'll just be bombarded with everyone's theories as to why the street chose this time to give out, and their opinions on what we should do with the hole now that it's here. That, fortunately, is the council's headache."

Mark nodded and exchanged greetings with several people, but didn't stop to talk to any of them. When they reached his four-wheel-drive vehicle, he held the door open for her. Once they were inside, he explained his gesture. "When I met your grandmother, she made it clear that she expected to be treated as a lady. I've never forgotten the lesson."

Kim liked being in this powerful, masculine vehicle with Mark Stockton. He completely filled his side of the seat, but didn't impose on her space. "My grandmother's that kind of woman," she said as she straightened her skirt. "I keep teasing her that it's the age she was raised in. She tried to convince me I didn't have to take the bull by the horns, but I went to school with a bunch of rednecks. Now that I think about it, Josh was one of them. I'll have to take him to task about that. Josh and his friends believed that the only girls who had a right to the swings were the ones who fought for them. I liked swings. I learned to fight.''

Mark brought the vehicle to life. ''Your grandmother's a gentle woman, but there's a strength to her that has gotten her just about everything she set her sights on. Once she's made up her mind about something, the rest of us had better let her have her way.''

Because Mark had turned his head away from her, Kim was able to study his profile. The man's face was built with strong lines and angles and just enough flesh to soften the impact. She decided, without having anything more than these few minutes to base the decision on, that Mark was born to be a lawyer. ''You're right. She has a great deal of strength. You wouldn't think she'd need that considering the way her husbands doted on her, but I think it was being widowed with three small children that forced her to be strong. Grandmother doesn't talk much about that time. Someday I'd like to get her to write down her life story. If I can get her to hold still long enough, that is.''

Mark's jaw tightened. ''How is she doing? She'd like me to think she doesn't feel any different than before she broke her hip.''

''I can't be sure. She still thinks of me as her little girl. I'm going to have to keep an eye on her to make sure she isn't trying to hide any worries I can help with.''

Mark drove slowly through the town. The buildings were two-stories tall or appeared so at first glance. About half of them had fake fronts above the street level. The brickwork was authentic and, according to the old stories, had originally been built as protection against Indian attack. Most of the commercial buildings bore plaques identifying them as having been blacksmith shops, assay offices, or dry-goods stores in the 1800s. Although the businesses now operating in them were those most likely to appeal to the tourist trade, the historic exteriors remained. Kim felt as if she had never left. The streets looked narrower than they had when she was a child, the buildings smaller. Still, very little had changed.

"I love this town," Kim said softly. "When I was a little girl I loved having the freedom to go anywhere I wanted because it was so safe. Knowing everyone and having them know me. Then when I got older I thought it was the most boring place in the world. Now I finally understand and appreciate the forces that created Camp Oro. I think I know why Josh stayed here. I wonder how many others did the same."

Mark signaled and waited until he was off the main street and pulling up to the right of the museum before speaking. "We're so blasé as young people aren't we? We feel it's beneath us to show enthusiasm for certain things. It's only as we get older that we're able to give our curiosity free rein again."

Kim had known Mark Stockton less than an hour and yet it already seemed that in many respects they operated on the same wavelength. "I'm glad I'm not a teenager anymore," she told him. "It's better to be comfortable with oneself." She reached for the door handle but didn't quite get it open.

Because she was concentrating on Mark and he on her, neither of them noticed a figure passing in front of one of the second-story museum windows. The figure stopped, turned around and leaned against the window, watching.

"What happens now?" Kim was asking Mark. "How long is it going to take before I can use my car?"

"I wish I had an answer for you. Look, the phone at your grandmother's house is still hooked up isn't it? I can give you a call once I know what the city council has in mind. Better yet, maybe you should attend the meeting. There's sure to be one called to discuss and, if we're lucky, deal with this."

"I'd like that. I still don't understand what the problem is. Gravel can't cost that much. Just dump some down the hole—"

"Do you have a minute?"

"I guess so. I'm late enough now that I don't think a few more minutes will make that much difference." A workman was starting to mow the museum lawn. The sound made it necessary for Kim to lean toward Mark.

"You grew up in Camp Oro."

"Until I was in my late teens. Then my father remarried and we moved to San Francisco."

"Then you understand the town's history."

"I think I do. Mark, I was a child when I lived here."

"But you do know that Camp Oro was founded during the gold rush."

"Of course."

"That the creeks around here were extensively prospected."

"Of course."

"And that mining kept many people from starving during the depression."

"The depression?" Kim repeated. "No. I—"

Mark nodded. The corners of his mouth lifted just enough to give him away. He was enjoying being thrust into the role of teacher. His explanation of what had happened in the 1930s was factual and yet presented with just enough emotion that Kim was able to understand the desperation that had driven men to dig up their backyards during the uncertain time. "The city fathers couldn't sanction the digging of mine tunnels under the streets," Mark explained. "But because it had to be done if people were going to survive, the politicians turned their backs. They pretended they didn't know that the ground under the town was being honeycombed with tunnels. There wasn't much gold left around here by then, but for some people, that was all they had."

"That's what happened this morning? One of the tunnels dug during the depression collapsed?" Kim tore her eyes off Mark's face, seeking a foothold in the present by watching the lumbering pace of the riding lawnmower. But the 1883 brick county courthouse turned museum was another tie to the past. She could sense men, their faces pinched with concern, digging inch by inch as they searched for the illusive precious metal. What did it matter to them that their tunnels might eventually undermine the town? They had hungry children to feed.

"There have been several attempts to chart the mines dug both during the depression and earlier," Mark continued. "The mines constructed in the 1800s were sources of pride. We've been able to document most of them. But during the depression, it was another story."

"The one that caved in today—" Kim turned back toward Mark to finish her thought. "I wonder if any of my relatives had anything to do with it. What if—" Kim broke into a delighted grin. "Mark! What if my grandfather dug that tunnel? But no. I don't suppose so. It was Dow's property, not my grandfather's. Just the same—"

Mark's eyes were on her face, not the excited gestures she was making. "There's probably no way you'll ever know that. Like I said, most of those tunnels were dug surreptitiously."

Mark's words brought Kim back to earth. "I know. I was just indulging in a little whimsy. It's always bothered me that my grandfather died so long before I was born. All I know is what Grandmother told me. All those wonderful things. I feel a little cheated." Once again she reached for the door handle and opened the car door. "Mark, I'd appreciate anything you can tell me about what the council is planning to do. And if going to the meeting will help, I'll do that. I want it made clear that something has to be done. My grandmother has made a difficult decision. She wants the house sold. She doesn't need things to be any more complicated than they are already.''

"I talked to her about the house a couple of times. I thought she might change her mind. I wanted her to have the opportunity to do that."

How lucky her grandmother was to have an attorney who saw her as more than just a client. "I thought the same thing," Kim said as she got out of the car. "But she's made up her mind. I'm not going to argue with her."

"You think you're going to be able to handle all the details? Get it ready to sell?"

"I think so," Kim told him. "The house is sound. It doesn't need anything done to it structurally. I've started—" Kim paused as she gave Mark what she hoped was a confident smile. "I've started going through things, getting them ready to put in storage or give to Dad and my aunts. I keep getting sidetracked, though. Going down memory lane."

"I'm so scared she'll find out," Margaret had said, "Don't let her, Mark. Please."

It wasn't going to be easy. Not now that Mark had met Kim Revis and discovered a woman who appealed to a side of him that had nothing to do with law and ethics and representing one's client. Keeping his emotional distance from the woman leaning in the window might very well be impossible. "Just as long as memory lane doesn't trip you up, Kim. We romanticize the past. We forget things like miners tunneling under a town so their children won't starve."

"I know." Kim straightened. The morning light was filtering through the massive oak and walnut trees ringing the museum. A current of gold touched her hair, turning auburn into shining copper. The planes and angles of her face blurred under the bright light.

This wasn't an ordinary woman. She was smoke and shadow. A presence as illusive as she was compelling.

What had gotten into him? Mark was a respected attorney who, in addition to having his own practice in Grass Valley, was on retainer to the town of Camp Oro. He'd been asked by one of his oldest and dearest clients to guard Kim Revis from the truth, not to allow his imagination to take flight.

Mark forced himself to speak. "Do you have any idea how long you'll be here?"

Kim shook her head. The light that had settled on her hair danced with the gesture. "After I've done my study, I want to stay on to oversee the installation of the security system. I don't know how long that's going to take."

"Probably longer than you'd like. You're not going to get a quick decision from that bunch. Your study? I take it you'll be spending a lot of time in the museum, becoming familiar with it."

"That's the first step."

"Yeah. I guess it has to be. Kim, good luck."

"Good luck? Is there a problem?"

Mark started to frown but composed himself. He'd come too close to a slip a moment ago. He had to change the subject. However, he also believed he had to give her some inkling of what she was walking into. "That's not for me to say. Just— They're strong individuals, Kim. Keep your eyes and ears open."

"Is that advice? Or a warning?"

"Maybe neither. Maybe both. I'm just saying you're not a trusting little girl anymore. The town has changed."

"I know, Mark," Kim said as she backed away. "Nothing really stays the same, no matter how much we might want it to."

Because she was concentrating on what Mark had said, Kim headed for the museum without really looking at her surroundings. If she had, she might have noted the shadowy figure pulling back from the second-story window.

Chapter Three

The three steps leading into the Comstock Museum were broadly spaced. Beyond the cement stoop was a twelve-foot-high hardwood door, so weathered that the original carvings were barely discernible. Turning the handle took strength.

The carpet under Kim's feet had been beaten into submission by thousands of feet. It stretched the length of a dark hallway with a ceiling higher than the door she'd come through. Lighting was provided by gas lamps set at infrequent intervals down the length of the hall. A woman with sagging cheeks and curious eyes stared at her from behind a solid circular desk just inside the door. Kim took quick note of the "ordinary" or high-wheeled bicycle on display on the opposite side of the entry, at the base of a wide staircase that led to the building's second story.

"Would you like to sign the guest book?" The soft question echoed in the oversize foyer.

Kim kept her voice low to prevent her words from reverberating. "I'm looking for Rogan Coffers. I have an appointment with him."

"Oh." The woman's interest in Kim went up a notch. "His office is to your right. Through those doors. They stick sometimes."

This was one of those times. Kim guessed that settling of the old brick building and uneven climate control was responsible. As she stepped into the staff work area, Kim's eyes were forced to compensate for leaving the dark corridor and entering a room with a large window through which the morning sun shone. A thin young man looked up from the copy machine he was using.

"Rogan Coffers?" Kim asked. The man she'd spoken to over the phone had sounded older.

"Hardly." The young man's laugh was brittle. "His office is around the corner there. The director gets his own turf, you know."

Because Kim didn't know whether she was expected to say anything in response, she simply smiled and headed in the direction the man had indicated. Like the hall, this room had an extremely high ceiling. And Kim was concerned about the haphazard stacking of the aged manuscripts and books that she noticed as she walked. If she was a betting woman, she'd wager that cataloging of artifacts was haphazard and not up-to-date. Still, Kim would wait to make a judgment until she'd seen the system at work.

At least this door opened without sticking. Kim caught the scent of pipe smoke clinging to a strange cool damp smell.

A tall but sparsely built man, dressed in a navy-blue suit, sat behind a massive oak desk. He held a pipe in one hand. He was talking on the phone. "We've had that agreement challenged before. Yes. Of course he can contest it, but we've been assured it's binding. No. I'm not interested in meeting with the executor. All right. I'll talk to you tomorrow."

The man who Kim guessed was in his early fifties hung up the phone and leaned back in his chair. Its springs protested weakly. "Yes?"

The man did not look pleased to see her. "I'm Kim Revis. And I'm sorry if my being late has disrupted your schedule."

"Ms. Revis. Sit down."

Kim's first impression of Rogan Coffers was that a museum was the perfect setting for him. His hair, what there was of it, was more gray than brown. Someone had gone to great effort to try to cover the bald spots. His suit, although expensive, didn't fit him particularly well. His hands very possibly were softer than hers. Right for someone who spent his days in contact with fragile antiques. But it was the pipe that rooted him firmly in his surroundings. Rogan Coffers looked the type to find a position as a university professor, or at the helm of an extensive if not progressive museum.

As Kim sat down, Rogan said something about wondering if there'd been a mix-up on the time for the meeting. "I had a great deal to keep me busy," he was saying. "Your being late wasn't that much of an inconvenience, however, I hope this doesn't set a precedent."

Kim quickly explained about the cave-in and her necessary conversation with the city attorney. "I'm sorry. I should have tried to reach you," she wound up. "But there really was no opportunity."

"A cave-in?" Kim had the man's full attention. "Where?"

Kim explained. "I don't know what's going to happen. I guess it's up to the city council, but—"

"They're incompetent." Rogan leaned forward. "Where does the tunnel go?"

"I have no idea. I wasn't thinking about that."

"You were talking to Stockton. What does he have to say?"

"Not much," Kim hedged. If she trusted first impressions, which she tried not to do, Rogan Coffers wouldn't have scored very high on her list. "I don't think anyone knows what to think yet."

Rogan leaned back, crossed one leg over the other and puffed deeply on his pipe. "I'll have to drive by and take a look at it. I hadn't heard, but then I've been quite busy since I got here this morning." Rogan recrossed his legs. "I'm certain it has the locals agitated. It isn't often they have this much to talk about."

Rogan was still talking. "Excuse me for being critical about the town and its people. It's an occupational hazard. Ms. Revis, we're in the never-ending position of trying to explain that, although the museum is located in Camp Oro, it is not an instrument of the town. The town doesn't dictate policy for us, and we make a point of remaining removed from its politics. Yes, we focus on local history and being located in an historic town has increased our credibility within museum circles. But our funding base covers a four-county area. And of course there's assistance on the federal level."

"I'm aware of that."

Rogan's voice, like the receptionist's, echoed off the high ceiling. "We have enough political dynamics existing within the museum system. Diverse personalities all vying for attention. We don't need to involve ourselves with the way this town is run."

"I see." According to her contract, Kim was an employee of the museum board and as such on a par with the director. It was time for that fact to be established. "When I called, you said you were going to try to set up a meeting with the other museum employees concerned with security. Is that still possible today?"

Rogan glanced at his watch. "I suppose. Not that anyone's going to be too happy about this. I asked our security guard and the business manager to sit in. His concern, if I can nail him down at this late hour, will be the cost of whatever you propose. There's—" Here Rogan's smile became brittle. "There's also Anthea Norval. She's our volunteer special activities director."

"Is she involved with security?"

"Yes and no." Rogan spoke without taking the pipe from his mouth. "Mrs. Norval's concern is that the security system not interfere in any way with public access to the building. She's a businesswoman in her own right. Very influential. It's hard to say no to Mrs. Norval."

Kim found it difficult to accept that explanation for allowing the woman to sit in on the meeting, but said nothing. In the week since she'd first heard from Stephan Jarvis, he'd called twice more. The Comstock Museum had been robbed again; he wasn't sure exactly when the thefts had taken place. A complete English, hand-engraved coffee-and-tea service and the museum's only Gatsby chair were now missing. Kim had asked if that was all that had been taken this time, but the board members weren't sure. All they knew was that they were frantic and frustrated.

As Kim sat across from Rogan waiting for him to locate the people she would be meeting with, she turned Stephan's words over in her mind. A tea service could be spirited out under someone's coat, but a Gatsby chair? Unless there was no one watching the doors, or whoever was supposed to be doing that was in on the theft, Kim had no idea how a chair could have been removed. Granted, her responsibility was to upgrade the museum's security system, not play detective, but she was determined to do more listening than talking about the thefts. If the thief was a museum employee—or even a board member—she wasn't about to impede the police investigation by saying more than was absolutely necessary. Perhaps, simply be being here, she could learn more than a man in uniform might.

Kim gave herself a mental head shaking. She was knowledgeable about electromagnetic locking devices and transmitter/sensor combinations, not detective work. She was here to assess, come up with a comprehensive plan and oversee installation of the selected security devices.

Rogan got to his feet. "They're still here. We'll meet in the conference room." As he escorted Kim out of his office and down the hall, he asked about the Wells Fargo History Room and the National Maritime Museum, both San Francisco institutions. Kim satisfied his curiosity while taking note of the tintype photographs gracing both sides of the hall. Most of the pictures were either of mining day Camp Oro or early logging operations. A cracked and faded photograph of Lake Tahoe piqued her interest as to how and when it had been taken, but there was no opportunity to ask questions.

Rogan was standing in front of yet another door, his hand on the doorknob. Instead of opening it, he faced Kim. "I'd like to get one thing straight between us. Hiring you was the board's idea. It was not what I recommended. They went over my head."

Kim said nothing. Although she was tense, she was glad this moment had come. Rogan had let her know that he considered the board's move an intrusion on his authority. She gave Rogan what she hoped was a controlled nod and stepped past him.

In the sparsely furnished cool room two men and a woman sat waiting at a battered conference table. Introductions went so quickly that Kim was given little opportunity to gain more than a fleeting impression. "Good luck," Mark had warned. The words came back to her now.

The woman was Anthea Norval. She was as imposing as her name. The middle-aged man in a loose fitting, rumpled shirt and stained jeans was introduced as the museum's lone security guard, William Lynch. Garner Dillon was a muscular man with a blatant sensuality made even more obvious by his skintight knit shirt and the dark slacks clinging to his muscular thighs. Garner was, Rogan explained, the museum's business manager.

"I was on my way to the annex when you reached me," Anthea started before either Rogan or Kim sat down. Slowly she fastened the gold buttons on her immaculate wool blazer. "I'd been lead to believe we were going to meet at 9:00 a.m. Now I'm gong to have to rearrange my entire day."

Stuffy. Self-important. Kim stopped the instant analysis. The fiftyish woman had a right to be irritated. "I'm afraid the delay was my fault," Kim said, and then gave a thumbnail sketch of the way her day had begun.

"So you've met Mark Stockton," Anthea interrupted before Kim was finished. "What do you think of the man?"

"What do I think of Mr. Stockton?" Kim repeated. "I don't believe in giving first impressions much weight. However, he impressed me as a take-charge type."

"You're astute, Ms. Revis. He certainly is that. Mark my words, the town's going to be in trouble if they don't keep him in line. It's no secret that he already runs the council. They do whatever he says."

Garner's snort was sharp enough to break Kim's concentration. The business manager flashed his perfect teeth at her. "You don't like the man because he plays a better game of hardball than you do, Anthea. One thing you need to understand, Ms. Revis. Personality conflicts are the name of the game around here. Everyone has their own ax to grind, their own nest to feather."

"Ms. Revis is not interested in your uncalled-for remarks," Anthea was saying. "I want it on record that I believe this concern with security is long overdue." She shot the silent security guard a pointed look before returning her attention to Kim. "If our business manager wasn't so tightfisted, we'd have more than one man, who should have been retired years ago, safeguarding our priceless antiques."

"That isn't your field, Anthea," Garner shot back. "Your function is to do what little you can to keep the museum in touch with community interests and concerns. Do you know what her group's major accomplishment this year has been? We now have a slide show of women's contribution to local history. That little presentation has been known to pull in five or ten people at a time."

"That's a total misrepresentation of the organization's accomplishments and you know it!" The perfect lady, Anthea's hands remained folded in her lap.

Kim glanced at Rogan, hoping that the director would order an end to the bickering, but he was looking at his watch. "I don't want to take any more of your time than necessary," Kim started. "Mr. Dillon, I—"

"Garner."

"Garner, I will want to meet with you later regarding the museum's finances. Once I've familiarized myself with the physical plant, I'm going to be formulating several options. I work for a museum myself. I understand the economics of an operation financed by grants and contributions."

"It's tight. Too damn tight for electronic wizardry."

Kim hadn't expected so sharp a retort from Garner. "Like I said," she repeated firmly, "we're talking options. I'm not going to be of much assistance unless I understand what the museum can and can't afford."

"Garner's right. It can't afford much," Rogan interjected. "We have an extensive collection. Acquisitions, restoration and storage has been our thrust. We are not interested in turning the place into a fortress. You have to understand our reputation."

Kim did. She also understood something else. "It isn't going to be much of a reputation if the museum is depleted. If antiques continue to be carried out the front door."

"Maybe it's the back door." Garner leaned back in his chair, hands clasped behind his head. The gesture expanded his chest. When Garner glanced at Kim, she realized he'd made the gesture for that purpose. "Maybe they come through the skylight and pass the antiques to their accomplices waiting on the roof. Oops. I forgot. No skylight."

Was Garner making fun of her? "This is not a joking matter. The losses now have a total value of thousands of dollars."

"If you want a dollar breakdown, I'm working on that," Garner pointed out. "At least I can give you a market value for the missing artifacts that have been reported to me. That's one of our problems. A major problem. There is no strict accounting of everything the museum has acquired over the years."

"You're certainly good at that," Anthea interjected. "Making lists. And quit flexing your muscles at Ms. Revis. I'd appreciate it if you played your games on your own time."

Kim blushed, but it was obvious that she was the only one upset by Anthea's comment. Garner flashed his perfect teeth. "Just because you can't get to first base with me, Anthea— You're young, Ms. Revis. Why did the board hire you?"

Anthea laughed a brittle laugh. "You took the words out of my mouth, Garner. Excuse me for saying this, Ms. Revis, but I remember you as a girl. It's hard for me to realize that Margaret's granddaughter is now a careerwoman. However did you get to be a security expert, if that's the right term."

"You're a friend of my grandmother?" Kim asked.

"Not exactly. After all, Margaret is older than I." Anthea ignored Garner's snort and went on. "Is that why you're here? Your grandmother recommended you?"

"No. In fact, my grandmother didn't know I was coming here until after I'd been retained by the board. She wouldn't have tried to pull strings for me. However, I doubt if I would have made time in my schedule to take this job if I hadn't grown up here in Camp Oro.''

When Anthea continued to give Kim a skeptical look, she explained that she'd had a double major of business and history in college, supplementing an academic scholarship by working part-time for the Golden Gate Museum. She'd expanded that to full-time work upon graduation and two years ago had been promoted to one of several assistant director positions. ''I've also worked on updating security systems for three area museums and recently acted as a consultant for a jewelry store,'' she finished up.

''Sounds boring,'' Garner proclaimed. ''No wonder you're not married, burying yourself in the archives that way.''

Kim chose to ignore Garner's comment. Instead she turned toward the still-silent security guard. ''I need an understanding of what security measures are currently being used.''

''Not very damn many.'' William Lynch cleared his throat, but when he continued, his voice still sounded seldom used. ''One man can't keep one hundred thousand square feet of building safe. There're maybe five hundred people come through those doors every day during the summer. I can't watch 'em all.''

Kim almost told William that it wasn't her intention to put him on the defensive, but thought better of it. Someone was stealing from the museum. It might be random light-fingered visitors, although she doubted that. It might be an organized effort made easy by paying off the lone security guard. And William Lynch could be involved more deeply than that. ''Who has the blueprints to the building?'' she asked. ''They would help me a great deal.''

''What's going to help is putting an end to this insanity.'' Anthea straightened the cuffs of the silk blouse under her blazer. ''We're not going to get the donations we need if patrons believe artifacts here aren't safe.''

"How are they going to know?" Rogan asked. "It hasn't made the paper."

Before Kim could ask how they'd managed that, Anthea spoke. "It's essential that our reputation remain unblemished. What you may not understand, Ms. Revis, is the unique situation here. We do more than act as a repository for artifacts. We actively solicit heirlooms."

Kim knew donations were essential if a museum was to build a sizable collection, but going out and asking for donations had to be handled carefully, if at all. Still, the management practice of Comstock Museum wasn't her concern. "Has anything been taken that was recently acquired?" she asked. "What I mean is, is there a possibility someone might come in and ask to see something from the family collection that's disappeared?"

A quick exchange of glances answered Kim's question. "And what's going to happen when that person comes in?" she asked.

"We tell them the item they have entrusted to us is currently in storage," Anthea answered.

Shock washed over Kim. She understood the museum's reluctance to admit its vulnerability, but to deliberately mislead people . . . "And this has the approval of the police department?" she managed.

Garner supplied the answer to that question in clipped tones. "That's not their concern. We want them to stop the thefts. We do not need them to tell us how to run the museum. Ms. Revis, Camp Oro doesn't have its own newspaper, and the Grass Valley paper doesn't routinely cover Camp Oro police business."

"But a museum is a public institution. People have a right to know."

"We prefer to work with the police chief, not the newspaper," Anthea interjected. "There are enough opinions expressed within these walls without outsiders becoming involved."

"Including the interests of certain people who should be concerned with special activities and not what kind of security system we can afford."

Kim ran her fingers through her hair, but the gesture didn't shake free the knot in the pit of her stomach. Once again she turned toward the museum director, hoping he would defuse the two. Rogan looked as if this was the last place he wanted to be.

Still, Kim didn't have to sit and listen to this endless argument. There were things they needed to hear from her. Briefly she explained that she would be considering the effectiveness of everything from light beams and door switches to ultrasonic and passive infrared devices. Her suggestions would be just that, suggestions. The final decision would be up to a committee consisting of board members and employees. "Much of my recommendation will be based on finding someone locally who can do the necessary installation," she finished. "The most sophisticated device, even if the museum could afford it, would be worthless if there's no one in the area with the expertise to install it."

"That's assuming you can get the board and employees to agree," Garner snorted. Without giving anyone the opportunity to either confirm or deny his statement, he rose to his feet. He was smoothing the taut fabric over his thighs as he continued. "Much as I'd like to continue this discussion, I have another meeting. If you're in need of transportation, Ms. Revis, I'd be happy to take you. Anywhere."

Kim drew a quick comparison between the business manager and the wolf at Little Red Riding-Hood's door. Thankfully she didn't have to dream up an excuse for not accepting Garner's offer. "I'm going to have Rogan give me a tour of the museum," she explained.

Anthea and William were getting to their feet as well. Ignoring Garner, Anthea pointed out that she needed to make an appearance at her shop. She left while Garner was still checking the contents of his briefcase. Kim was aware of William's cool, wary eyes on her, but the security guard said nothing. He was still watching when she and Rogan left.

Rogan was explaining that the second floor, which was accessible only by stairs, was divided into different sections, each one representing a specific historic era. "My time is short. I don't have time to give you more than a superficial tour. Maybe later—"

They'd retraced their earlier steps and were starting up the stairs when the receptionist stopped them. "Ms. Revis? I have a message for you. It's from Mark Stockton. He'd like you to call him at this number." The woman handed Kim a piece of paper. "He said to make sure you got the message."

"He called here? What else did he say?" Rogan asked.

"That's all, Mr. Coffers."

Rogan grunted. "How did Mr. Stockton know you would be here this morning?"

Kim didn't know why her relationship with Mark should be of any concern to the museum director. Still, she could hardly tell him it was none of his business. Briefly she explained that Mark had driven her this morning. Then she brought the conversation back to her reason for being here. "You said the only access to the second story is by these stairs. There isn't an elevator for disabled access?"

Rogan explained that the building's age and physical design precluded the installation of an elevator. There was an upper-level door leading to a fire escape, but that was kept locked and would trigger an alarm should anyone try to use it. Rogan's explanation of the second-story displays was cursory. Back on the ground floor, Kim was shown collections of mining exhibits, early photography equipment, tools and weapons. The displays devoted to silver artifacts and mint-condition Victorian bracelets rivaled those she'd seen in metropolitan museums and held her attention for several minutes. "The building's a basic design," she said as they reentered the ground-level hall. "There's just the one door, isn't there?"

Rogan pointed out that there was a fire door at the rear of the building, but like the one upstairs, it was tied into an alarm system. "There aren't any side doors or separate entrances for staff. Unless someone wants to set off the fire alarm, they have to go through the front door."

"Don't the windows open?"

"The last time the museum was painted, the windows were painted closed. Not only is it all but impossible to free the windows, but the screens have been nailed in place. Granted, that isn't the most effective system in the world, but it stops kids from trying to sneak in at night."

"Has that happened?" Kim watched as Rogan tamped fresh tobacco into his pipe. "Have kids ever broken in?"

Rogan shook his head. "Not successfully. I understand that some of the local youngsters consider it quite a challenge. But the museum grounds are patrolled at night. Between that and the local police, when they're on duty, we've been successful in keeping the kids away."

"The police. In other words, William Lynch isn't the only security personnel you have."

"Not strictly speaking." Rogan opened a door to show Kim the museum's historic library. He nodded to a couple of women working among the shelves but didn't speak to them. "William works days. He spends most of his time stationed at the front door, although occasionally he will follow a group around if he feels they might be, shall we say, opportunistic. At night the door is locked, and we've felt we were secure with only external night patrols. At least we felt secure until the past few months."

"That's when the thefts began," Kim finished for him. "The museum has a substantial foundation. Is there a basement?"

"No." Rogan paused as he studied his pipe. "My one vice." He patted his flat stomach as he returned the tobacco pouch to his back pocket. "I watch my weight and I don't drink, but a pipe helps me to relax. Shall we return to my office. That's the only place I smoke in the museum. I wish we did have a basement," Rogan said as they entered his office. "It would remedy some of our storage problems. As it is, we have a great deal stored in other locations throughout the county."

Without waiting for an invitation, Kim seated herself in the chair she'd used earlier. Although she hated cigarette smoke, there was something pleasant about Rogan's pipe. "Have there been any thefts from the storage buildings?"

"No." Rogan's eyes strayed to his watch. "We rent space from commercial storage firms that have their own security systems. Very few people know about the existence of these storage units. That's what has me convinced the thefts we're experiencing are being done by the public and not an inside job as Stephan seems to believe."

"Why is that?"

"Because the only place that's being robbed is the one the public has access to."

Kim thought about pointing out that it would be next to impossible, even for an employee, to steal from a storage vault protected by a modern security system, but kept silent. Until she knew which employees had access to what collections, she was going to ask as many questions as possible and reveal as little as necessary. She questioned Rogan about any possible pattern in the thefts, but because the museum was staffed in large part by volunteers and no routine checking was done of what was on display, it was hard to determine when a particular object had disappeared.

"What happened twice was that a volunteer was explaining a display to a visitor and noticed that something was missing. We have glass cases for the smaller, most valuable items and rope barriers to keep visitors from touching the displays, but obviously that hasn't been an effective deterrent."

Kim's mind whirled with possibilities. She had to remind herself that she wasn't a policewoman. Still, it was within the realm of her responsibility to ask if the glass cases had been effective.

"Up until ten days ago they were. I came to work Monday morning last week to find a case smashed and several pewter pieces missing."

"Monday?" Kim repeated. "Was anyone working over the weekend?"

Rogan shook his head. "Not on Sunday. It's policy that no one stay in the buildings after working hours. Either William or I lock up in the evening. And we always leave at the same time. He has his invalid brother to fix dinner for, and my wife and I have engagements most evenings, so neither of us are inclined to work overtime. Our leaving together is standard practice and acts as a check-and-balance system."

Kim turned that over in her mind. William was openly hostile, and it hadn't been Rogan's idea to hire her. She wasn't likely to get much cooperation from either man. "How many people have keys?"

Rogan was staring at her, his pale eyes giving away nothing of what he was thinking. "Just William and myself. And if you're thinking that either William or I could come back at night or on Sunday, don't forget the alarm system. It is activated after hours and turns off automatically Monday morning. It would alert the police even if either of us attempted to get in. Ms. Revis, we couldn't get insurance without that."

Kim could have apologized or told Rogan she wasn't questioning anyone's integrity, but she didn't. "Museums are like banks," she said. "Most thefts take place during the day."

"I'm aware of that." Rogan leaned back in his chair for a moment then suddenly straightened. "I've been the director here for almost six years, Ms. Revis. There's never enough money for all the staff we could use. That means I wear many hats. Although the budget is Garner's responsibility, I'm the one who the newspaper focused on when we were audited last year. According to preliminary reports, there were discrepancies in our bookkeeping methods. Those were later clarified, but I'm the one the fingers of doubt pointed at. Garner survived unscathed. As he always does."

Kim nodded, hoping the gesture would encourage Rogan to continue. It was obvious that Anthea didn't like Garner, but this was the first inkling she'd had of how Rogan felt about the business manager. "I take it the budget is on the line."

"Oh, yes. There's always money for Anthea's little pet projects. Never mind that the budget committee hasn't seen fit to give me a raise in two years." Rogan ran a hand over his eyes. "I won't burden you with our internal politics, Ms. Revis. Let's just say that the business manager makes almost as much as I do."

"Oh." Kim had been prepared to give finances priority when making her recommendations. She hadn't realized she'd also be asking people who resented and distrusted one another to work together for the good of the museum. "About the blueprints," she asked, determined to move the conversation away from the petty to what was essential.

"I'm not sure I can get my hands on them right away." Rogan glanced at the watch on his bony wrist. "I have other commitments. Wait here. I'll be back."

Kim kept a smile pasted on her face until Rogan closed the door behind him. Then her tired muscles begged for relief. She leaned back, pressing a hand to her forehead. What she sensed at the Comstock Museum went beyond anything she'd experienced before. Working here was going to be an emotional strain, a strain made even more difficult because she had no one in Camp Oro to confide in. She wasn't about to burden her grandmother with this.

"Quit feeling sorry for yourself, Revis," Kim warned herself aloud. "That isn't your style."

There wasn't much on Rogan's desk to hold her attention. She flipped idly through several professional journals but didn't look at the two letters awaiting his signature. She started to get to her feet but wound up reaching for her purse instead. A moment later Kim was dialing Mark's number. He picked up the phone soon after she identified herself to his secretary.

"How are you holding up?"

For the first time since walking through the museum's doors, Kim laughed. Some of the tension seeped out of her. The cold room warmed. What was Mark's office like? What was on his desk? What had been on his mind when she called? "You tried to warn me."

"I don't know much. Just rumors that all is not one big happy family. The reason I called was—are you going to need transportation? I'm at your disposal this evening."

Her own private chauffeur. "I don't know," she had to admit. "I don't know what I'm going to be doing tonight."

"What about now?" the soft, rich voice asked.

Kim no longer smelled Rogan's tobacco. Instead her senses registered the memory of soap and spiced after-shave. "I need to talk to the police, but right now I'm waiting for the director to get back."

"I'm serious about being available tonight." Kim could hear Mark say something to someone and then he continued. "A word of advice. Actually two words of advice. If you want to get out of there today, don't ask Rogan about his wife. She has as much clout as your grandmother and would like the world to appreciate it. And watch yourself around Garner."

Kim laughed. "He certainly thinks a lot of himself. And his effect on women."

"I'm sure of that. He's a brilliant man. Arrogant and brilliant and frustrated."

"Frustrated?"

"Garner and I went to high school together. It came as a real shock to him when he learned that the world doesn't revolve around him."

"Oh." Kim pressed a hand to her forehead. Despite Mark's voice, Rogan's office with its high ceilings, massive desk and small, painted-shut window were making her feel trapped. She didn't want to have to deal with Garner Dillon's complex personality or Rogan Coffers's marriage on top of everything else. She didn't want to face-off against a powerful businesswoman or a hostile security guard.

And she didn't want to have to ask herself why the eerie feeling of unease that had haunted her at the cave-in had followed her here.

Chapter Four

Whoever had been cutting the museum lawn was finished, and the air was filled with the sweet aroma of freshly mowed grass. It was all Kim could do to keep from skipping the half-dozen blocks from the museum to the police department. If she hadn't been tempered by the years of projecting a certain image in San Francisco, the happy, carefree child who'd grown up in Camp Oro would have resurfaced.

The town had changed and yet a great deal remained the same. The grocery store had moved into a larger building adjacent to the one it had occupied when Kim was a child, and a drugstore now occupied the old space. What had once been an historic residence across from the museum was now a bed-and-board. A vacant lot had been taken over by the local garden club and now provided a parklike setting where residents and visitors could relax surrounded by roses and other plantings capable of surviving the two or three snowfalls Camp Oro got a year. Kim had readied herself for the changes years and weather would have to have made on the brick buildings that lined the main street. She was pleasantly surprised to see that the buildings' owners were keeping the structures true to their original condition. Kim kept to the right side of Pioneer Street because workmen had erected scaffolding around a restaurant and were in the process of replacing old mortar between the bricks.

It was incredible. Fifteen years ago Kim had seen not an historic landmark, but a quiet town with little to interest a girl given to flights of fancy about living on a huge ranch surrounded by horses. Now she was peeking in the windows of specialty shops for quilters, antique collectors, wine connoisseurs, crystal fanciers and those attracted to gold jewelry. Kim noted an old-fashioned soda fountain as well. Although it might not provide the most well-balanced meal, she was looking forward to having lunch there.

Even with modern cars parked in front of the businesses, Kim was able to make contact with the past. Camp Oro had begun as a collection of tents that were gradually replaced by wooden buildings. It wasn't until the town had burned down twice that brick buildings came into vogue. Once the sidewalks had been made of wood, but almost a hundred years ago they had been replaced with sandstone. The sandstone was worn down in many places. Kim was concentrating on her footing when she noted that the man coming toward her was wearing boots.

For a moment Kim lost contact with today. She would look up and see, not a tourist, but a cowboy just in from the range. He would tip his hat at her, the pioneer woman in her Sunday dress. She would smile shyly at him, and he would show up later at the church social. They would share her picnic lunch. He would tell her about months spent herding cattle. She would let him walk her home. Weeks later, if he was still in town, they might share a shy kiss.

Smiling at herself, Kim shook her head and focused on the owner of the boots. Her sense of anticipation faded. She'd wanted to look up into Mark Stockton's eyes, not see a beanpole of a man with a small girl straddling his neck.

Kim's only consolation was that no one could have guessed what she had been thinking. Besides, Mark wouldn't have been a cowboy. She was trying to decide whether he better fit the role of circuit judge or the owner of the town's largest gold mine when her progress was slowed by a couple of well-dressed men emerging from the largest Pioneer Street business.

"She's going to be in this afternoon. At least it wasn't a wasted trip," one was saying to the other.

"I guess," the other grumbled. "All I know is, I don't want to waste my time talking to the hired help. Anthea knows what I want."

"Relax. She's always gotten you what you wanted before, hasn't she?" the first asked. "She isn't going to fail you now."

"She better not. Especially not at the prices she charges."

"What do you care?" The first speaker pulled his companion closer to the building so Kim could pass. "You want the best, you're going to pay through the nose. Anthea delivers."

It was all Kim could do to pretend she wasn't interested in the conversation. She smiled vaguely at the two men and then turned her attention to the window display to the left of the door. A half-dozen earthenware pitchers decorated with elaborate paintings dominated the display. Painted on the window were the words Norval Antiques. The two men had crossed in the middle of the street and were heading toward the wine and gift shop. Kim watched until they went inside. Then, acting on more than casual curiosity, Kim stepped into Norval Antiques.

The business was easily the biggest on the street and if Anthea was responsible for its success, she was to be commended. Not only was it well stocked, but the merchandise was artfully displayed and included some fine antiques. The shop would have to draw customers from outside the immediate area if it was to remain in business. Obviously, judging by the man with the southern accent in the process of making a substantial purchase, it did. Kim had one question, one she wasn't about to ask Anthea or anyone who worked for her. How was the woman able to get her hands on the quality and amount of merchandise offered here for sale?

Kim wasn't any closer to an answer by the time she left the shop. With her mind crowded with possibilities, she turned off Pioneer Street and headed toward the newer brick building housing the city hall, fire and police departments.

She was waiting for the middle-aged woman in the main office to get off the phone when a door at the rear of the room opened and a two-hundred-and-twenty-pound man in a police uniform came out. For a moment Kim and the man stared at each other. The policeman smiled first. "Kim. Kim Revis. Would you look at yourself!"

"Charles!" Kim's grin was a twin of the one being directed at her. "I don't believe it. You're a policeman?"

"Wonders never cease, do they? Not bad for a kid who thought he was going to spend his life repairing cars in his dad's shop." Charles motioned for Kim to follow him to the back of the room. Two minutes later Kim was sitting in Police Chief Charles Horne's office, still trying to absorb the fact that someone who'd been two years ahead of her in school was now the police chief in their hometown. Not only that but Charles had married one of Kim's childhood friends and they had two sons. Charles had no reservations about fatherhood or the only town he'd ever lived in. However, his enthusiasm didn't extend to the museum staff. "It's a hell of a mess," Charles responded after Kim told him why she was in Camp Oro. "If you've met with those characters, then you have a fair idea of what I'm talking about."

On Charles's desk were two pictures. One of two young boys photographed in costumes and background that duplicated old wanted posters. The boys had obviously inherited their broad noses and prominent chins from Charles. The second photo featured a slim, attractive woman dressed in a dance hall costume. She was responsible for the boys' thick black hair. Sandy still looked like someone who didn't take life too seriously. "I'd been warned even before I met the staff," Kim explained, glad that the police chief had turned out to be someone she could be open with. "By the town attorney."

"Mark. Yeah. You'll either like or hate that man. He isn't one of those lawyers who never lets you know what's going on inside him. Mark says what he thinks. I've always been honest with him and he with me."

"I hope so. He hasn't said anything about when I'm going to be able to use my car again."

"That's because it isn't up to him. He'll do the best he can by you. And if he can't help, he'll let you know."

"That's good to know. The reason I wanted to talk to you—well, I suppose I should confine myself to the job I've been hired for, but I'm wondering if I might be on a fool's mission."

"You wanna explain?"

Kim took a moment to collect her thoughts. "The thefts—it might not be visitors."

Charles leaned back in his chair and clamped his hands behind his head. His hands were those of a mechanic. Funny, Kim thought, she'd never pictured Charles as doing anything except following in his father's footsteps. But he had, and she reminded herself that nothing could be taken for granted. "You want my opinion?" Charles asked. "Might doesn't cover the half of it. Look, Kim, Mark called me not more than an hour ago. I think he guessed you'd be coming here."

"He did?"

Charles smiled. "Don't let anything Mark Stockton does surprise you. He's a jump ahead of most people. He said— well, let's just say he suggested that I cooperate with whoever the board had hired. And now I know that it's you—we need to be up-front with each other."

"I'm glad to hear that."

"I could name three, maybe four people I'd watch what I say around. Kim, right now I'm damn glad the Grass Valley paper hasn't gotten wind of this. Because if it did, what I've been able to accomplish so far would make me look like the fool of the year."

After being called Ms. Revis all morning, Kim appreciated hearing her first name. Still, she wasn't quite sure what to say in response.

"What those fool reporters wouldn't know, and what I wouldn't bother telling them, is that I'm getting absolutely no cooperation from the staff. That director they have is so blasted busy doing whatever he's doing that he can't find time to talk to me."

"That isn't right."

"Maybe. Maybe not." When Charles shrugged, Kim was afraid his shirt seams might split. "I keep telling myself I shouldn't be surprised. After all, they've got their own security guard, if you can call William a security guard, and they contract with the county to have someone check them a couple of times a night. The town and the museum, well, let's just say it's been an uneasy alliance. The museum doesn't depend on local tax money so they figure they don't owe the town much. Maybe they're right. After all, the museum acts as a big draw for the rest of the town."

"But—they're losing valuable artifacts."

"Exactly. You'd think they'd want the holes plugged up, wouldn't you? If they are worried, either they don't want anyone touching it, or they're doing something to stop the thefts on their own. I guess they are doing something. After all, they hired you."

"The board did," Kim started and then decided Charles should know everything. She relayed the essence of what the director had said about it not being his idea to have her here, mentioned that the business manager was being less than cooperative, and commented that she wasn't sure what Anthea Norval's connection was. And finished by saying, "Mr. Lynch acted as if he hated everyone in the room."

"He probably does. Calling that man a security guard is a joke. There's training he could be getting through the police department. He's asked about it a couple of times. But the museum has never budgeted the money for that. I don't know." Charles shook his head. "If you want my opinion, they've either got to get William certified or get rid of him."

Kim and Charles talked for another fifteen minutes. Charles candidly told her that his investigation was stalemated. So far none of the stolen merchandise had shown up in the county. He'd asked other law-enforcement offices throughout the state to keep their eyes out for the list of antiques he'd given them, but that was a long shot. Fingerprinting was an exercise in futility because of the number of people in and out of the museum. "A couple of the board members said they were going to take matters in their own hands. They weren't too happy with me when they said that. If you get a decent security system installed, maybe that'll do the job."

"Maybe." Although it wasn't quite noon, Kim felt as if she'd been on the go for days. "And maybe, if that happens, we'll never find out who's responsible."

Charles shook his head wearily, reminding Kim of a fighter at the end of a match. "I've said it before. I'll say it again. It's an inside job. It sounds as if you're thinking the same thing."

"I'm not sure," Kim hedged. "I just got here."

"True. Look, maybe we can work together on this. You say you're looking for someone who can install a decent system. I think I can steer you in the right direction. If you'll keep your eyes and ears open..."

Kim didn't need Charles to fill in the rest. She got to her feet and stuck out her hand. "I'll let you know. Anything, I'll let you know."

"That's what I figured," Charles told her on the tail of a hearty handshake. "At least now I have someone inside the museum who's going to give me a straight answer. You're staying at your grandmother's place? I'll have Sandy give you a call.''

Lunch consisted of two scoops of ice cream followed by a stop at a small bookstore specializing in local history. By the time she and the owner had exhausted the subject of the cave-in, she'd been in the shop for an hour. By then Pioneer Street was almost wall-to-wall people. Kim was still some distance from her useless car when it became obvious that the cave-in was responsible for the increased traffic.

Since there was nothing she could do at the museum until Rogan and Garner had time to talk to her, Kim decided to go home. If nothing else, she could begin what needed to be done to ready her grandmother's house for sale. Kim hadn't given a thought to taking another look at the hole, but when she heard arguments over whether more asphalt had cracked off since morning, she slipped around an older couple for another look.

Nothing had changed. The cave-in still fascinated her. Stifling a sigh that sounded too much like a gasp, Kim clenched her fingers and forced herself to move even closer. She couldn't be sure; maybe the hole *was* a little larger than it had been earlier.

''They ought to put a light down there,'' a man nearby said to no one in particular. ''That way we'd be able to see what's happening.''

''Give them time. It just happened this morning.''

Kim wasn't interested in what else was being suggested. As she'd done earlier, Kim crouched low to give herself a better view of the dark hole. The presence of so many people helped. Yet, it wasn't enough.

Come here. Just a little closer.

''They've got to cover it up right away. Some kid's going to fall in.''

''I think it's a shame. This is the most interesting thing that's happened to Camp Oro in a month of Sundays.''

Kim was on her feet and backing away rapidly before she'd regained her balance. She brushed against a man, gave him an apologetic smile and hurried away. She'd made a wide circle and was beside her car before she took a conscious breath. No matter how crazy it sounded, Kim wasn't going to risk another look at what everyone else seemed to be able to take for granted. She forced herself to walk, not run, up the lane leading to the house where she'd grown up.

Why was this happening? And why—? Kim stopped her questions. The dark hole had unnerved her this morning. The feeling had disappeared when Mark Stockton arrived. Now it was back again.

The sight of her grandmother's rose garden restored her equilibrium. Margaret had spent hours trimming and caring for the roses with her granddaughter chattering nearby. In the fall they would watch squirrels in search of nuts in the walnut tree. In the winter Kim would watch the heavy clouds forming to the west, asking again and again if her grandmother thought it was going to snow.

The seasons, the love of a grandmother and father, those things were reality, not whispered words from a hole in the ground.

Kim had talked to her grandmother on the phone last night about what Margaret wanted to have placed in storage and what should be kept out for the movers. Relying on the partial list she'd been given, Kim devoted her afternoon to filling boxes and recapturing memories. She was in the middle of cleaning out a cupboard when the doorbell rang.

Mark's smile wiped Kim's mind clear of her nostalgic mood. "I thought you might have gone back to the museum," he said.

Kim shook her head but didn't bother with an explanation. She was more interested in why Mark was here. "My first visitor," she said as she let him in. "I did get hit up for some candy the Little League was selling, but I don't think that counts."

"Did you buy?" Mark noted the boxes stacked by the front door. He was even more aware of the old shirt sagging over Kim's shoulders and the long shirttail that covered almost all of her well-worn shorts.

He shouldn't be here. Yes, he had a legitimate reason for his visit, and as Margaret Revis's attorney, he might be able to convince himself that he was here on business. But one look at the long expanse of leg, one instant lost in her cool hazel eyes, and Mark gave up lying to himself.

He was here because he, the private man behind the professional, wanted to see this woman.

Kim was telling him about a little boy with a huge baseball mitt tucked under his arm and sales tactics no one could refuse. "I don't even like chocolate-covered raisins. Would you like some?"

"Maybe." Mark nodded at the boxes. "You've been busy."

"I'm feeling a little stymied." Kim was sitting on a couch with a handmade throw over it. She curled her bare feet under her and started kneading her calf. The gesture pulled Mark away from everything except her and his reaction to her. "I didn't get as far as I wanted to at the museum. I was given the cook's tour, but I'm a long way from being able to formulate any kind of security system."

"How did it go? Did anyone give you a reason to be nervous?"

"Nervous? Why should they?"

"Good question." Mark forced his attention back to the room. For a moment the distraction accomplished what he needed it to. Quickly, before Kim distracted him again, Mark asked his question. "Will you have to spend much time at the museum? I mean, how much poking around will you have to do?"

"Poking around? I'm not sure I understand what you mean."

Mark made himself laugh. "Maybe I don't, either. I was just wondering—the museum can be quite a distraction. I thought you might be interested in the collections. Your grandmother thought—"

"I wasn't hired to look at the collections, Mark. I have a job to do, but until I get some cooperation—"

"So you decided to do some work here."

Kim nodded. "I still don't feel right about doing this. These are my grandmother's things. The little girl in me wants her living here, not in some sterile apartment in Grass Valley."

"Nothing stays the same, does it." A radio was playing softly in the kitchen. Several windows were open letting in smells and sounds. Mark wondered if he would have noticed such things if Kim hadn't been in the house, making him more aware of everything. "Your grandmother's a wonderful, practical woman. She made the adjustment. I hope you can do the same."

"I know. I will." Kim stopped working on her calf. She smiled openly and with the gesture Mark forgot everything he knew about the professional woman he'd met this morning. And what Margaret had wanted him to find out. "It's just going to take a little time," she finished.

Mark explained that he'd gotten off work a little early because his parents were planning a trip to Lake Tahoe. He wanted to make sure their motor home was ready to go. "My father is one of the world's great procrastinators. He puts off until next week what should have been done yesterday. Mom called in a panic because they were having trouble with their water tanks, and Dad was working himself into a lather. I shouldn't complain. I'd much rather tinker, even with my dad leaning over my shoulder, than prepare a brief."

"I'm sure your dad appreciates it."

"I'm sure he does. In fact, I wouldn't be surprised if he put Mom up to it. Responsibilities." Mark nodded at the boxes. "There's no getting away from responsibility where our families are concerned, is there?"

"I don't mind. You didn't say. What are you doing here?"

"You're going to need transportation."

"I'm aware of that. Did the council decide to take my advice and throw gravel in the hole."

Mark's laugh echoed. "There's one thing you'll have to learn, Kim. Nothing moves quickly in this town. However, a special meeting has been set for tomorrow night. I hope you'll be able to attend."

"You'll be there?"

"Command performance. I'm paid well for my services. I'm not going to deny that. In exchange—" Mark shrugged his shoulders. "In exchange, the town believes they own me lock, stock, and barrel."

Kim knew she shouldn't say anything. After all, even if he was her grandmother's attorney, she'd just met him. However, it was important to her that they be honest with each other. "This morning someone said that the council does what you want it to."

To her relief, Mark laughed. "I've heard the rumors. Kim, the council is made up of volunteers. They're not required to know the town's legal obligations. That's what I'm there for. If it seems as if I'm guiding policy, it's only because I don't want this town placed in an awkward legal position. When I take a stand, it's a firm one."

"You don't have to explain that to me. The Golden Gate Museum has a lawyer on retainer. I've seen him in action. Anyway, thank you for stopping by. You could have called me about the meeting."

"True. But I couldn't have gotten the car to you that way."

"The car?" He was smiling; this smile was less open and yet every bit as appealing as the ones he'd given her before. "What car?"

"The car parked at the end of the driveway. I wanted it to have air conditioning and a good radio."

"I have no idea what you're talking about."

"I know you don't." Mark was nodding as he spoke, but instead of supplying answers, he got to his feet. He walked over to an open box and looked inside. "Dishes. What are you going to use while you're here?"

Kim explained that she'd packed the good china but was going to leave the everyday dishes out until the last minute. Mark's silence on the matter of a car didn't bother her. If he wanted to draw out the suspense, she was willing to play along. "I'm having a wonderful time," she explained as she joined him. "There are so many memories here. If you have time, I'd like to show you something."

"I have the time." Mark straightened. He lifted his hand and for a moment Kim thought he was reaching out to her. He didn't touch her, and Kim was left with the question of whether she'd imagined the gesture.

Unnerved, Kim led the way into her grandmother's bedroom. In a distracted voice, she explained that her grandmother's second husband had made the bed while Margaret was quilting the bedspread. "Every time I come in here I think about the love that went into this room. I just can't get used to the idea of it being anywhere else."

"Your grandmother's made up her mind."

"I know she has. And I'm going along with her decision. It's just—"

"It's just what?"

Kim had been studying the intricate stitching in the spread. Now she turned in response to Mark's gentle question. "I've been in here most of the afternoon. I think I've let the museum get to me. I've been looking for— Something's missing. At least I can't find it. I don't know how she's going to take that."

Mark moved farther into the room. "What's missing?"

Kim lifted a ceramic box off the dresser and sat on the edge of the bed. Then she upended the box. Pieces of jewelry tumbled onto the spread. "Grandmother didn't believe in spending money on fine jewelry, but Dow loved to buy her costume jewelry. I loved dressing up in her necklaces and brooches."

Mark had sat down nearby; his weight pulled Kim toward him. His strong fingers sorted through the beads and chains. "That's quite a collection."

"It's incomplete. Something, the most important piece, is missing."

"You're sure?"

Kim nodded. She spread the jewelry on the cover, hoping that she'd just missed the pin before. "I'm afraid so," she sighed. "Grandmother had this exquisite rose-shaped mourning pin. It was made of jet, absolutely black and opaque. Except—there was a thin white slash across one end of the stone like a lightning bolt."

He hadn't expected it this soon. "A mourning pin?"

"It came from my grandfather's side of the family. A keepsake. Grandmother said Jeromiah gave it to her right after they were married. Apparently women in mourning wore such pins as their only jewelry in the late 1800s. Jeromiah wanted her to have it. It was—Grandmother always turned quiet when she was looking at it. Except for her wedding ring, it was the only piece of jewelry Grandfather ever gave her."

Mark continued to stare at the jumble of jewelry between him and Kim. Anything but this. He could handle any conversation but this one. "Maybe you don't have to tell her. You don't want to upset her. It's bound to show up."

"Not tell her?" Kim frowned. "Mark, Grandmother and I have always been honest with each other."

"She's older now, Kim," Mark said softly. "She's had to make a lot of changes lately. Hard decisions. I'd just hate to see her upset unnecessarily."

"You really think I shouldn't say anything?"

"Kim, I know your grandmother pretty well. She's much more than a client to me. My mother's parents lived in the Midwest. I seldom saw them. My father's mother, well, she wasn't a particularly warm or outgoing woman. Your grandmother has shown me a great deal about caring and commitment. I guess what I'm saying is, if I can spare her, I will."

"What a beautiful thing to say." Kim blinked rapidly. "All right. I won't say anything. Not unless I have no choice. But I've looked everywhere I can think of. Mark, that was the only piece of jewelry Grandmother didn't want me to play with. It meant so much to her. Her only reminder—"

"Then don't disturb her memories."

Mark waited until Kim had collected the jewelry and put the pieces back in the box. Then, feeling as if he was standing at the edge of a cliff waiting for the gust of wind that would throw him into space, he got to his feet and offered Kim his hand. She took it and allowed him to help her up without questioning what was happening. They'd walked through the house and were outside before either of them said anything.

Mark took the only way he could find out of his mood. "You're going to have to drive me back to Grass Valley. Either that or I'll have to walk."

He was standing only a few inches away, keeping her close to the wonderful things he'd said about her grandmother. Kim had to struggle to keep up with the turns in this conversation. "You aren't going to tell me what this is all about, are you?"

"Nope."

A week ago Kim had been up to her ears in the budget considerations. One marathon meeting had lasted until one in the morning because Kim wasn't about to back down on her request for shock sensors to be placed behind several priceless paintings. She'd been called bullheaded and a few less savory things, but in the end she'd prevailed. Now she was standing in front of her grandmother's house dressed in an old shirt and shorts with a man who wanted her to walk barefoot down the driveway. And Kim was a breath away from doing just that. "Shouldn't I get my purse?"

"Purse? If it makes you feel more comfortable."

"And shoes."

"Shoes? Are you a tenderfoot?"

"Yes," Kim shot the comment over her shoulder. She hurried back up the steps and disappeared inside the house. Mark stood waiting for her, knowing nothing except that, despite the danger, this was the only thing he wanted to do today. When she rejoined him, he was so lost in thought that he didn't think to look at what she'd put on her feet.

Brush and trees had been allowed to grow unchecked for several years. The driveway was so narrow that it was impossible to get a car up it without branches brushing the sides. Their hands were swinging within touching distance of each other. The only sound that Kim noticed was that of Mark's tennis shoes hitting the gravel. A branch slapped her shoulder; she wondered what her reaction would be if their fingers touched.

They didn't. Instead Mark identified a few shrubs during the two minutes it took for them to reach Kim's stranded car. Because she remembered all too well her reaction to the cave-in, Kim made sure that Mark was between her and the hole.

She paid little attention to where they were going and would have walked past the Honda if Mark hadn't stopped her.

"I don't know how long you're going to be stranded," he said. "I wish I could give you a deadline, but that isn't possible. In the meantime, you're going to need transportation."

Kim leaned forward so she could see inside the car. "What do I owe you?"

"Nothing. Just put gas in it."

"But—"

"I know the owner of the rental car agency. He owed me a favor. No money changed hands."

"But—" Kim stopped herself. Mark had gone out of his way to do her a favor. She could at least show her appreciation. "Thank you. I knew I was going to have to do something. I just hadn't decided what that something was to be."

"You'll have to take me home."

"Oh. Of course. You have the keys?"

"Yes ma'am. But first—first, I'm starving."

Kim's ice-cream cone had been hours ago. "I could fix you something. I haven't done much shopping yet, but—"

"We're going out to dinner."

Kim glanced down at her bare legs. "The Ritz?"

"Not a bad idea. Unfortunately, Camp Oro doesn't have a Ritz."

Kim's mood swung wildly. If Mark had asked her to sit cross-legged on the hood of the car while they ate chicken with their fingers, she would have agreed gladly. "What did you have in mind?"

"Pizza. Chinese food. Steak."

They wound up having hamburgers in a family-style restaurant on the outskirts of Grass Valley. Mark did most of the talking. He explained that his parents must have been injected with gypsy blood. Now that they'd retired, they were always on the road. He had a younger brother living in Los Angeles. According to Mark, Phil must have a short circuit somewhere to have moved to the city. Mark didn't mind visiting his brother there, especially if Phil had Raider football tickets, but it would take an earthquake to move him south. "Phil's living the bachelor life to the hilt. I don't know how he finds time to work, with all the parties he says he goes to. I've given up trying to keep track of the women in his life."

Kim picked up a French fry but didn't put it in her mouth. Mark came from a warm, closely knit family. He hadn't said so in so many words, but the love he felt for his parents and brother was obvious. "L.A.'s a good place for single people. At least that's what I hear."

"I've heard the same thing. It's just not for me."

"Why?" she asked gently.

"Why aren't I interested in the singles scene?" Mark took the fry from Kim, dipped it in catsup and popped it in his mouth. "I've never given it a try. Maybe I'd change my mind if I did. Kim, I think I'm a workaholic. I know that's one of the things I've been accused of. I take my responsibilities seriously. Too damn seriously sometimes."

"But you do have a personal life, don't you?"

Mark nodded; it was the better part of a minute before he spoke. "Not as much as my folks want me to have, but it suits me. How did the rest of your day go?"

Kim admitted that designing a security system for the museum was going to be the least of her problems. Dealing with four distinct antagonistic personalities was going to be the real test. "But I have someone in my camp. The police chief. Charles and I grew up together. While I was driving here I wondered whether any of the old gang was left. It helps to know I can be honest around Charles, and he's going to be honest with me."

"I'm sure it helps. And wait until you see his boys. They come into the office sometimes. The littlest one just learned how to walk. He isn't safe anywhere. You'd like him. Everyone likes Boomer."

BECAUSE THE AIR CONDITIONING had been turned on in the restaurant, Kim was chilled by the time they left. She walked briskly out to the car and flexed her legs, restoring circulation. She had no idea how long they'd been inside, only that they hadn't run out of things to say. It seemed as if no matter what direction the conversation had gone, they'd both had something to contribute.

Mark was in no hurry to get back in the rented car. Instead he pointed at an auto dealership located across the road from the restaurant. "Biggest dealership in the county. At least that's what their ads say. I wouldn't buy anything there if I were you. Some of that man's practices— Let's just say that I get my share of phone calls from dissatisfied customers asking if there's any way they can get out of the deals they've gotten themselves into with Friendly Eddie."

Kim pointed out that she wasn't in the market for a new car. "Are you supposed to tell me something like that? I mean, what if I repeated it somewhere?"

"I trust you not to. Besides, it's not like the man's cutthroat tactics aren't general knowledge."

They were getting into the rented car when an expensive new Buick pulled out of the dealership's lot, crossed the road and pulled up alongside Mark.

"Slumming, Mark?"

Because the lighting in the park lot wasn't the best, it took Kim a moment to recognize Anthea Norval. Mark still had his hand on the car's door but had turned to face the woman. "It's a decent restaurant, Anthea. I didn't feel like spending the whole evening getting a meal."

Anthea's cool laugh sent a quick chill down Kim's spine. "Don't get defensive, Mark. Ms. Revis. I didn't recognize you. I told Charmaine that if Mark was half the man he wants everyone to believe he is, he'd find a way to spend some time with you. However, I didn't think even he could work this fast."

Kim nodded to acknowledge Anthea's presence but didn't attempt to enter the conversation. Anthea was explaining that she'd been on her way home when she'd spotted Mark. "I didn't recognize the car. But I recognized your walk. And your build. I heard that the town council is meeting tomorrow night. You work fast.''

"The mayor called the meeting, Anthea.''

Anthea shrugged off Mark's explanation. "At your insistence, I'm sure. I'll be there as I'm sure you will. What are you going to recommend, Mark? Maybe there's a way you could charge people to see the cave-in. Heaven knows the town budget needs every boost it can get. I just wish you and the council would get it through your heads that you can't support the town by placing the burden on the backs of local businesses. You're going to drive business away if you keep on raising the business tax.''

"It was raised once in the last seven years, Anthea.'' Mark's voice, which had been a light touch inside the restaurant, now alerted Kim to another side of Mark's nature. There was no doubt in her mind that Mark didn't want to talk to Anthea.

With a shrug, Anthea dismissed Mark's comment. "You don't mince words, do you? If nothing else, I always know where you stand. Maybe you'll give me an answer to something.'' When Mark said nothing, she went on. "Everyone knows the council is in your hip pocket. What I'd like to know is when you're planning on turning your considerable energies to the museum.''

"I have no interest—''

Anthea snorted. "Come on, Mark. A man with your kind of drive, I'm surprised you haven't started making inroads already. I'm going to be honest with you. Your involvement with the museum would not have my approval.''

Mark shrugged. "I'd rather gathered that. Besides, I'm not interested. I have my practice.''

"Ambition, Mark, ambition.'' Anthea tapped her forehead. "What do you want, a judgeship? A political career? I'm not the only one who's watching for you to make your move.''

"It's going to be a long wait then.''

"We'll see." Anthea began to put up her window. "We'll see."

"That woman," Mark muttered, once he and Kim were on their way. "There isn't a word that comes out of her mouth that isn't calculated."

"What was her point?" Kim asked.

"She's just digging. Trying to feel me out. Pushing buttons to see if she can get me to say something I hadn't intended."

"Is she right? Would it be to your advantage to get involved with the museum board?"

"Kim, the last thing I'm interested in is clawing my way up any ladder." His tone softened. "I like what I do. I'm content to spend my working life as a lawyer."

"Then why would—"

"Why would Anthea think different? Because she's an ambitious woman married to an ambitious, unscrupulous man. She doesn't believe there's any other way of living."

"I'm sorry," Kim said after a moment of silence. "I wish we hadn't run in to her."

"So am I. But I should have expected it."

"How could you?"

"The auto dealership. Her husband runs it."

MARK'S HOME was in the hills above Grass Valley. The road leading to his house was narrow and not particularly good, but Kim noted that the homes along it were large and the lots well maintained. Mark's house, almost hidden by pine trees, had been built in the 1930s and extensively remodeled. It was obvious that Mark was proud of the results. "I could have spent a lot less money buying a newer home, but Anthea's right about one thing. I love a challenge."

"I love the surroundings." Because Mark hadn't gotten out of the car, Kim took her cue from him. "It's so natural."

"I have a deck and yard in back. I just wish I had more time to enjoy it. Kim, I enjoyed tonight."

Wasn't he going to invite her in? He'd just told her about the work he'd had done in the kitchen, the updated wiring and plumbing. "So did I. Having a car I can use is going to help."

Mark opened his door. The desire to invite Kim into his home was strong. He wanted to show her the den with its brick fireplace, and the way he'd opened up the living and dining room to created a feeling of spaciousness.

But he didn't dare. He was a man who put loyalty to his clients first, so there would always be something he had to keep from Kim Revis. And if they became any closer than they were right now, he didn't know how he would be able to do that. "Call me when you get home," he told her. "I'll feel better knowing you arrived safely."

"Of course."

He wasn't imagining the questions in her voice. Still, Mark helped Kim out of the car and walked her around to the driver's side. As she slipped behind the wheel, he felt a little of the tension go out of him. He'd done her a favor by providing her with transportation and taking her out to dinner. It was the least he could do for the granddaughter of a client.

It was the only thing he dared to do, under the circumstances.

Chapter Five

A little after eight the next morning, Kim left the house and walked down to where she'd left the rental car. She hadn't told Rogan that she'd be there early, but she'd been awake since six and, although she could have spent some time going through her grandmother's possessions, she was too restless for her own company.

Kim didn't know whether to view last night as a beginning, or simply tell herself not to read too much into their shared meal and the pleasant trip out to Mark's place. True, he'd called a half hour after she left to make sure she'd gotten home, but he'd limited his end of the conversation to a reminder of the upcoming town council meeting.

Except for children walking to school, Camp Oro was almost deserted this time of the morning. Although it was a little chilly, Kim drove with her window down, savoring the fresh smells and nodding at a couple of young boys riding skateboards on the sidewalk. Seeing them took her back to her own childhood and served as a reminder of how safe growing up in Camp Oro had been. The only difference was that she'd ridden a bike instead of a skateboard.

The woman volunteer Kim had met yesterday was setting up brochures when Kim walked in the door. Kim had meant only to acknowledge the woman's presence, but the volunteer stopped her. ''I wish I'd known yesterday. You're

Margaret's granddaughter. That woman. She talked me into coming here, and now I'm hooked."

"Grandmother can be like that."

"Don't I know it." The woman smiled. "I don't mind. I just wish Margaret could get here more often. Years ago she used to be here all the time. But then she stopped coming. I guess other things took up her time."

"I'm not surprised," Kim said by way of explanation. "She's involved in too many things for her own good. You wouldn't know where Mr. Coffers is, would you?"

The woman frowned. "I've been in one of the storage rooms. I'm sorry. You might try down the hall."

Kim headed toward the conference room, her footsteps echoed. Before she'd gone more than ten feet, she felt cut off from the only other person sharing this part of the museum with her. She should have waited, come here when there were visitors to take away the silence.

The conference room was empty; for a moment Kim fought an impulse to turn and walk back out the way she'd come. It was ridiculous. Just because the lighting in the room was poor was no reason to wonder what might be in the shadows. Shrugging off her unease with a shaky laugh, Kim closed the door behind her and retraced her steps. She found the volunteer's presence comforting, but she couldn't stall what had to be accomplished today. No one was in the room outside Rogan's office. Kim slid her hands down her thighs, unnecessarily straightening her skirt. It was time to see if Rogan had changed his mind about having her here.

Rogan was on the phone. Kim thought hostility and not surprise touched his features when he looked up at her, but the mood lasted such a brief period of time that the look was gone before she could be certain. Rogan pointed to a chair and then returned to his conversation. Kim didn't pay much attention to what he was saying, something about an upcoming conference and Rogan's inability to commit himself to attending.

"Meetings," Rogan muttered after putting down the receiver. "Meetings because someone thinks there has to be a meeting. Always something taking me from my work. You're here early. What can I do for you, Ms. Revis?"

Kim reminded Rogan that he had promised to find the building's blueprints for her. "I have to have them if I'm going to know where structural beams and the wiring system are. I was hoping I could get started today."

"I wish you'd called." Rogan began shaking old pipe tobacco out of his pipe. "I just had a few minutes to look yesterday. I didn't find anything. I told Stephan that springing you on us when we're so busy—"

Kim almost pointed out that the museum director should know where important documents were stored, but held her tongue. The man was already hostile toward her. It wouldn't do to further fuel his mood. "Then I guess the next best thing would be for me to meet with the security guard. I'd like to know what he considers the most vulnerable areas."

"William isn't here."

"He isn't? What time does he get to work?"

Rogan consulted his watch. "Visitors don't usually start showing up until about ten. I don't punch a time clock for William. Ms. Revis, I know you believe you have a job to do, but I have a full schedule today."

The only thing Kim wanted to do was get out of Rogan's office, but if she let herself be dismissed, it might set a dangerous precedent. "I understand." She made herself smile. "I have a fair idea of how much responsibility lies on your shoulders. I thank you for your time, Mr. Coffers. If you find the blueprints this morning, I'll be in the building."

Rogan was no longer playing with his pipe. "What are you going to do?"

For the first time since she walked in, Kim felt she held the upper hand. "I need to familiarize myself with the physical plant."

"We did that yesterday. I showed you around."

"You gave me a cook's tour." Again Kim made herself smile. "I appreciate that. I also understand that your time is at a premium, and what I need to accomplish will be time-consuming." Kim slowly got to her feet. It was important that Rogan believe she wasn't at all bothered by his dismissal of her. "If you're interested, I'll give you a report on my preliminary findings. Of course you're so busy—"

"I'll make time for you this afternoon."

Kim wasn't ready to give herself a pat on the back, but she did believe she'd made her point with the museum director. She was an independent consultant. She didn't have to wait around for the staff to find time for her.

An hour and a half later Kim had a much clearer concept of the pluses and minuses of the Comstock Museum from a security perspective. Because the museum had only one public entrance, Kim would be recommending an electro-magnetic locking device for the door. She still hadn't come to a final decision about recommendations for protection of specific displays. That would have to wait until she'd talked to the guard and business manager, and seen the wiring blueprints. She'd been looking for both William and Garner while wandering through the museum but hadn't seen either man.

She was debating whether she would have to ask Rogan to find the men for her when Garner appeared at the opposite end of the hall. For a moment he stared blankly at Kim. Then, his smile unfolding slowly, he acknowledged her presence. "I've been outside," he explained as they met in the middle of the hall. "My eyes haven't adjusted to the dark. If I'd known you were going to be here— Where's Rogan? I thought he was supposed to be helping you."

Dismissing her uneasy reaction to the way the large man dominated the dark hall, Kim explained that Rogan was busy. Garner's hair was damp, and he smelled of Ben-Gay. It must be nice to have the kind of job that allowed a workout in the middle of the business day. "I was hoping you and I would have time to discuss things."

"What kind of things?" Garner leaned forward, giving Kim a whiff of breath mint. "If I may make a suggestion—" He rested his hand on Kim's shoulder. "Now that we don't have to put up with the others—"

Kim slipped out from under his hand. There was so much strength in him— "You made it clear yesterday that the budget for security is limited. I need to know what kind of money I'll have to work with."

"On a gorgeous day like this? Wouldn't you rather sit out on the lawn?"

Kim would but not with this too-confident man. "There are national grants specifically earmarked for museum security," she pointed out. "Given the record of thefts here, I don't believe you'll have trouble qualifying for them."

Garner leaned away. Kim was all too aware that he was looking at her only from the neck down. "I hope you know how long it takes to process those grant applications. And there are so many strings attached to those grants—"

"Are you saying you aren't interested in applying?" At this moment Kim would welcome anyone who walked down the hall. She'd prefer to keep this man at a distance.

"Kim, I can apply for grants in my sleep. I've done it enough times."

"Then—"

"Let's talk reality. Even if I put in an application this morning, it'll be months before a decision is reached. In the meantime, we've paid your retainer and have nothing to show for it."

"The museum will have even less to show for it if nothing is done. There's no way these thefts can be kept out of the news much longer. When that happens, people are going to be asking why the staff did nothing."

"We haven't done nothing. We hired you."

"You didn't. The board did."

Garner's plastic smile turned to stone. "You're a hard lady."

"Just realistic, Garner. Are you going to have time to sit down with me and talk finances?"

"Not today. Maybe not until next week."

Kim bit back a retort. She was well within her rights to point out that if he had time for a workout, he had time to meet with her. But any more antagonism between her and the business manager wasn't going to solve anything. Still, she had to make her point. "I don't believe this can wait until next week. When would be the best time for you tomorrow?"

"Evening. Over drinks."

Kim pretended to consider Garner's offer. In truth, that was the last thing she wanted to do. "I'm sorry. I'm busy. We could come here early tomorrow morning. Maybe around seven?"

"I never get to work that early. This museum might pay my salary. It doesn't own me."

"When then? Could you make it around eight?"

Garner wasn't interested in that time, either. He finally agreed to meet with Kim in the afternoon. He repeated his suggestion that it would be more pleasant for them to hold their meeting in a cocktail lounge. "You're single. I'm single. Don't forget that."

Somehow Kim managed to refuse graciously. She returned to the foyer and was about to ask the volunteer whether she'd seen William when the phone rang. After a moment, the woman turned the receiver over to Kim.

"I was going to leave a message for you," Mark was saying. "I have to be in Camp Oro this afternoon. If there's anything you need—"

He was thinking of her. Somehow that made the whole day better. "I appreciate the offer. But you've already done so much by providing me with a car."

"I don't want you stuck at that place without transportation. It's going all right?"

"Fine." Kim was mindful of the receptionist.

"Your grandmother called me this morning."

"She did?" Kim took note of her practical tennis shoes. Someday, somehow, she'd like to be dressed up when she saw Mark. "What did she want?"

Mark's answer was slow in coming. "Not much. We got to talking about getting some of the furniture to her. She says the stuff she's using is driving her crazy. Maybe, I was thinking, there might be some way we could get some workmen to carry at least her bedroom set out to the road. They could take that over and set it up for her."

Kim forced her thoughts on to practical matters. Yes, she didn't see why they couldn't get someone to get the bedroom set around the cave-in. Since she didn't know anything about the local labor force, she agreed to leave that up to Mark. "We can talk about it tonight," she offered. "If you want, I could cook dinner." They could sit out on her grandmother's porch and get to know each other better.

"Tonight? There won't be time."

"Why not?" Kim didn't care what the receptionist might be hearing. "Don't you want—"

"Unfortunately the town council meeting is tonight."

How could she have forgotten? Laughing to cover up her embarrassment, Kim thanked Mark for reminding her. It wasn't until he'd said goodbye that Kim faced reality. Being around Mark did things to her she didn't understand. It would be much safer to see him in a roomful of people.

LIKE GARNER, William Lynch said he was too busy to meet with Kim. "You should have asked me earlier," he said when she finally located the guard in the mining exhibit room. William nodded at two middle-aged couples. "I've got to keep an eye on those folks."

Kim was ready to dispute that claim, but if she did, the visitors might overhear. "I really need your input," she stressed. "I'm sure you know more than the others about what I'll be dealing with."

"I do. Not that they'd admit that."

The police chief had said something about William requesting security training and being turned down. Maybe that explained the tight line he was holding his mouth in. "I'm the one you'll be working with," Kim stressed.

"Maybe."

"What do you mean, maybe?"

"Maybe we'll be working together. Maybe we won't."

Almost before she knew she was going to say them, the words were out. "There's no maybe to it, William. Your cooperation is imperative."

"Is that so? That's a new one."

Kim managed to get the older man to commit to a meeting at four in the afternoon. "Are you sure you'll be there?" Kim questioned. "You were late this morning."

"I'll be there." The security guard wasn't looking at her. "I had business to attend to this morning. Business you wouldn't understand. Ms. Revis, I've got work to do." He turned away, putting an end to the conversation.

KIM DECIDED TO FORGO the temptation of another meal at the ice-cream parlor. Instead she ran into the grocery store for a few items and then parked as close to her driveway as possible. To her surprise, she found only a trio of elementary-school-age boys around the cave-in.

"Aren't you supposed to be in school?" Kim asked as she was getting her groceries out of the car.

"Our teacher said it was all right," explained a boy with enough cowlicks to drive any barber to despair. "He said it was part of our history lesson."

Kim doubted that, but it wasn't her job to herd the boys back to school. Besides, their loud voices, bumping and pushing, and off-the-wall suggestions about what had caused the street to cave in almost distracted her from the hold the maw had over her. Although they hadn't solicited her opinion, Kim explained that a dynamite blast had been ruled out as a cause. "There are old mine tunnels all around this part of town," she explained. "One of them collapsed."

"Yeah?" The largest of the three boys dropped to his knees a few inches from the opening. "Do you think there's gold down there?"

Kim placed her groceries on the hood of the car and stepped forward. The boys' enthusiasm was catching. She'd once been their age. But it was only a hole in the ground, not a prop from a Stephen King movie. "Probably. I don't know how much. Not enough to make us rich."

"You don't know that. There could be millions down there."

"There could."

"Just waiting for someone to pick it up," the boy with the cowlicks offered. "You know what I'd do? I'd buy me a car. An Indy race car."

"What would you do with it?" the boy who'd been quiet so far interrupted. "You can't drive. And there's nowhere in this hick town you could go that fast."

"I wouldn't live here. I'd move to Chicago."

"Chicago?" Kim asked. "It gets pretty cold there in the winter."

"I like the cold. And their football team." The boy leaned on the barrier, staring into the dark. "I wonder how cold it is down there."

"Probably not too cold," Kim offered. The conversation delighted her; for a few minutes she felt ten years old again. "It isn't that far down."

"I wonder if anyone's been inside."

Kim didn't think so. "I think they're waiting for a decision on what to do with the hole."

"I know what I'd do with it," the boy leaning over the opening said. "I'd let people explore it. Wouldn't that be something? Just like Huck Finn and Tom Sawyer."

"That was a cave," Kim tried to explain.

"So what. Boy, I'd love to go down there. Wouldn't you?"

"I don't know," Kim started to say, but the boys weren't interested in her answer, and she certainly wasn't going to tell them that, for her, climbing into the hole wasn't a simple matter. The three were already arguing over the best way to lower themselves into the opening.

How wonderful it was to be young and full of enthusiasm. Still, as much as she enjoyed the company, Kim was concerned because the boy kneeling next to the hole was inside the barriers. She was searching her mind for a tactful way to get him to retreat when Mark pulled up in his Blazer. Still smiling, she joined him. "We're having a discussion about whether there's enough wealth for all of us down there," she told him. Mark was wearing new slacks, a pale green shirt and a darker green tie. He looked wonderful.

"Phillip Dunham, you get away from there. Can't you read?" Mark gave Kim a wink before heading toward the boys. "I know what your dad would do if he caught you here."

"How do you know my dad?"

"I know everything. Now unless the three of you are so brilliant that you've already graduated, I suggest you hightail it back to school."

Kim watched the three boys depart. She was a little sorry that their fun had been interrupted. "You're a spoilsport."

"I know. I also know that something's got to be done before some kid hurts himself."

"Does that mean—" Kim risked another look at Mark. His smoke-green eyes now sparkled. She wouldn't be at all surprised to see him tear off his tie and lower himself into the hole. In fact, the child still lingering in her wanted him to do exactly that. "Are you going to recommend that they repair the street?"

"You know it isn't my job to make recommendations, Kim. Despite what Anthea said, I do not control the council. What are you doing out here? Playing hooky?"

"I might as well." Kim hadn't been able to place enough distance between herself and Garner Dillon. But any space between her and Mark felt like too much. "It's a repeat of yesterday. Everyone keeps putting me off."

Coming out to Camp Oro this afternoon had been a mistake. True, he had a professional reason for being here, but that reason faded before Kim's influence on him. He couldn't deny that trying to sleep after waving Kim off had been an exercise in futility. Mark, who practiced the ethic of weighing every word, every movement, had done something completely spontaneous last night. He didn't want to talk about it; he didn't even want to think about how good it had felt just to be around Kim. "Putting you off?"

"Stalling. You said you had business out here. What is it?"

In a tone he didn't recognize, Mark explained that he would be meeting with an engineer in less than a half hour. "I don't know what we're going to find, but I don't want to go into that meeting tonight knowing no more than I do now about what's down there."

"You're going to climb down there? Really?"

"That's the general idea. Al's pretty excited. I think it's the most interesting thing he's done in a year."

Kim started to fold her arms, but when that didn't feel right, she let them drop back to her sides. No! When push came to shove, the truth was, she didn't want him in that deep, cold hole. "In your suit?" was the only thing she could think of to say.

"No. Not in my suit. I was on my way to city hall to borrow something from the public-works crew. I saw the boys. And you."

"Oh." Had there been an extra emphasis on the last two words? Because everything Mark said affected her in ways she didn't understand, Kim was unable to answer her own question. "Do you . . . you don't have any idea what you'll find?"

"A little." Mark squatted, picked up a stick and started drawing a crude map on the dusty street. "I talked to a local historian this morning. He'd already done the research so it was easy for him to explain. What caved in, as far as Dennis knows, was the main artery. Supposedly there's a fork a few feet farther on. Dennis believes that one of the forks heads due north while the other angles off toward your grandmother's property."

Kim dropped to her knees. Her fingers traced the end of the second fork. "How far does it extend?"

"Dennis isn't sure. Maybe as much as three or four hundred feet."

"I wonder—" Kim rose quickly. "Do you think it's possible that it goes as far as to the house?"

"I have no idea." Mark straightened.

He was standing too close to her. There was no way Kim could think straight while he was doing that and, although she didn't yet understand why, being able to concentrate on what he'd told her was important. "Mark? Let me change my clothes. I want to go down with you and the engineer."

"You—no."

"No?" Despite the danger to her nervous system, Kim squared her shoulders and turned to face Mark. "Why not? You're going down."

"I have a responsibility to gather as much information as I can. You have no reason to be down there."

"Curiosity." This was her talking? Every time she thought about the cave-in she felt chilled. If she had the sense she was born with, she'd heed the warning. Still— "It affects my family's property. It's causing me more of a problem than anyone else."

''Not valid reasons, Kim. I won't jeopardize your safety. Besides, if you were injured, you might sue the town.''

Exasperation effectively eliminated most of the distracting effect Mark had on her. ''I'll tell you what. Give me something to sign that'll absolve the town of all blame. Mark, you're talking to someone who has survived the big, bad city. This—'' she jabbed a finger at the hole ''—is a piece of cake.''

''Absolutely not,'' Mark repeated. ''If I make an exception with you, then other people are going to want to go down.''

Mark had a valid point, enough of one to silence Kim's arguments. She was still upset enough that when he told her he had to go pick up a pair of coveralls, Kim simply shrugged and went to pick up her groceries.

She set them back down again as soon as Mark was out of sight. Then she reached into the Honda's glove compartment for a flashlight. For the better part of a minute, Kim leaned against the car, lost in thought. Fighting a million emotions. She understood that Mark was concerned for her safety. The lawyer in him was doing the talking. What he didn't understand was that she had a monkey on her back and getting rid of that was a lot more important to her than whether she got dirt on her clothes. Kim had no doubt that the three boys would have eventually talked themselves into going down into the tunnel. If they could do it, so could she.

Still, it was another minute before Kim actually pushed herself away from the car and faced what had been mocking, and challenging, and even threatening her. ''Think you've got me buffaloed, don't you?'' she asked the hole. ''Think I'm chicken, don't you?''

There was no answer.

In a way, Kim wished there had been. That way she could have let fear make the decision. But she was staring down at a simple, shadowy hole leading to an ancient tunnel. There was nothing mysterious or sinister about that. Dozens of men had dug channels just like this one; surely none of them had been kept awake nights with thoughts of clammy hands reaching out of the dirt.

This was insane! All she had to do was crawl on her hands and knees to the edge of the hole, lower herself over the side and jump to the earthen bottom. Piece of cake.

Of course Mark would be angry, but she would be ready to come out by the time he arrived with a ladder or whatever he and the engineer were going to use.

Kim couldn't concentrate on Mark. When all was said and done, her decision was based on nothing more than a need to prove something to herself. To put her unreasonable fear behind her. Without thinking about it further, Kim lowered herself into the hole.

It was colder underground than she'd thought it would be. Still, because the sky was directly overhead, Kim was able to keep contact with the world she knew. After a minute, her eyes adjusted to the gloom. Behind her, dirt and debris hid much of the tunnel, but she was facing a perfectly preserved corridor. It was at least three and a half feet in diameter. The soil was packed clay. Kim picked up a chunk of concrete and jabbed at the wall. It was like trying to chip away rock. "Good," Kim said aloud. Her voice echoed. "Good and solid." She almost believed her words.

Kim dropped to her knees, snapped on her flashlight and beamed it into the corridor. As far as she could see, the opening continued at the same height. She was only going to go a few feet, just far enough that she would have some idea what the miners experienced.

At first Kim couldn't hear because of the pounding in her chest. But as cool silence surrounded her, she grew a little more comfortable with her surroundings. She was passing her self-imposed test; the boys, and the brave girl she'd been, would be proud of her. Twice more she tested the walls of the tunnel to convince herself that it was hard packed.

When she turned around, she could no longer see the opening.

"Just a few more feet," Kim muttered. "The fork has to be here somewhere." Twenty feet farther on she found it. Both forks appeared to be identical, but, because her sense of direction told her that the one to the left was more likely to head toward her grandmother's property, she went that way. The tunnel slanted downward slightly and then leveled out. The air was stale but not bad enough that Kim couldn't breathe in comfort. Almost in comfort, Kim amended. Her nerves were totally alive, and she had to keep talking to herself. Otherwise, the thing called fear that continued to claw at her throat might gain the upper hand. If it did, she might start screaming.

Kim would have turned back if the sides hadn't begun to widen out. After another twenty or twenty-five feet, she was entering a room. The sense of space eased her somewhat. She guessed that whoever had dug the tunnel had come across enough evidence of gold that he'd concentrated his digging on this area.

She was now in a space as large as a small bedroom. The ceiling was high enough that she could almost stand upright. Still, Kim remained on her hands and knees. The room bothered her; there were too many shadowed spots. The walls were rough cut as if someone had hacked in one spot for a while before turning to another. Kim turned her flashlight on an area of the wall close to her, her untrained eyes seeking some sign of gold.

Nothing. Kim sensed the long-ago miner's frustration, his despair and fear. Most of all she sensed fear. Self-control? It was elusive, almost nonexistent.

Kim began to scramble backward. She'd been a fool to come here. What was she trying to prove? That she could hold her own with some preadolescent boys? She was trying to turn around so she could head back the way she'd come when her flashlight beam revealed something in a far corner of the room. Kim swallowed down whatever was trying to spread itself through her and held the flashlight trained on the corner. Something was definitely there. Something—

Oh, God! Kim forgot to breathe. Her heart thudded painfully; her pulse pounded in her temples. "It can't be!" Her voice surprised her. Kim tried again. "Stephen King? This isn't some sick joke of yours, is it?" After swallowing, Kim tried to speak again. This time she couldn't get the words out.

There was no mistake. She was looking at a skeleton.

Kim had no idea how long she stood frozen in place. She couldn't breathe; she couldn't think. A skeleton! Not in her worst nightmares—

Gradually Kim gained mastery over her fear. She was a professional, not a frightened child. She'd crawled into the past. What she was looking at had happened years ago. It couldn't touch her now.

Still, she would give anything not to be where she was.

Slowly, not sure where the courage came from, Kim inched forward. Now that she was closer, her curiosity surfaced. Who? How? When? The skeleton was remarkably intact. She saw that it was human and adult sized. There were a few remnants of clothing clinging to the bones, but the clothes had so disintegrated that she had no idea what the man or woman had been wearing when he or she had died.

Something glinted under the glare of Kim's flashlight. She was first startled and then curious. She crept closer until, if she was so inclined, she could have touched the skeleton. A rusted pocketknife lay a few inches beyond the finger bones.

"Who's in there? Whoever you are, you're not supposed to be."

Kim jumped. A cry died in her throat. Mark! "What—" she tried. She tried again. "It's me. Kim."

"Kim? Damn it, I told you—" The voice was coming closer.

Kim didn't know what prompted her to grab the knife and stick it in her pocket. Maybe, she told herself later, she just wanted some souvenir from this experience.

Mark wasn't alone. With him was a wiry, slightly built man dressed, like Mark, in faded green overalls. The men were wearing hard hats with powerful lights attached to them. As soon as they entered the room, Kim and the skeleton were bathed in light.

Chapter Six

Mark's eyes and thoughts went, not to the pile of bones in the corner, but the wide-eyed woman looking at him. He didn't even notice the skeleton. For now there was only Kim. Anger, protectiveness, and something he either didn't understand or didn't want to admit washed over him. He should be furious at finding her down here. Instead he wanted to pull her against him and hold her until he had convinced himself that she was safe. Then... Mark wasn't going to deal with what he wanted to do after that.

"You're not supposed to be down here."

"It's too late for that, Mark. Sue me if you have to."

Mark still wanted to embrace Kim, but it was easier to let himself be angry. "I might. What if the tunnel had caved in?"

Kim was sitting cross-legged on the dirt. Her slacks were soiled. "I checked it," she was telling him. Her breathing was ragged, making a lie of her simple words. "It's solid."

"You don't know that. It could—"

"Mark! I don't want to argue with you." Kim nodded to acknowledge the man with Mark, but didn't take time to speak to him. "I found something."

The wiry man had moved around Mark and was leaning over the skeleton. "Would you look at that." Al whistled. "This is straight out of Edgar Allan Poe."

"I—I wonder what it's doing down here." It was easier talking to the other man than trying to face Mark.

Mark crawled alongside the engineer. He didn't speak, but Kim could hear his breathing. Startled by his angry reaction, she looked at him, but his thoughts were hidden from her. "Mark? Do you have any idea who it might be?"

"No."

The room had seemed to warm when Mark entered it. With the clipped word, it cooled again. "What's wrong?" Kim asked.

"Wrong? Nothing's wrong."

You're lying to me. "I wonder how long it's been here?" Kim said because she needed to fill the silence. "Years. Do you think he might have been a miner?" She directed her question at the other man.

"It's anybody's guess at this point, Ms. Revis. Makes you wonder, though, doesn't it? I mean, people don't usually crawl off into a tunnel to die. I wonder— Do you think it could have been murder?"

"Al. You're letting your imagination get the best of you." Mark's voice was sharper than he wanted it to be. But despite being known for his ability to think in a packed courtroom, he was unable to think past the stark reality of what they'd found. Anything, anything would have been better than this.

"Maybe." Al Strausberg touched the skeleton's foot but didn't try to move it. "But if he had a heart attack or something, why didn't someone come down after him?"

Kim wasn't interested in the engineer's theories. Mark had backed away from the skeleton and was peering into the tunnel that extended beyond the room. Kim crawled after him. She waited until they were side by side, staring into the long, darkening corridor. "You don't like this, do you?" she asked gently.

"No. I don't."

"What is it?" In another heartbeat, she would touch him. "Don't you like enclosed spaces?"

Mark could have lied and told her she was right, but he couldn't do that. He first removed his hard hat and then drew the flashlight out of Kim's fingers. Al was engrossed in the skeleton. Mark could tell Kim—no, he couldn't.

Someday his silence would trap him; Mark had no doubt of that. The only question was, when. But that time hadn't come yet, and what time he had with Kim Revis was suddenly very, very special to him.

She had a raw courage that fascinated him and a bullheadedness that maddened him. She was intelligent and strong and rooted in reality. She had inherited her grandmother's gentleness as well as her complexity. Margaret was one of his favorite clients, and her granddaughter was quickly becoming just as important to him.

Kim was waiting. He sensed her anticipation, her hesitancy. Although they were in shadow, he knew she was turned toward him. If he reached out, he would touch her cheeks. Her mouth was only inches away.

Mark reached. His fingers tasted her cheeks and stayed there only momentarily. He was exploring, absorbing the warmth of Kim's throat, the strength in her shoulders, the long, smooth column of her arms.

She was trembling.

"Don't be afraid," he told her. His voice didn't carry.

"I'm not."

She felt it, too. The electricity building in them was being shared. He should turn from Kim now and return to safety, but it was already too late for that. He'd touched her, and her breath was on his throat, and he was drawn to her.

He couldn't tell her that. They didn't know each other well enough. Mark wasn't sure they ever would. But they could take this moment. Even with the county engineer a few feet away, he could draw Kim next to him and take a few moments of pleasure. Sweet sharing.

Kim was frightened. This fear was nothing like what she'd felt when she came across the skeleton. Now she was afraid of herself.

She felt something deep within her reach out for Mark. This need was beyond her capacity to understand, a power with a life and need of its own. She wanted to taste and touch and smell, and draw him to her. She needed his lips against hers, their arms reaching for each other.

A touch, a kiss, that's all it was. But in that touch and kiss, everything changed.

"What do we do? Call the police, I guess."

Al's question cut through the whirling of Kim's thoughts. She felt Mark turning away and watched as he put the hard hat back on. "The police. We don't have any choice, do we?"

"You don't want to?"

Mark's sigh sounded too much like a groan. He pressed his hand to his forehead. "I was just thinking, I wish we could leave whoever it is in peace. He was doing fine before we got here."

Despite the chance that Al might see, Kim squeezed Mark's hand. It was a beautiful sentiment from a man who lived his life surrounded by laws. "I agree," she said. "He's been here so long, it's a shame he can't stay."

"Talk about sentimentalists," Al laughed. "The next thing, the two of you are going to bring flowers. I wonder—how much do you think the police can tell about the cause of death?"

"What does it matter?" Mark left Kim and crawled close to Al. He trained his light on the skeleton, studying it. His face was in shadows. "They'll send it to the state crime lab. Something this old, it's not going to have much priority. There won't be any dental records."

"Too bad bones can't talk. Mark, why do you think he was left here?"

Mark took so long to answer that Kim's alerted senses became even more alarmed. "I don't know why he's here. Al, no one's been in this tunnel since the 1930s. No one's going to put those puzzle pieces together now."

Al was still throwing out possibilities regarding the skeleton while the three returned to the entrance to the cave-in. Kim followed Mark with Al bringing up the rear. She felt much more secure now that she was flanked by the men. Occasionally the knife poked against her hip, reminding Kim of what she was keeping from Mark. She already regretted her rash action, but now it was too late to explain why she'd hidden the knife.

That wasn't it at all, Kim admitted. She would have shown the men the knife if Mark's mood had been fathomable. But he was edgy and distracted. If she was responsible for that mood—

Mark and Al had lowered a ladder into the hole. Although she didn't need help, Kim accepted Mark's hand as she emerged. He held her against him so long that she became alarmed. When she looked up at him, Mark's mouth was smiling, but his eyes weren't. "Going down there, that was a foolish stunt."

"So you keep saying." There were two Marks, one passionate and exciting, the other distant and a little frightening. "It turned out all right."

"All right? Yeah. All right. Do you have everything you need for your report to the council, Al?"

"I think so. The tunnel's in pretty solid shape, but I don't know about the entrance. It wouldn't take much for the rest of this part of the street to collapse. I want to make a point of that. One question. Do you think we should mention what we found?"

"No," Mark answered quickly. "Look, there're going to be reporters there tonight. If word of this gets out, we're going to have a hell of a time keeping people out."

"But—" Kim began. She was interrupted before she could voice a protest.

"I'm reporting it to the police, Kim. They're the only ones who need to know." Mark's voice was lifeless. "I know what my duty is."

Kim stepped back and then forced herself to stop. She might be drawn to Mark. That didn't mean she was foolish enough to ignore the warning bell going off inside her. Until today she'd thought of Mark as an honest, straightforward man. Now a darker side was emerging. Until she better understood that side, she would be ruled with her head and not her heart. "I'm sure you do. I wasn't questioning your ethics."

"I'm glad to hear that. But something's bothering you."

"Bothering? Maybe so. The way you're acting—"

"How am I acting? Kim, I asked you not to go down there."

That was it? Mark's concern for her was the answer to his mood? "I'm sorry," she told him. "But I was letting the cave-in do a number on me. I had to conquer it. Can you understand that?"

"You were afraid of it?"

"Don't laugh at me. Please."

A cautious man would let Kim go to her house alone, but this afternoon Mark didn't want to be a cautious man. He decided to take the conversation in a safe direction. "I've been talking to Charles," Mark told her. "He said he was going to try to use some of his connections to help you go ahead with your work at the museum. I may be able to help, too. There are two, maybe three local firms that might be able to provide the electronics you're likely to need. I'm sorry. I meant to bring the list with me."

"You didn't have to do that."

"I know."

A sane woman wouldn't have anything to do with this moody man. But right now Kim didn't feel like being sane.

"I don't have much to do here," Kim told him. "I could follow you back to your office."

"You don't have anything else to do today?"

Kim explained about the meeting she'd set up with the security guard. "It's not until 4:00 p.m."

"Who else is going to be there?"

"Who? No one."

"I don't like that."

Kim wanted to brush aside Mark's concern. All she wanted was to concentrate on going to his office. Being with him. "He's all right, Mark. A little strange maybe, but nothing I can't handle."

"You don't know that. Charles said something. Both of you think the thefts are an inside job, don't you?"

"I don't know what I think at the moment, Mark. I don't believe in jumping to conclusions."

"But what you've learned points in that direction, doesn't it?"

"Yes," Kim had to admit.

"That's what I thought. Watch yourself around William. Do that for me, will you?"

There was only one answer Kim could give Mark.

AN HOUR LATER Kim had dropped off her groceries, changed her clothes and was sitting in Mark's office while he conferred with his secretary. He hadn't said anything more about the security guard and neither had she. It hadn't been necessary.

She was more than a little impressed with his office. It was located in a new building less than a block from the new courthouse. He shared the building with several other attorneys but wasn't in partnership with any of them. Two walls of his office were taken up with cabinets containing files while a bookcase on another wall contained an impressive array of legal manuals. His desk was a beautifully restored antique so large she didn't know how they'd gotten it through the door. In contrast, his telephone system was the most technologically advanced available. A stereo played softly in the background.

Kim had no intention of intruding on attorney/client confidentiality. She was only wondering if the list he was going to give her might be in sight when she glanced at his desk. He'd been working on several files; the folders took up most of the available space. Several loose pieces of paper lay on top of the folders. A message on yellow notepaper caught her attention. Margaret Revis had called a couple of hours ago and wanted Mark to return her call.

"I'm sorry you had to wait," Mark said as he entered his office. "I'm due in court tomorrow. Nervous clients. They've already called my secretary three times."

He was the consummate lawyer again. While she ran up to the house, Mark had turned in his overalls. He was in his environment, professionally dressed, in control. The man who'd made her rethink everything she'd believed about herself an hour ago no longer existed or, if he did, Attorney Mark Stockton had placed that man behind bars.

"Do you have to do much hand-holding?" Kim sank into a chair and folded her hands in her lap. He was calm. She could be the same—at least she could pretend.

"A lot. Actually—" Mark glanced at his desk, shrugged and turned back to Kim. "I'd rather have nervous clients. They're the ones who are thinking. If you ever find yourself up against the legal system, don't let your lawyer do your thinking for you."

Kim found it easy to laugh. "I have no intention of being on either side of the legal system. But if I do, I'll hire you."

"You haven't seen me in court. Maybe you wouldn't want me."

She'd been wrong; Mark wasn't enough of an attorney for her to forget what else he was. She stared at her hands and watched her knuckles turn white. The room filled with

Mark; he became the air she breathed. "You—my grand-mother called you."

Mark glanced at his desk and then picked up the message from Margaret Revis. "She says I'm never in my office."

"Are you going to call her?"

"Later." Mark dropped the piece of paper and rum-maged around until he found a sheet of legal sized paper and handed it to Kim. "Three companies. The first two I know. Their reputations are first class. I don't know much about the third one, but Judge Winters had them do some work for him, and he swears by them. I hope this'll help."

Kim took the offered paper, folded it and placed it in her purse. "It will. Thank you. You didn't have to go to that much trouble."

"I wanted to. Kim, maybe I have no right asking. All right, I have no right asking, but I'm going to anyway."

Kim waited; her heart wanted his question to be per-sonal; her mind knew otherwise.

"I don't want you going down in the cave-in anymore. I'd like to have your word on that."

He cares about my safety, Kim thought. This is more than concern for the town's liability. "I won't. I can't imagine ever wanting to," she was able to tell him honestly. The moment of intimacy built and Kim acted on it. "I wasn't going to. I didn't mean to sneak behind your back, but Mark—I'm going to sound crazy if I say this."

Mark stood and started around his desk. "Say it."

He was standing over her now, his presence both com-forting and challenging. Kim wanted him to understand some of the forces that motivated her. "I take pride in who I am. Maybe it sounds conceited, but I don't believe there are many things I can't accomplish if I put my mind to it. When I saw that hole—I was afraid of it. I said that al-ready, didn't I?"

Mark took her hands. The gesture was comforting and a great deal more. "What were you afraid of?"

"I don't know." Kim tried to laugh, but the sound didn't come out the way she'd wanted it to. "I think that's why I did what I did. I didn't know what I was afraid of, and that made me mad. It—" She looked at her hands. They were safely in Mark's; at this moment, everything about her felt safe. "Every time I looked at that damn hole I felt as if it was mocking me. It knew I was afraid."

"It's just a hole, Kim."

"I know that. Now. I told you I'd sound crazy. I just knew I couldn't let that thing get the best of me."

Mark nodded. He leaned forward, but the kiss she was waiting for wasn't forthcoming. Instead he brushed his lips against her forehead and then retreated. "I'll remember that about you. You aren't a woman to back down from anything."

"Do you understand?"

"Yes, Kim. I understand."

MUSEUM GUARD William Lynch was drinking coffee in the staff meeting room when Kim found him that afternoon.

"I've been looking for you," Kim explained in what she hoped was a friendly tone. "You're a hard man to find."

William turned slowly from his study of his coffee to look at her. Every move he made seemed slow. "I'm not hiding."

"I know you aren't. It's just a figure of speech." Although she and William were the only ones in the room, the air felt close and tight. Kim sat down near William, taking note of the ring of drying coffee staining the table. She hadn't forgotten Mark's warning but discounted it because she knew there were others in the building. "I'd like to talk about yesterday."

"What about yesterday?" William licked his finger and tried to rub away the dried coffee. The effort took the better part of a minute.

"Rogan, Garner and Anthea did a lot of talking. You didn't have much to say."

"There wasn't nothin' to say. Nothin' anyone wanted to hear."

"I don't agree, William." Mark had leaned toward her and made communication possible. Maybe the same gesture would work with the drawn-looking guard. "You're the one who's down in the trenches. Garner might be able to talk about finances, but you know the museum's vulnerable and strong points."

"No one wants my opinion."

"I do."

Kim waited. She could tell that William was thinking things over. To say more now might divert him from his thoughts. Finally he gave up his attack on the coffee stain. "Do you know what this makes me look like? Things are going out of this place under my nose. I do my job, Ms. Revis. Damn it, I try. But no one believes me."

"You're being asked to do the impossible." When William blinked, Kim went on. "This place is huge. It's full of artifacts worth hundreds of thousands of dollars. We'd all like to believe that people are honest, that their only reasons for coming here are to look at what's being displayed. But that isn't reality."

"Tell me about it."

"I know," Kim agreed. "There's only so much one person can do in a building with an almost nonexistent security system."

"Yeah? Then why is everyone blaming me?"

"Is that what you think?" Kim asked. She wanted to get down to the specifics of the building's vulnerability, but until she and William were working together, that would be impossible.

"That's what everyone thinks. Why shouldn't I?"

"Because that kind of thinking will only defeat us." Kim put her emphasis on the last word. She waited a moment and then went on. "We can't help what happened yesterday or last week. The only thing we can deal with is today and try to prevent another theft tomorrow. That's what I need you for."

William leaned back in his chair. His thin body seemed barely strong enough to complete the movement. His eyes were small and placed close together but capable of probing. Capable of judging. "You want us to work together?"

"Yes. I need you."

"Only one person needs me, Ms. Revis. And that one ain't you." William was on his feet before Kim knew it was going to happen. "Let me tell you something. You go talk to Garner Dillon and that man who calls himself a director. Ask them what they pay me? Barely a cent over minimum wage. Ms. Revis, I'm sixty-three years old. I've been working hard all my life. I used to make damn good money, but now that I'm old and stuck in this town, I'm being taken advantage of. I'm not here because I want to be. I'm working because I don't have a choice. Loyalty?" Spittle formed at the corners of William's mouth. His face reddened. "I'm the wrong person to talk about loyalty to."

Kim was on her feet, too. She'd reached deep down inside for courage already once today. She could do it again. "Maybe not," she acknowledged. "If what you say is true, you are being taken advantage of."

"I don't wanna talk about it, Ms. Revis. I've talked until I'm blue in the face. The cops around here, they laugh at me. I tried to get the training. No money, they kept telling me. No money. I'm not going to beg for a raise, and I'm sure as hell not going to bail out this damn museum. You think I should be fired, go head, get me fired."

"I can't." Kim was standing toe-to-toe with the man. He loomed over her, but he was so slight that she didn't feel threatened. "It's not my job to hire or fire even if I wanted to. And I don't," she emphasized. "What I want is your help."

"Listen." William rocked back on his heels and then leaned forward again. "I've got all I can do to hold body and soul together and take care of my brother. There isn't enough of me left to string up booby traps or whatever you're thinking of putting in here."

Kim allowed herself to be sidetracked. "What about your brother?"

"Nothing. None of your business." William started toward the door.

Kim stopped him. His forearm was bony, but surprisingly strong. "I don't agree, Mr. Lynch. You're angry and frustrated. It's not good to hold all that inside you."

"What do you know?" William pulled free. "Let me tell you something, Ms. Revis. You and this museum and those people looking down their noses at me, can all go to hell."

KIM HAD STOPPED reacting emotionally to the argument with William by the time she walked into her grandmother's house. The radio in the kitchen cut through the echo of William's angry voice but couldn't stop thoughts of what Kim had found out after the guard left. From the volunteer at the front desk, Kim had learned that William lived with his older brother. Toby Lynch was a step away from needing a nursing home, but William, through love or loyalty or some other motive, refused to give up responsibility for his care. William said little about his life beyond work, but the volunteer had a friend who worked in the local doctor's office where Toby went for treatment. It was so sad, the volunteer said. Those two old men living together with no one to help them and medical bills that wouldn't quit. Kim kicked off her shoes and headed for the kitchen. The telephone rang.

"Honey, I've been trying to reach you all afternoon. I called the museum, but they didn't know where you were." Margaret Revis sounded concerned.

Kim shook her head at the incompetence of whoever hadn't gotten the message to her, but didn't bother her grandmother with the details. "I was going to call you. So much has been happening."

"I'm sure it has. Kim, how is it going?"

"How?" Kim laughed, hoping her grandmother couldn't hear the strain she was feeling. "Let's just say it's been a three-ring circus."

"Were you at the museum today?"

Kim thought that a rather strange question, but answered anyway. "I got to see Mark's office. It looks as if you've chosen a successful attorney. What did you want to talk to him about?"

"What?"

Kim wished she could have taken the words back. Margaret's business with her attorney was none of her concern. Still, now that she'd started, she had to finish. Briefly she explained about noticing the telephone message while she'd been waiting for Mark.

"That man is so hard to get a hold of. I certainly hope you don't have to spend much time at the museum."

"It's my job, Grandmother." Kim sat down and reached for her aching instep. Something about this conversation wasn't right; she just wished she could put her finger on what it was.

"It's so stuffy in there. So much junk piling up everywhere."

"Artifacts. Antiques," Kim laughed. "At least have the good grace to call them by their proper names."

"But you don't have to wade through all that stuff, do you?"

"No. Of course not. Maybe, if I have time—"

"Don't bother," Margaret interrupted. "It'd just bore you."

"That doesn't sound like you. I met a volunteer who said you used to practically live there."

"Used to," Margaret repeated. "I can't be bothered any-more. I just... Well...I'd much rather have you out among people. What about dinner, dear? I'd love to see you."

Because she sensed something close to desperation in her grandmother's voice, Kim told her grandmother about the meeting tonight and promised to come see her tomorrow.

KIM ELECTED TO WALK to the historic building where coun-cil meetings were held. After the emotional ups and downs of the day, she was hungry for any kind of physical activ-ity. She was glad for a few minutes alone, watching the sun set around the now empty streets. She wanted to find a sense of peace. Unfortunately it didn't come.

The long, narrow building was rapidly filling with peo-ple. Although she would have preferred the anonymity of sitting in the back of the room, it was important that she sit where she could hear and participate. Next to her a couple of men were talking about yet another break in the town's ancient water system. "There's no way around it," one of them was saying. "They're going to have to raise the tax base. Either that or the town's going to fall apart."

"It'll never pass. People'll scream bloody murder. Taxes are high enough as they are."

"Not compared to other communities this size," the first replied. "I've seen this list from the council of govern-ments—"

"I've seen it, too," the second man interrupted. "You know what happened the last time the council tried to raise the tax base. They just about got thrown out of office. No one's going to try that again very soon."

"You know what the problem is, don't you? People here, they think they can support the town on the money tourists bring in. It isn't working."

Kim felt like an eavesdropper, but she couldn't help it. Camp Oro's problems interested her. Even though she was nothing more than an alumnus back for a brief time, she felt involved in the town. As more people entered the room, Kim glanced around. She recognized Charles and, beside the police chief, his slight, curly haired wife. Sandy grinned and smiled at Kim. Kim returned the smile, disappointed that there wasn't room close to the front for Sandy and Charles to sit next to her. Still, having Charles and Sandy in the same room made her feel as if she'd never left Camp Oro.

A door opened behind the area reserved for council members. Three men and a woman emerged and took their seats behind the horseshoe-shaped table. Then Mark entered the room.

Kim lost interest in what the two men next to her were saying. Mark was in his environment, a smiling, confident man leaning over the middle-aged councilwoman and eliciting a soft laugh from her. He patted another man on the shoulder and shook hands with Josh Bertrum as the mayor made his way to his chair.

Mark's eyes were sweeping the now packed room. He nodded a time or two, but it wasn't until his eyes found hers that their restless movement ceased. "Hi," he mouthed.

Kim wanted to look around to see if anyone had noticed their silent communication, but she needed to keep contact with Mark even more. She wanted to ask him if he'd called her grandmother, and if the police had gone in after the skeleton yet. More than that, she wanted to ask if he would come over to her place later tonight.

Kim barely noticed when the mayor used his gavel to silence the crowd. The recording secretary read the minutes of the last meeting, but that didn't hold Kim's interest. Her mind drifted while some ongoing budget items were discussed. Mark was leaning forward, concentrating on what was being said.

Someone was making room for himself between Kim and the man to her right. She glanced at him, and then blinked in recognition. Garner Dillon was pressing his hard shoulders against hers, infringing on her space. "Fancy seeing you here." Garner's teeth flashed. "Actually I knew you'd be here."

"Oh."

"Yeah. I saw you walking here. I'll bet you wouldn't do that if we were in San Francisco. Not safe, you know."

Kim, who was less than relaxed with Garner sitting beside her, only gave him a half smile.

Garner either didn't notice or ignored her reaction. "Big excitement. It's going to be interesting watching the council on the hot seat. I see even Rogan managed to show up." He nodded to indicate a spot behind him. Kim turned to see the director sitting three rows behind her. Sitting next to him was an extremely attractive, slender, middle-aged woman.

She turned back toward Garner. "I thought the museum didn't concern itself with town business."

"That's the public policy. However, it beats TV, and I knew you were going to be here."

"Oh." Kim took a deep breath, picking her next words carefully. "Are you interested in the cave-in?"

"Why not. I'd like to see whether the council can make up its mind tonight or if it decides to study things to death."

The next item on the agenda for the council was a report on the fire department's need for new tires for one of the two fire trucks. After a ten-minute discussion that centered around the lack of money for repairs or upkeep, the fire chief got his point across that the town really had no option if the fire department was going to stay in operation. Finally the councilwoman moved to appropriate the necessary funds.

"Money, or the lack of it, is the name of the game around here, isn't it?" Garner whispered. When he was done speaking, his body remained angled toward Kim's. His breath was too sweet, his body language possessive.

Kim shifted away uneasily. The mayor was speaking. The next and only other item on the agenda was a discussion of the damage done to Rich Gulch Street. "We were fortunate the last time," Josh Bertrum began. "That time it was the post office's parking lot. We didn't have to pay for the repairs. Now, not only are we going to have to foot the bills, but there appears to be organized objection to repairing the street. Harden, why don't you present your proposal."

Kim watched a thin, dark-haired man in a three-piece suit make his way to the microphone set up for the audience. "Community pride group," Garner muttered. "Bunch of busybodies with no idea what they're doing."

So this was the man responsible for the resistance to filling up the hole. Kim leaned forward, concentrating. "What does he do?"

"Investments, he says. Laundering money if the rumors are to be believed. Tough man. Hates being crossed."

Harden Langford's voice was soft, but the man was articulate. He occasionally referred to his notes as he threw out figures regarding projected increase in tourist trade should the cave-in be developed and billed as a local attraction. His estimate was that it would cost the town slightly less than a thousand dollars to construct a stairway, which would allow visitors into the hole. He'd consulted another engineer who, without having been into the tunnel, had assured the community pride group that there was no danger of the ground giving way as long as vehicles were kept off the road. Charging five dollars per person to go into the hole for a guided tour would significantly increase the town's revenues.

Harden stepped to a blackboard where a map of area streets had been drawn. "Traffic can be easily rerouted to California Street. There aren't any commercial businesses on that block of Rich Gulch. The one house on the south side of the street is so situated that a driveway can be constructed for them on California Street. I've already talked to the owner. He's amenable to the suggestion. I'm talking about a major attraction, Your Honor. A way of putting Camp Oro on the map and relieving its financial problems.

We aren't going to get another opportunity like this again. The whole town will lose out if we don't take advantage of it."

Several council members had questions that Harden answered confidently. If Harden's figures were to be believed, the town could easily bring in enough additional revenue that there wouldn't be a need to increase the tax base. Mark reported that the town's insurance company hadn't flatly turned down the proposal.

Kim rose to her feet and waited to be acknowledged. When all eyes were on her, she walked to the map and pointed out where the driveway to her grandmother's house began. She focused on Charles and Sandy, glad to have friends in the audience. "Mr. Harden is right that the house on the other side of the street isn't going to be adversely impacted if a new driveway is constructed. However, what he failed to point out is that presently the only way I can get to *my* house is by walking. And my car is trapped on the wrong side of the cave-in. What happened is an accident, destruction of a street that should be repaired, not exploited." She waited until she was sure she had everyone's attention and then continued her plea. "The accident has done more than inconvenience me. My grandmother, who owns the house, wants to sell it. As things stand, she has a worthless piece of property."

"Ms. Revis, what do you believe the property is worth?"

Intent on the point she hoped to make, Kim reacted only slightly to Mark's question. "I'm not sure. The home was built in the 1940s, and although it has been maintained, there has been no major updating. It sits on two acres."

"You say the property is for sale. If it were possible for the town to buy it, then would your concerns be resolved?"

"Why would the town want to do that?" Kim asked.

"I'm just trying to make the council aware of its options, Ms. Revis. If your grandmother received fair value for her home, that would leave the town free to use or not use the property as it saw fit. It's just a possibility. I'm not sure there's money in the budget for the purchase.''

"I don't understand. Why would the town want to buy a house it can't use? A home is to be lived in, not allowed to decay.''

"That wasn't my point. I've been looking at the town map. It's possible to cut a new entrance through the trees so the house could be reached from the street to the south. Once that was done, the council could elect to resell the house.''

Kim hated the thought of cutting down any trees for a road. "It would be much easier to simply fill up the hole and reopen Rich Gulch Street.''

"Perhaps. I'm speaking as an attorney, Ms. Revis. I would be remiss if I didn't pursue all options.''

Mark was right, of course, but Kim didn't see this as an option. Her grandmother's house should have someone living in it, not be closed up for however long it took the town to get around to building a long driveway that would alter much of the property's charm. She'd grown up exploring those woods. She didn't want that to change. And there was another issue, her car. She couldn't go without it indefinitely.

A member of the council asked Kim if she was pushing for a decision tonight. When she didn't immediately answer, the man pointed out that when they were discussing thousands of dollars, the council had a responsibility to the town to move slowly. Certainly she could use a rental car a little longer.

"I understand that,'' Kim managed. "What do you consider a reasonable amount of time? A week. Two.''

"Perhaps more,'' Mark supplied. "The community pride group's proposal needs to be carefully considered.''

"And my situation? Will it be given the same consideration?''

"Of course. Was there more you wanted to say?''

Frustrated, Kim could only shake her head and sit down. Although Garner praised the way she had handled things, Kim barely acknowledged him. She kept looking at Mark, waiting for something, anything from him. Mark, however, was telling the council about his exploration of the tunnel with an engineer earlier in the day. The engineer Mark relied on wasn't as optimistic as the community pride engineer that the tunnel, particularly around the cave-in itself, was structurally sound. From that the discussion turned to estimates from the public-works crew as to the cost of filling in the hole and resurfacing the street. The council threw figures back and forth for the better part of an hour, but came to no decision.

"I'm not a betting man," Garner said as the meeting was breaking up, "but I'll wager that they're leaning toward turning this into a carnival act. All they can think about is how much money all those supposed tourists are going to bring in."

Kim had to give Garner his due. She agreed that the commercialization of the cave-in sounded like a circus to her, too. "Someone needs to challenge Harden Langford's statistics. There's no way he can determine how many people are going to come see a hole in the ground." She slung her purse over her shoulder. "And if he thinks I'm going to roll over and die, he has another think coming. I've just begun to fight."

"A fight? Yeah, I guess you're capable. Just remember something, Kim. Sometimes you get thrown in a ring with someone a hell of a lot bigger than you. If that happens, you'd better bail out before it's too late."

Kim shrugged off Garner's comment. A moment later she was refusing his less-than-subtle invitation to join him at the local tavern for a drink. Garner was backing away when Charles and Sandy joined her. "Welcome back," Sandy said after the two women finished hugging each other. "There's nothing like jumping in with both feet, is there?"

Kim had to agree. "Do you usually come to these meetings?" she asked Sandy.

"Not too often. It's too hard to find someone who'll keep an eye on the boys. Look, I've got to get back to them, but we have to get together while you're in town. The stories I could tell you about that bunch we ran around with— Why don't I call you tomorrow?"

Kim nodded. "Sounds good to me."

A minute later Kim was drinking in deep breaths of cool night air. People were gathered outside the meeting hall talking, but Kim wasn't interested in attempting to join any of the conversations. It hadn't taken her long to gain an understanding of small-town politics. Unless she knew which side of the fence people were on, she was well-advised to keep her opinions to herself. And she didn't think it would do any good to wait for Mark. The last she'd seen of him, he was surrounded.

Camp Oro was different by night. With cars and shoppers gone, Kim was able to bridge the gap between the present and the gold rush days. Replicas of gaslights cast gentle shadows over the buildings. Kim's shoes made no sound as she wandered aimlessly down the sidewalk looking in the windows. She stopped at a shop featuring gold jewelry that had been vacant all the time she was growing up. As soon as she saw the window display of a miner crouched over a stream, she lost all thoughts of what she'd been doing a few minutes ago.

Her grandmother had been born and raised in Camp Oro. A seventeen-year-old beauty with love in her heart and dreams of a life with her older, successful husband must have looked in a shop like this one. Maybe Kim's grandfather had come into a Camp Oro store to buy a wedding ring for his bride. Although Grandmother had never said, Kim imagined her grandfather was a romantic with dreams of being able to provide for his cherished bride. Maybe one night years ago he and Grandmother had walked down these night-quiet streets planning their future.

Their dream life together had begun well. Yes, Grandmother had borne her children when she was very young, but at least there'd been no money worries. Grandmother had been able to dress her babies in the finest clothes and set her table with fine china. Certainly she'd worried about childhood illnesses and perhaps chafed at the restrictions caused by three small children, but she'd been loved.

Lost in her thoughts, Kim was unaware of the man following her. Despite the crowd, he'd taken note of Kim's leaving. Now he was aware of her aimless steps. He heard her soft sigh.

The sound tore through him.

It wasn't supposed to be like this. Life, at least the life he'd managed to create for himself, was supposed to be painted in blacks and whites. Some people he allowed to get close to him. Others he didn't. And now a certain woman had come into his life, and because she belonged amid uncertain shades of gray, he didn't know how to deal with her. The town's texture was different simply because Kim was in it.

"Kim? Are you all right?"

Kim wasn't startled. She turned slowly, gathering her thoughts. Her grandfather must have been a man like Mark. Both men knew what they wanted out of life and how to go about accomplishing those goals. "I was thinking."

"About the meeting?"

"No. When I think about how long this town has been here—" Kim wrapped her arms around her waist and looked up at Mark. "Where do you stand?"

"Stand? It isn't my role to take sides."

"I guess not."

"I'd like to know what you're thinking."

"Thinking? So much has happened lately." Mark had removed his tie; his jacket was thrown over his shoulder. He looked, like she felt: like a person without past or future.

"You were sitting with Garner."

"Garner? He said he watched me walk to the meeting. I had no idea—Mark?" Kim was still looking up at Mark. She couldn't take her eyes off him. "Do you think it would be to Camp Oro's benefit to let the town buy the house?"

"What do you think?"

If any other lawyer had asked the question, Kim would have applauded his tactics and given him a practical answer. But even if he didn't agree with her, Kim wanted Mark to understand the forces at work inside her. "That's what I've been thinking about, about what created this town, the continuity between past and present. A sense of dignity. Mark, there's a lot of life left in my grandmother's house. If the town happens to have the money to buy it, how long would it take for that other road to be built? Would the project be put on the back burner?"

"It's a possibility. If you're afraid that's going to happen, fight for what you believe."

"Do you mean that?"

Mark backed away until he was leaning against a brick wall. "I'm not going to give you legal advice, Kim. But if you believe in something, you should fight for it. Life isn't worth much if we don't have passion for it."

Mark's words were undoing her. Kim could handle a cool, logical attorney discussing facts and dismissing emotion. But the attorney was gone now; only the man remained. "Garner said something," she managed. "This—what the community pride people are proposing—could turn Camp Oro into a circus."

"It could."

"I'm not going to be a party to that, Mark. Maybe I'll lose the fight, but at least I am going to fight."

"You can't fight if you aren't here, Kim."

"I know." At sixteen, Kim had moved to San Francisco with her father and new stepmother. She'd absorbed the magic of the city by the bay. Encouraged by her stepmother's commitment to her own career, Kim had looked inside herself until she knew what she wanted in the way of a career. Until tonight she'd believed herself happy.

"When you came, I was thinking about my grandmother as a young woman. My grandfather bought her a gold band when they got married. Mark, she had to sell that ring in order to feed her children. He—there wasn't a will and when he died, everything got tangled up in the courts. I don't know what I'm saying," Kim groaned. "I guess—I'm thinking about all the things we don't have control over, the way life carries us along. Tonight—" Kim let her arms drop to her sides. "I just want to think about what's good in life."

"What's good in your life, Kim?"

The threads of logic that held Kim together unraveled. She was nothing except a woman standing on a deserted street with a man who asked impossible questions and waited for impossible answers. You, she almost told him. You're one of the good things in my life. "This town. The pride I feel here. The sense of peace. Doing a job I'm proud of. Being healthy."

"You didn't mention a man."

"No. I didn't."

"Is there a man in your life, Kim?"

"No."

Why had he asked her that? But even as he asked the question, Mark knew what the answer was. He could come to regret this. In a sense he already did. But just as she was living in the moment, so was he. Tonight they could touch. Tomorrow he would deal with the consequences.

Chapter Seven

"Sometimes it feels as if I've never left." Kim was staring up at the flag flying over the visitors' information center. "None of the buildings have changed. This used to be an insurance office, I think. But it was the same color. And the metal hitching post has always been here. I remember..." Kim smiled up at Mark. It was important to her that she share her mood with him. "I used to pretend that I had a horse. I would tie him here. Then I'd walk down the street and back again and get on my steed and we'd gallop off into the sunset. Being a child in this town, it was so good."

"You sound as if you miss that."

"Maybe I do a little," Kim admitted. She linked her arm with Mark's, using the contact to put behind her the professional he'd been earlier in the evening. Kim felt on shaky ground. She had no way of knowing whether Mark shared her mood, whether he wanted their relationship to change focus. Still, maybe because it was night and she was back in the town of her childhood, she needed to explore the possibility. "I said Camp Oro hasn't changed, but I think maybe it has. There's an energy here these days. There aren't any empty buildings anymore. I like the feeling."

"So do I. That's why I agreed to be the city attorney."

"You're part of that energy."

"I take that as a compliment. I care about what happens here." He was looking down at her, the night sheltering whatever was in his eyes. There was no reason for her to feel this way; certainly she didn't need a man to protect her. But having Mark touch her was doing things to her she couldn't deny. Good things.

"You're good for the town," she whispered. "You—you're good for me."

"We don't know each other. You don't know me."

He was right. "I know you're a decent man."

"I hope I can live up to that. Kim, I'm only human."

"I know that. I'm glad you followed me here," she said softly. "I like the idea that we see the same things, feel the same things when we look at Camp Oro. There's something going on between us."

"Maybe too much."

"Do you believe that?"

Mark's lips were on her temple. His hands settled around her waist. "I can't answer that, Kim," he told her. "It's something we need to talk about."

"Not now. Please," Kim asked. It had taken all her courage to say what she just had. She wasn't sure she was ready to go on.

Mark laughed. The sound vibrated through Kim's body and made it difficult for her to remember anything except his presence. Still she had to try. "When I saw you there tonight—I hardly recognized you."

"I looked different?"

"Not that. But—" His slate hair was coarse to the touch. "I think I'd forgotten your professional role."

His professional role. For a moment Mark had been able to forget that, too. The time didn't last long enough. "That's why I'm here," he told her, although that was only part of the story. The rest was being told through his hands and eyes. "Do you understand what I was doing back there?"

"The stand you took? Yes. Mark, this isn't the first time I've been a part of negotiations. I know what's involved."

A kiss. They could share that before— "I don't like the position this places me in," Mark said softly. "It isn't what I want to be doing."

"Mark? We all do things we don't want to."

"Yes. We do. Fortunately, when we're aware of what's happening, we can balance that out with other things." Another kiss, this one longer.

"I'd—" Kim tried again. "I don't want to talk about that tonight. I thought I wanted to be alone after the meeting. All I wanted was to try to sort out my feelings. I don't feel that way anymore."

"I'm glad. I guess—" Mark ran a finger from Kim's temple into her hair. "A lot has happened to you since you got here. I wish it didn't have to be like that."

"Mark. When I was five years old, my mother died. She'd been sick a long time. Leaving me inch by inch. This—" Kim waved her hand in the air "—is nothing."

Mark's hold tightened. "That, having your mother die, made you strong."

"If I'm strong, it's a legacy from her."

Mark nodded. His gentle smile let Kim know she'd been right in telling him what she had. It did almost as much to her nervous system as his kiss had. Kim waited for him to say more. Instead Mark wrapped his arm over her shoulder and led her away from the silent buildings. A couple of cars passed them on their way home from the meeting. Neither Mark nor Kim acknowledged them.

They were walking around the cave-in now. From a distance they looked like nothing more than close friends with their arms wrapped around each other. When Mark spoke, the words weren't ones mere friends would share. "Margaret told me about her daughter-in-law, how your mother kept her illness from the family as long as she could. But when she couldn't anymore, she turned it into the greatest battle of her life. She didn't cry. She didn't try to blame anyone.''

"I was very young, Mark." Kim glanced over at the stretch of dark that was the entrance to the tunnel. She could have asked Mark about the skeleton now, but she didn't. "I was spared a lot of that. But I knew something bad was happening. My father— My grandmother stepped in during that time and gave me the security I needed. I said I learned strength and courage from my mother. I think maybe I learned even more from my grandmother.''

"Hearing that would make your grandmother proud.''

"I know.'' Kim could smile for Mark. "I have told her.''

Mark looked down at the black hole they were slowly circling. "Is your grandmother to blame for the fool stunt you pulled down there?''

"It wasn't a fool stunt. I faced my fear. Got it out in the open. Put it behind me.''

"That's really the way you see it?''

"That's the way I see it," Kim said with her arm around Mark and his warmth easing through her. "No lectures. I'm not interested in them. Mark, there isn't much I feel I can't face head-on. Going down there might not be the smartest thing I've ever done, but I'm glad I did. And—nothing bad came out of it.''

Tonight was for forgetting the outside world. For creating emotional bridges. The short trip from the street to where Kim lived proved the perfect transition. Within a few feet of leaving Kim's stranded car, they entered a shadowed lane with trees and bushes insulating them from everything except a narrow ribbon of night sky. Some people might have been unnerved by the sound of leaves brushing against each other or the quick hoot of an owl, but Mark sensed only peace. A short peace, but peace nonetheless.

Kim Revis, not the night, was responsible for that mood. Days, sometimes weeks passed with Mark being aware of very little except work and a few hours stolen away from that work. He was devoted to his parents, but they lived their own lives unencumbered by the routine of earning a living. Clients, other attorneys, secretaries, police officers, city officials were part of Mark's world. He moved easily among them but they, like he, were only chess players in a massive, never-ending game. The faces and voices might change as people darted in and out of his life. The treadmill never altered its course.

Until tonight.

As Kim unlocked the door, Mark felt his awareness expand. The shapes in Kim's living room were sharp and clear. He was aware that the air had a crisp, clear taste. He was even more aware of the way Kim handled her body. She was utterly graceful, a small, self-confident woman moving about the room as if she'd never lived anywhere else. When she turned toward him, he absorbed her slight smile, the way her fingers angled toward her thighs, taut calf muscles altering the line of her slacks.

They hadn't come here to discuss the council meeting, her job, the future of the hole that held her car prisoner, even her grandmother. They were here, Mark believed, because they didn't know enough about each other and what he wanted to learn should be accomplished in privacy.

"I haven't found the mourning jewelry I told you about," Kim was saying. She was standing near the lamp she'd just turned on. She didn't move toward Mark and yet he felt her invitation. "I found a picture of it, though. In a scrapbook. I think my father took it. Would you like to see it?"

Although he didn't, Mark nodded. The photograph was faded and a little out of focus. It showed the rose-shaped pin against a backdrop of velvet. Kim was right. The jet stone was unique. "Where have you looked?" he asked.

"Everywhere. I wonder if Grandmother put it somewhere. I keep thinking I should ask her, but if she hasn't...if it's lost..."

"Maybe it isn't that important to her."

"Maybe. She called me this evening. She was asking questions about my job. Some of the questions didn't make much sense. Mark, how did you become her lawyer?"

Mark chuckled. "I'd just started practicing. Something came up that put me on the opposite side of the fence from Harden. Your grandmother liked the way I handled myself."

"That sounds like her." Kim started to stretch. For a moment she felt light-headed. She reached for Mark.

"Are you all right?" Mark asked, with Kim soft and warm in his arms.

"Fine. I just got a little dizzy."

"It's been a long day for you. Both emotionally and physically."

"I'm used to long days. So are you."

"Yes." He couldn't release her. Neither could he simply go on doing what he was. The man who could face a hostile witness without a qualm had no idea what to do with his hands. "Kim? What do we do now?"

"What? I don't understand."

"Don't you?" Mark cupped Kim's chin in his palm so that she was looking up into his eyes.

"Yes." The word was almost inaudible.

"What do you want from me?"

Mark should have never been a lawyer. If he had been a longshoreman or a logger, he wouldn't have asked that question, and she wouldn't have had to answer it. Kim could deal with reality; she prided herself in her ability to do just that. But this was a question she'd never been asked before. Her body knew the answer. Her heart was hesitant. "I don't know," she started. That wasn't enough. He had to have more. "We're together. Doesn't that tell you something?"

"It doesn't tell me enough. Kim, there's something I have to say. I'm only going to say it once, but it's important that you understand."

With her hands touching Mark's waist, Kim waited.

"This is the lawyer in me talking. I want to be with you. When you were talking about growing up in Camp Oro I felt as if I'd shared that with you. But I didn't. We have an appreciation of this town in common, but that might be the only thing. If you come to that decision, I want you to let me know."

This was insane. They were discussing taking their relationship another step as if this was an automobile they were trying to make up their mind about. Kim couldn't treat what was more emotion than logic that way. "I'm glad you're here tonight."

"Is that all?"

"I think, for now, yes."

Mark stood where he was for perhaps five seconds and then drew Kim against him. One moment she felt powerful against him; the next she'd turned soft and fragile. The split fascinated him as did everything about Kim Revis. She'd worn a summer-weight sweater in pale yellow. The fabric moved easily under Mark's fingers but kept her flesh from his searching fingers.

They kissed. They touched. They murmured things outsiders would never hear. Kim felt herself growing lighter as if whatever lived and breathed within her had taken leave of her body. She was aware of what Mark's hands and body were doing to her, and yet that part of her remained separated from thought and emotion.

There was need; yes, there was need. There was the desire to give herself to this man, to share and explore. If Kim had been younger and more innocent, she would have let those emotions dictate her actions. But she was no longer a girl. She was a woman, and no matter how much she might rebel against what she'd become, that woman ruled her.

This had to be right between her and Mark. When and if they took that step toward intimacy, there would be no going back. There would be no pretending that the greatest act of sharing hadn't taken place.

When the time was right Kim would want Mark to make love to her. But not tonight. Not when there was still too much emotion and not enough logic. Not until she'd come to terms with what he was capable of doing to her self-control.

"I don't think—"

"You don't want?"

"Oh, yes. I want. But Mark—" She was still clinging to him. She couldn't let go of him yet. "I'm afraid I want too much. Do you understand what I'm saying?"

Mark didn't want to understand. With all his heart, he wanted freedom from responsibilities and promises. He wanted to spend the night with this wise, gentle witch. But if he allowed that to happen, Mark wasn't sure what would be left of him. "You want me to leave?"

"No." Kim gripped Mark tighter. Even as she spoke, she pressed against him, taking what she would need to get her through the night. "I don't want you to leave. But—" Angry at herself for the confused messages she was giving both of them, Kim pulled back. She stood alone, feeling starved. "You scare me. I scare me."

That Mark understood. "It's powerful, isn't it?"

"Too powerful. I don't want it to be like this. I want . . . Mark, I don't know what I want."

He could touch her. He could give her one last kiss before leaving. One last embrace. "You're going to the museum tomorrow?"

"I have to."

"Let me know when you're going there."

"Mark." She was holding on to him and turning him half crazy. "I have to handle this myself."

MARK DIDN'T WANT to walk past the cave-in. The mocking blackness wouldn't let him forget what stood between him and Kim Revis. It was ironic somehow. He'd walked out of her house feeling the promise of what might be and the wisdom of not jumping into something they couldn't retreat from. Although he wasn't comfortable with his body and wouldn't be for hours, Mark had felt he'd done what was right. Until he came to the barriers placed by the public-works crew and what lay beyond reminded him. There was no hiding from doubts and questions. From knowing he should have never come here.

It was too late. He'd begun a journey with Kim. He couldn't do anything but continue the journey, even if it all blew up in his face.

KIM DIDN'T BOTHER with a light. Needing the anonymity of night, she slipped out of her clothes and reached for her nightgown. The strength had gone out of her legs. She sat down on the edge of the bed and leaned forward, resting her head in her hands, breathing deeply until she was capable of facing the scope of her emotions. Her body ached with the need for what it had been denied. Her heart still thudded uneasily. Still, she didn't regret sending Mark away.

Unless something she couldn't possibly foresee sprang up between them, the time would come when things would be right. When that happened, Kim would give Mark a great deal. Her heart had already begun a journey it had never been on before.

Kim leaned back. Her hand brushed against the clothes she'd left there earlier in the day. Without thinking of what she was doing, Kim felt in the pocket for the object she'd put there. She held the small, solid weight in her hand, absently running her fingers over the rough surface.

At length she got up and turned on the lamp at the head of her bed. The handle was bone. She thought there was a tiny carving on the once-white surface, perhaps something to identify its owner, but the years had made their impact, erasing whatever its owner had done to it. The blade was badly rusted and resisted Kim's efforts to open it completely.

She should have told Mark about this. They could have shared speculations about its source, and maybe Kim would better understand Mark's reaction to the skeleton. She could understand revulsion. Certainly, she'd felt a moment of that herself. But Mark wasn't a man to turn from what was grim.

Maybe—Kim dropped the knife into the palm of her right hand, feeling its weight—maybe she should turn it over to the sheriff. As soon as the thought surfaced, Kim dismissed it. She was an historian. She wanted to research the knife's history herself.

KIM'S FIRST ACTION, once she was out of the shower the next morning, was to call her grandmother. "So much happened last night," she began. She had wanted to keep the news about the problems the cave-in could cause to selling the house from her grandmother, but better the story come from her than a newspaper. "You wouldn't believe what that Harden man is trying to force on the council. You were talking about our getting together for dinner? I'd like to try for tonight. That way I can explain what happened."

"I'd love that, my dear. What do you have to do today?"

Kim had to think for a moment. "More meetings at the museum. I'm afraid it isn't very exciting."

Margaret's sigh was a little too close to a groan. "I'll be so glad when you're out of that musty place. Call me this afternoon, dear. We'll make our plans then."

Although she wanted her next call to be to Mark, Kim forced herself to attend to business. When she called the museum to make sure it wouldn't be a wasted trip, Rogan Coffers answered the phone. She started to ask if he'd come across the building's blueprints when he cut her off. "Forget the blueprints. All hell's breaking loose here this morning."

Kim tried to get more out of the director, but he repeated his contention that he couldn't possibly deal with her mundane request right now. In the background she could hear an excited conversation. "You'll be there?" Kim managed to get in.

"I don't have any choice, do I?" Rogan asked before hanging up.

Kim slipped into her practical tennis shoes, hurried with her makeup and closed the door on what had and hadn't happened last night.

Garner and Rogan were already there when Kim entered Rogan's office. The tension in the room was a living thing, made even more powerful when William pushed in behind her. The guard didn't look at the others. Instead he leaned against the closest wall. "Figures," he muttered. "Figures."

Kim didn't bother asking William to explain himself. "What happened?" she asked Rogan.

"We've been hit. Again."

Somehow Kim had known this was what had been behind Rogan's short words earlier. "What was taken?"

Garner answered her question. "We're not sure. Inventory is being taken right now. The case held depression glass."

There was a chair waiting, but Kim decided to stand. "How did they get into it?" she asked, wondering if "they" was in the room.

"It's broken. Pieces of glass all over the place. The worst thing—" Rogan glanced at Garner. When he turned back toward Kim, he was blinking rapidly. "It wasn't found by one of the employees. If only we'd discovered it before— We'd just opened the doors when Delores Witherspoon came in with her grandchildren. The kids were visiting and Grandma was going to spend the day working on the kids' education. I'm surprised you didn't hear her at your place."

Was Rogan blaming Delores Witherspoon for calling attention to the theft and vandalism? Kim could hardly believe that. "What else did she see? Where is Mrs. Witherspoon now?"

"Gone," the business manager explained. "She stomped around here for a few minutes, pulled Rogan and me out of the conference room where we were working and then bundled up the kids and hightailed it out of here. She said she wasn't going to have her precious grandchildren stay where a crime had been committed." Garner laughed but his tone was grim. "To hear Mrs. Witherspoon tell it, you'd think a murder had been committed here."

"It isn't funny," Rogan interrupted. The director stabbed his pipe in Garner's direction. "You know where she's heading now don't you?"

"How many guesses do I get?" Garner's sharp tone echoed the director's. "First stop, the police department because she probably figures we aren't smart enough to do that on our own. From there she proceeds to the nearest telephone where she starts calling everyone within a hundred-mile radius."

"Including the newspaper office."

"You knew that it was only a matter of time," Kim began.

"We don't need the publicity. Not now. Hiring you was supposed to put an end to things. Our reputation—"

Kim understood. Rogan's anger was caused, not by what had been stolen, but by the fact that the thefts could no longer be kept out of the news. "I'd like to see where it happened."

"What for?" the business manager threw at her. "It's broken glass, some things pushed aside and others missing."

"It's my job, remember."

"Job. This keeps up and none of us is going to have a job. What we need to do is figure out what we're going to say when the reporters show up."

Kim wasn't in a mood to be put off. She'd had to contend with that from Garner and the museum's director for too long as it was. Ignoring Garner, she asked William if he would take her. The guard grunted but pushed himself away from the wall.

They were out in the hall before William spoke. "Run over to one of the storage units and pick up some canopy bed they've been repairing. That's what they tell me to do when I show up for work. I hightail it out there, and when I come back, everyone's yelling at me." William's long arms swung angrily. "They must think I should live here. Stay here all night. Not for any more money, though. Hell, no. Not for any more money."

Kim was having trouble keeping up with William's long strides, let alone his rapid speech. "Have you called the police?" she managed to ask.

"Of course. I'm no fool, Miss. I know what I'm supposed to do." William stopped just outside one of the ground-floor rooms at the far end of the hall. He let Kim go in ahead of him. "There wasn't no one on duty when I called, but the city hall lady said she'd call Charles at home and get him here pronto."

Glass lay on the floor and on the velvet at the base of the display. By the amount of empty space, Kim guessed that a considerable number of artifacts had been removed, but an exact count would have to wait until inventory had been taken. Kim was an advocate of shatterproof glass but could understand that a museum like the Comstock had set up many of its displays before the improved glass had been developed. She leaned forward, trying to determine how much force had been necessary to break the glass. Not much, she decided.

"No one heard anything?" she asked William.

William hadn't moved. His hands were knotted at his side. His eyes were alive, too alive. "It happened at night, miss. No one was here to hear anything."

Kim wasn't convinced that the theft had taken place at night. For one, how had someone gotten into the museum after the doors were locked? Also, if someone had managed to circumvent the alarm system, why hadn't they taken advantage of the empty building to do more than grab a handful of items? Kim was trying to decide whether to propose that theory to William or concentrate on trying to defuse his anger when Garner joined them. The handsome business manager's lips were pulled taut against his teeth.

"Let me commend you, Kim. I didn't think you'd be up and around for hours."

Kim had no idea what Garner was talking about. But she was patient enough to wait for him to explain himself.

"Come on. You can't believe I don't know about you and Stockton. I saw him take off after you last night."

"That was last night," Kim emphasized. "We're talking about now. At least I am."

"And you're saying I'm not?"

"I don't know what to think." William was still glaring at her. Kim forced herself to ignore him. "I wanted to talk to you yesterday about the budget I'd have to work with. You were too busy to have time for me then."

"What are you talking about?"

"About plugging up the holes." Kim jabbed a finger at the case. She shouldn't be angry about the senseless violence. It was her job to bring the museum's security system into the twentieth century, not pass judgment. But yesterday this case had held items that once meant something to their owner. Now they were probably being shipped out of town to be sold on the black market. "I've been here three days, and so far I haven't been able to accomplish much of anything."

"Maybe that's because you're being sidetracked by the city attorney."

"What I do on my own time has nothing to do with the job I was hired for. The job I'm trying to do."

Garner moved closer to Kim, ignoring the security guard. Kim had been aware of Garner's carefully sculptured muscles. Now, with him standing only a few inches away, she felt the impact of the power inherent in those muscles. Garner wasn't that tall, but beneath his suit was coiled strength. If he placed his fingers around her neck—

Garner was still speaking. His words almost, but not quite, pulled Kim free from her thoughts. "If you were hanging around anyone else, I wouldn't say anything, but Mark Stockton has his nose in everything. Too damn much for his own good."

Kim cast around for an excuse to back away from Garner. She glanced at the guard, but William's stony eyes left no doubt of his opinion of her. Mark had warned her not to trust anyone.

After a deep breath, Kim broke her silence. She chose her words carefully. Establishing her position clearly and quickly was essential. "The only thing I want to discuss with you right now is the budget I'm going to be operating with. If I can't be assured of cooperation from you, I have no choice but to go to the board."

"Good bluff, Kim. I've got to hand you that."

Garner's hand hovered over a shard of glass. In a heartbeat it could become a weapon. "It's no bluff," she told him boldly.

"No. I don't suppose it is." Garner rocked his body slightly and brought his hand even closer to the glass. Kim's eyes were riveted on his fingers. Her body tensed, ready for flight or fight.

She didn't have to do either. With a loud grunt, Camp Oro's police chief entered the room. Kim felt herself go weak but fought off the sensation. She'd never been at a crime scene before. She was simply reacting to that.

"You took your time getting here," Garner was saying.

"So I've been told. I was with Rogan Coffers while he tried to round up a list of what was in the case. Interesting collection of stuff." Charles Horne dismissed Garner and concentrated on the glass. "Has anyone touched anything?"

"I don't know," Garner countered. "Probably the lady who found it. And her grandchildren, too, for all I know."

"What about you?"

Kim wasn't imagining the tension between Charles and the business manager. She moved to stand beside Charles, not just because he was an old friend, but because she couldn't dismiss what had passed between her and Garner. Garner was making it clear that he knew better than to get his fingerprints all over something. Charles grunted again before turning his attention to the security guard. William repeated what he'd told Kim about having been sent on an errand as soon as he got to work.

"It was all right when I left last night." As he'd done in Rogan's office, William propped his frame against a wall. "I've been trying to remember when I was last in this room. Late in the afternoon. And I sure didn't hear anything."

"Anything?"

"Glass breaking."

"Yeah. Of course—" Charles stepped over to the heavy door and closed it. "With this closed, someone could drop a rock on that glass and no one would hear. You can't be any more specific about the last time you were here?"

William either couldn't or wouldn't cooperate further. He was willing to help Charles dust for prints, but he wasn't sure what good that would do. "It hasn't gotten us anywhere before. It isn't going to be any different this time."

Charles sent William out to the police car for the fingerprinting kit. Garner had been a silent observer to the conversation. Now he dismissed himself. "You want me, I'll be in my office. I've got a financial report to prepare. Give me an hour, Ms. Revis. I'll have everything you want."

Kim waited until Garner was out of the room before letting her sigh escape. "Problems?" Charles asked.

"I don't know," Kim said honestly. "Maybe it's just me. But, Garner makes me uneasy."

"He makes me want to give him a swift kick. Thinks he has the answers to everything. Thinks too damn much of himself if you ask me. I was out of town for a couple of days last year. When I came back Sandy told me that Garner had called her twice. Can you believe that? It's a good thing it wasn't anything more than a phone call."

Kim was willing to let Charles go on about his opinion of the business manager. She appreciated her old friend's candid comments. If he didn't believe she would keep his confidences, he wouldn't have said anything. "Do you have any new theories?" she asked when he ran down.

"Not really, but don't tell anyone that." Charles handed Kim the list he'd gotten from the director. "I don't know what half of this stuff is. I guess it's a list of everything that was in the case, or as near as anyone knew. Now we have to determine what's missing." Charles sighed again. "This is so damn frustrating. I swear, I've got a better chance of identifying that pile of bones we hauled out of the tunnel yesterday."

Kim tried to smile. "So, you did get that done. What happens now?"

"Now it goes to the crime lab. My deputy and I hauled it out before that meeting. Mark says you're the one who found it."

Kim nodded. "I suppose I should have been shocked, but I wasn't. Surprised, yes. Repulsed, no. Is there any chance they'll be able to find out who it was?"

"Are you kidding?" Charles laughed. "Those crime lab guys should have a field day with that relic, but I'd be surprised if they come up with more than the sex and a rough estimate of when whoever it was died. Another in a long line of unsolved crimes.''

Kim heard footsteps approaching and rushed her question. ''Do you really think it was a crime?''

''Makes sense to me. Someone dies of natural causes, other people make sure the body gets a decent burial.''

The footsteps belonged to Anthea Norval. The businesswoman and dedicated museum volunteer swept into the room with another woman close behind. Anthea's companion was vaguely familiar, but Kim was unable to remember where she'd seen her before.

Anthea's tone left no doubt of her reaction to the latest theft. ''It's all over town already,'' she told the police chief. ''Mrs. Witherspoon is holding court down at the post office, telling everyone about the terrible thing she found. I told Rogan there's no way we can keep this out of the news now. Charmaine's been trying to tell Rogan we can't have this kind of publicity, but it hasn't done any good.''

The other woman smiled her perfect smile. ''Husbands don't listen to their wives, Anthea. You should know that.''

That's where Kim had seen the woman before. She'd been sitting next to Rogan at the town council meeting. Before Kim could decide whether this was the time to introduce herself, Anthea focused her attention on the glass case while Charmaine stood back where there was no danger of broken glass getting in her heels. Self-absorbed, Kim decided, glad that no one was privy to her thoughts.

Anthea was giving Charles a list of the missing pieces without having to consult the paper the police chief had shown Kim. ''There was an indigo compote in the Thousand Eye pattern. I have clients who would kill for one in perfect condition. I can't believe that's missing.''

Anthea sounded agitated, but Kim heard no genuine shock, no true disbelief. Was that the way someone who knew more than she wanted to let on would act?

Kim didn't try to answer the question. She wasn't a detective. But Anthea had access to the entire museum, an insider's knowledge of the artifacts, and a business that depended on a steady supply of antiques. And all signs pointed to an inside job.

"You're sure about this?" Charles was asking. "You know to the last piece what's missing?"

"Do you have to ask, Charles? Who spelled it out to you the other times we were robbed? I swear, I don't know what's going to happen. If someone doesn't do something—"

Kim turned her attention to Charmaine Coffers. The impeccably dressed woman was nodding in agreement. Charmaine exuded money, or if not money, at least a healthy taste for it. Her husband, on the other hand, looked and dressed as if he had too much on his mind to concern himself with physical appearances.

Kim had no idea what the two had in common.

Chapter Eight

Kim sat in on the interview with the newspaper reporter. She had to hand it to Rogan. If the man had had any doubts about his ability to carry off an interview, he hid it well. He, along with the other staff members, were appalled that such a brazen theft could have taken place. Rogan didn't deny that there had been other thefts. Neither, however, did he allow the interview to head in a direction that might lead to that question. Instead the suggestion was made that if Camp Oro had a larger police force this might not have happened.

Kim was surprised that the reporter didn't ask why a security expert was already on the scene when the robbery occurred. However, before the interview was over, she believed she understood. All Anthea had to do was drop a hint to the effect that her husband was a major advertiser for the newspaper. Anthea had the utmost confidence that the reporter would handle the story without sensationalism and would make it clear that the staff was on top of the situation.

As soon as the reporter left, Garner returned to inform her that he had the museum's books ready for her. The two huddled over finances for several hours while Garner explained, in boring detail, how finances would have to be juggled from one area to another. Plans for updating the heating/air-conditioning system would have to be delayed. Another project Anthea had been campaigning for would have to be either scrapped or a fund-raising program implemented. If Kim wasn't insisting on such an extensive, to say nothing of expensive system, none of this would be necessary.

"You play hardball, Kim," Garner grumbled when she stood firm. "A sweet young thing like you—"

"I'm not a sweet young thing. I'd think you'd have figured that out by now."

"You don't care whose toes you step on, do you?"

Kim refused to take responsibility for the pinch the museum was going to feel. She wasn't advocating for a complex electromagnetic locking device throughout although that was what she would prefer to see in place. Instead she explained that wireless transmitters for the most valuable collections, simple detection light beams and door switches weren't that expensive and would be far better than nothing. Shatterproof glass would replace the fragile cases now in place. And at the top of her list was updating the status of the security guard and providing him with the same training given the local police force.

Garner balked at the last. "What do we need that for? If we have all this other high-tech wizardry in place, we won't need a guard."

"You couldn't be more mistaken," Kim countered. "The visibility of a human guard deters most opportunists. Garner, these are the suggestions I'll be making to the board. The final decision is up to them."

"Yeah." Garner got to his feet. To her relief, he didn't come closer. "And you know they're going to go along with whatever you recommend. I might as well save my breath."

Although it was well after noon by the time Kim finished with Garner, she was too on edge to eat. Instead she drove to Grass Valley. She had hoped to see her grandmother but was informed that Margaret was out. No one was sure where she was or when she would return.

Kim spent the afternoon meeting with the three security firms Mark had told her about. One of them was proud of the low false-alarm rate of his product but knew less about its long-term effectiveness than Kim did. Kim easily dismissed that one. However, the other two understood her needs and were willing to work under her direction. Kim arranged a time to meet at the museum with them in preparation for estimates that she would turn over to the board along with her recommendations.

By then Kim had a pulsing headache, but at least she'd made progress. She made a fruitless phone call to Cobblestone Manor and left a message for her grandmother to call her. She thought about dropping by the museum to ask Rogan if he'd come across the blueprints yet, but changed her mind when she saw a TV camera crew interviewing Anthea on the museum lawn.

The only thing she really wanted this afternoon was to see Mark.

She also knew better than to drop in on him unannounced. Tonight, she promised herself. Tonight they would be together.

Kim was driving past the police department on her way home when she spotted Mark's Blazer parked out front. Puzzled, Kim parked nearby and went inside. She could hear Mark's voice before she knocked on Charles's office door.

"That's more than I thought they'd come up with," Mark was saying. "You're sure there won't be anything else?"

"I doubt it," Charles said. "We wouldn't even know what we'd do if I didn't have a friend working for the crime lab. I told him where it came from, got him all steamed up and he pulled out all the stops. It's really something, isn't it?"

"What's something?" Kim asked as she entered. Charles smiled. Mark didn't.

"What we found out about our miner. Or at least what's left of him," Charles explained. He waited until Kim had sat down and then handed her a computer printout. "John Doe" had been a male in either his late thirties or early forties. The date of death, based on the condition of the bone marrow, was estimated to have been the mid-1940s.

"The forties?" Kim questioned. "But the tunnels weren't used after the thirties."

"It's got to be a mistake. That's what I've been telling Charles." Mark took the printout from Kim but didn't look at it. He and Charles had been talking about a half dozen things in the twenty minutes he'd been here. She could have come in while they were saying something else. Anything else. "They've got to put down something so they won't look bad," he said, wondering if any of them could possibly believe that. Kim was watching him. He had to change the subject. "I've been trying to reach you. I must have left at least three messages with Rogan. Are things really the hornet's nest gossip is making it?"

Kim didn't bother to ask how Mark had heard of the latest theft. The man either had spies or learned things by osmosis. "The cat's out of the bag, all right," she acknowledged. "But at least Garner has come through with the financial information I need. I'd like to have a larger budget to work with, but I understand the museum's limitations. Now if I only felt as if the other employees were working with and not against me."

"What happened?" Charles asked. The police chief retrieved the computer printout from Mark and slipped it into a file. "I got a couple of prints, but they come from the cleaning crew. I've had my deputy doubling up on his night cruises around the museum, and I get by there several times during the day myself. Damn. This is making me look bad."

Mark quickly reassured Charles that he was doing every-thing possible. The museum was a private entity handling its own security. The residents of Camp Oro understood that.

"Maybe." Charles looked as if he was carrying the weight of the world. "But the rest of the county doesn't. And I can't count on the newspaper and TV to spell out the mu-seum's position in my town."

Kim understood Charles's frustration. She explained that she was advocating training for William and, if her pro-posal was accepted, she would need Charles's help in get-ting the security guard into the police academy. Charles promised to add his weight to the proposal.

Kim wanted to tell both Charles and Mark about her meetings with the security firm, but she felt she'd inter-rupted their meeting too much already with museum busi-ness. Besides, her stomach was rumbling and her headache growing.

She rose to her feet but didn't risk another look at Mark. There'd been nothing in the brief look he'd given her to take her back to last night. Maybe... maybe he regretted what had happened.

Kim pointed at the file containing the information on the skeleton. "What happens now?" she asked. "I feel as if I haven't done right by that poor man."

"There aren't any missing persons' records from the 1940s, Kim," Mark told her. "And you've got enough to worry about without this."

"Maybe." Kim's head throbbed, but she couldn't let go that easily. "But if the tunnels were closed down in the 1930s and he died in the 1940s—"

"Let it rest, Kim." Mark turned away from her. "Charles, you'll write something up for me? If the council knows you're opposed to leaving the cave-in open, it'll have an impact."

For a moment Kim could do nothing but stare at Mark's broad shoulders. He'd dismissed her. He might have been polite and civilized, but the dismissal was there nonetheless.

She shouldn't feel so insecure, so off balance. So hurt.

Kim headed for the door. "You're going?" Mark asked.

"It's been a long day."

"I'll see you, Kim."

Kim. Why did her name coming from him have to have such an effect on her? "I'll see you, Mark. Charles? Say hi to Sandy for me, will you. Tell her I'd still love to get together with her, but right now—" Mark was looking at her; his expression unreadable.

Kim's resolve to dismiss Mark lasted halfway to her car. Something was wrong. Something she couldn't understand and he obviously wasn't going to explain.

She rested her aching head on the steering wheel. Her stomach was telling her that food was required. Her head was holding out for aspirin. Her heart—Kim had no idea what her heart needed.

"Kim?"

His voice. Against all reason, Kim responded. "What?"

"Are you all right?"

Yes. No. "I have a headache. And I'm starved."

"Kim. We need to talk."

His simple words struck Kim like a physical blow. He was going to tell her he didn't want to see her anymore. He was going to ask her to pretend that last night hadn't happened. "What about?" she made herself ask.

"About what happened today. I know." Mark raked his fingers through his hair. "You're going to tell me to stay out of your business, but Charles has the same concerns."

Kim couldn't keep up with this conversation; it wasn't what she'd been expecting. "About what?"

"About your safety. Kim, you represent danger to someone. An end to a lucrative career."

"Because of the security system? But Mark—"

"Don't. Just listen to me. Whoever it is knows the rug can be pulled out from under them at anytime. But someone so desperate that he or she goes on stealing even after you show up isn't thinking clearly. That someone might believe that getting you out of the way will solve their problems."

The tone of Mark's voice made Kim feel cold. "Not many people knew what I was doing here before the interview at the museum. And there weren't very many people there."

"I know."

Although she hadn't given him much of a reply, Kim had nothing else to say. She'd wanted something personal from him, more than just concern for her safety. But that was all that he'd given her. She had to accept that.

"Go home, Kim," he was telling her. "You need to take care of yourself."

And you're not offering to be part of that. "All right," Kim managed. She blinked. Her eyes felt hot, dry and too big for her face.

He was touching her. His fingers were light on her forearm, but Kim clung to that warmth. "I want to be with you tonight," he whispered. "I hope you believe that."

"I . . . do."

"But . . ." Mark debated. He couldn't tell her the truth, but it wasn't in him to lie, especially not to her. "I have to see your grandmother tonight. If it was anyone else—"

"My grandmother? I've been trying to reach her all day. We were supposed to have dinner together."

Mark went tight inside. Danger was suddenly a word away. "I'll remind her."

"Don't." Kim worked on a smile. "It'll just upset her."

KIM WAS HOME before she faced the question. If Mark and her grandmother were going to be together this evening, why hadn't she been asked to join them? The question got in the way of making a decision about what to have for dinner. Instead Kim swallowed a couple of aspirins and took refuge in the shower. Then she pulled a short lounging gown over her body. She was drying her hair when the phone rang.

It was Mark. He was with her grandmother. "Margaret has herself all worked up over what she read in the paper and has been hearing on TV. The TV's playing it big. I've been trying to tell her there's nothing for her to worry about, but I'm not doing very well. Maybe if you let her give you some grandmotherly advice—"

Kim had a better idea. She suggested that Mark bring Margaret over for a simple meal and some conversation.

In the forty-five minutes it took Mark to drive Margaret to Camp Oro and help her up the driveway, Kim dressed, opened windows and curtains, dusted, washed the break-fast dishes, ran outside for some roses to put on the table and started making hamburgers.

"You didn't have to do this," Margaret exclaimed as soon as the hugs were over. "You had such a busy day. I told Mark to tell you not to bother, but he insisted."

Mark had already begun tearing up lettuce for their salad. "That isn't all I said. Tell Kim the rest."

Margaret ducked her head. She tried to smile but was only partially successful. "Honey, I—I let my imagination get carried away. I started thinking of all kinds of things, like you might come to work early some morning and find rob-bers in there. If they did anything to you—"

"Oh, Grandmother." Concerned by her grandmother's obvious nervousness, Kim hugged the frail woman. "You've been watching too many TV programs. And even if I did surprise our cat burglar—" Kim struck a kung-fu stance. "He'll be sorry he messed with me."

Margaret laughed. Kim had expected the exchange to re-lease some of the tension she'd sensed in her grandmother, but the air of strain continued. Kim gave Mark a puzzled look, but he merely shook his head and gave her a warning look. "What have you been up to?" Kim tried to change the subject. "Anything exciting going on today?"

"No. No," Margaret muttered. "I had a quiet day."

"You did? I tried to call you."

"Oh." Margaret looked confused. "I might have been over at my neighbor's. She's all worried about her medical insurance. I was trying to explain things to her."

Kim remembered to nod in response to the explanation, but she couldn't manage a smile. She'd been told that her grandmother was out for the afternoon. Either the receptionist was wrong, or Margaret Revis had lied to her.

Dinner was tense. Margaret filled Kim in on her activities since the last time the two had been together, and Kim told both Mark and her grandmother about the progress she'd made in developing a plan to present to the board. But Kim felt as if they were all tiptoeing around something.

Believing she knew what it was, Kim finally brought up the subject of the town council meeting. "I read the newspaper report," she explained. "It tells part of the story, but not everything. I wish—I suppose I shouldn't be so impatient, but I'd like to see the council come to a decision. Especially the right one."

Margaret nodded and tried another smile. "Be patient, dear. These things take time."

"I know that. I just don't like you not knowing what's going to happen. I mean, we were all set to put the place on the market, and now this—I just can't believe the council would consider buying you out. I mean, where are they going to come up with the money?"

"Valid question," Mark interjected. "You've done more packing? I don't remember seeing that many boxes."

Kim told Mark that he was right. If her grandmother weren't here, Kim might have said something about his powers of observation when she'd thought herself capable of distracting him. But tonight was for her grandmother, for being honest with the dear woman.

"So many things," Margaret mused. "People collect so much stuff. Most of it we don't need."

"But it comes to mean a lot to us, doesn't it?"

Margaret nodded. "I didn't think so until I moved. Now my possessions— Isn't that silly?"

Margaret would find out about the missing jet pin. Kim could remain quiet, as Mark wanted her to, and subject her grandmother to a frenzied search later or break the news gently, now. "I wasn't going to tell you," Kim began. "I mean, you have enough on your mind what with this cave-in business. But—there's something missing. I've looked everywhere. I hope, maybe you have it."

"What?" Margaret asked. Behind Margaret, Mark shook his head violently.

"Your jet pin. Everything else is here. I hoped maybe you had it."

"Oh, honey," Margaret started. She shot Mark a look but turned back toward Kim before the glance registered with the younger woman. "I haven't thought about that in forever. I'm so sorry you put yourself out."

"I don't mind that. You have it, don't you?"

"No, but don't worry about it."

"Don't worry about it? Grandmother, the history behind—"

"History? Kim, the quality wasn't that good. Jet's supposed to be perfectly black and that piece had that little bit of white in it."

"I know." Mark was staring at her. Kim tried to ignore him. "But it meant so much to you."

"It was such a morbid custom, wearing jewelry to let everyone know you were in mourning."

"You didn't used to think that way." Kim was confused. She'd been so sure that her grandmother would be upset. She was, but what she was saying— "I'll look some more," Kim offered weakly.

Margaret sank deeper into her chair. "I can't remember the last time I saw it. Years maybe. Honey—" She turned toward Mark.

Mark's voice was without warmth. "Let it go, Kim. It isn't important." Before she could say anything, Mark changed the subject. For several minutes Kim listened to him talk about an upcoming trial.

Finally, though, she'd had enough. She didn't mind Mark taking control of the conversation, but he was trying to take them from things that needed to be said. Margaret didn't want to talk about the jewelry. All right. Kim would honor that.

But she'd invited her grandmother here because Kim didn't want Margaret to be concerned with her safety. Margaret was still pale, still nervous. Kim wanted to try to set her grandmother's mind at ease. As smoothly as possible, Kim turned the conversation back to her reason for being in Camp Oro. "Charles has asked for my help. I feel like a private detective," she explained as she began clearing the table. "The problem is, on those TV detective programs, they know what they're looking for. I probably wouldn't know a clue if I tripped over one. All I know—" Kim almost said something about William's quick anger but thought better of it. "Rogan's so stodgy. He goes at his own pace and nothing I say or do hurries him along. His wife—have you met her?"

"That's one worthless woman." Margaret's tone left no question of how she felt about Charmaine Coffers. "I've seen her name on more committees than I care to think about. Her father was the mayor of Grass Valley for forever. You should remember him, but maybe he wasn't that important to you. He made a ton of money, and Charmaine never lets anyone forget it. People can be so gullible. She's always being asked to back some cause or another simply because she represents what passes for society in this part of the state. But to get a lick of work out of her—forget it."

Mark and Kim both laughed. Their eyes met and for a second Kim believed that things were right between them.

Mark pointed out that with Charmaine's expensive tastes it was lucky her father had lots of money.

"I have no idea what Charmaine sees in Rogan, other than the fact that his family was wealthy enough to associate with hers," Margaret observed. "Then, maybe I don't want to know. You said Charles has asked you to help with the investigation. Do you think that's wise?"

Kim gave her grandmother a warm smile. "It makes sense. After all, I'm there a lot. Don't worry," Kim went on when Margaret's expression turned serious. "I'm never there after hours, and Mark has already warned me not to be alone with anyone. He's doing enough worrying for the two of you. Not that any of it is necessary."

"You feel safe there?" Margaret asked. "Completely safe?"

Kim didn't, but she wasn't about to tell her grandmother that. "It's a three-ring circus. People all over the place."

"Really?"

"Really." Kim stopped working long enough to give her grandmother a hug. "You know what a set of lungs I have. One holler and I'd have everyone in the place on the run."

Margaret smiled, a real smile this time. "I'm so glad you invited us here tonight, honey. This is wonderful."

Kim sat down next to her grandmother. Dishes could wait. Moments like this were precious. "Charles is just a yell away, not that I'm going to need him. I'm so glad you were able to come. When I couldn't get a hold of you today... Oh? What did you think of our little hole? This is the first time you've seen it, isn't it?"

"Our little hole? The cave-in?"

The tension was back again. Once again Kim was looking into the eyes of an uneasy woman. This time she was certain she understood. "I hope you'll tell me something," Kim began gently. "I didn't ask what it cost you to move into the manor because you'd probably tell me to mind my own business. But you need the money from the sale of the house, don't you?''

"It wouldn't hurt. But no, I don't need it.''

"Then—'' This made no sense. Mark was clearing his throat again. But Kim decided to force the issue and see what developed. "Are you sure? There isn't a person alive who doesn't have money concerns.''

"I'm fine, honey.''

"I hope so,'' Kim relented. "It's just that I know where I got my stubbornness, don't I, Grandmother?''

"We aren't stubborn. We just know what needs doing and go about it.''

"Maybe.''

"Honey, I want you to listen to what I have to tell you. Listen and believe.''

"I will,'' Kim whispered. She was both worried and relieved. Worried because she had no idea what her grandmother might say. Relieved because it was time for honesty.

"This house—'' Margaret spread her arms. "It meant a great deal to me. There are a thousand memories— I wasn't sure how I would feel about coming here tonight knowing I can't live here anymore.''

"I know. It's hard.''

"Yes.'' Margaret was still smiling. "But I'm practical. If nothing else, I'm practical. Life has taken a turn I didn't expect.'' She pointed at her hip. "I can't go on living here. It's as simple as that. And it makes no sense to try to hold on to the house. I could have waited until I died and left that up to my relatives, but I refuse to do that to them. At least this way you and I can work together, Kim. You'll have to do most of the work, but at least I'm here to back you up.''

Kim blinked back tears. "You're a good woman. Practical. But there's no rush, you know. You're going to be around for many more years.''

"Maybe.'' Margaret shrugged. "Probably. But, Kim, I'm not afraid of dying. Your mother was a wonderful teacher.

Face what has to be faced, but don't let anything defeat you.''

What a wonderful belief. Before she gave herself time to think about the wisdom of what she was saying, Kim told her grandmother about going into the cave-in. ''It's what you said. Not letting anything defeat me. I know. I shouldn't have. Mark's already given me the lecture. But, Grandmother, I'm glad I did. Now I'm not afraid of it. There was a skeleton in there. Can you believe that? An honest to goodness skeleton. It's the strangest thing. The crime lab said the man died, it was a man, long after the old tunnel was shut down.

Margaret Revis was white. ''I—know. I mean, Mark told me about it.''

Kim was shocked, not because Mark had told Margaret, but because of her grandmother's reaction. Margaret was trying, too hard, to smile. ''What's wrong?'' She grabbed her grandmother's hand. ''I'm sorry. I didn't think that would bother you. Believe me, I wouldn't have kept on going if I'd thought there was any danger.'' Mark's eyes were on her, strong and relentless, not telling her nearly enough of what he was thinking.

''I wish you hadn't done that,'' the older woman went on, after too long a silence. ''You could have been hurt. Anything could have happened.''

Kim felt as if the house was closing in on her. Things were happening that she didn't understand. ''It didn't,'' she said softly. ''And, honest, finding what I did didn't bother me that much. I mean, he has as much right to be down there as I did. More. I just wish—'' Kim got to her feet and walked to the window. It was dark now but, because there was a half-moon out, she could see the outlines of pine trees and rosebushes. Being here felt good; miles away and a lifetime separate from what she'd experienced in San Francisco. ''It's a shame we'll never know anything more about him and what he was doing there." Kim turned back around. Her grandmother had aged years in a few seconds.

"What is it?" Kim hurried back to her grandmother and dropped to her knees. "Don't you feel well?"

Margaret sent Mark a beseeching look. "I—my hip's bothering me. I'm sorry, honey."

"I should have thought— The walk was too far for you. Give me a minute to make a bed. You can spend the night here."

"Oh, no. I have a breakfast meeting. I need to get home."

"But—"

Over Kim's objections, Margaret maintained that she was strong enough to walk back to the car. Mark backed up his client's request. "It's what she wants, Kim. We'll take it slow."

A few minutes later, Kim was walking with Mark and her grandmother down the dark driveway. Margaret was leaning against Mark and holding on to Kim's hand. She kept up a constant chatter about planting the rose garden in the rain, arguing with a surveyor over the boundary lines when Rich Gulch Street was resurfaced, her concern that the city water system was on its last legs. Her conversation rambled.

"I'm sorry," Kim whispered to Mark once her grandmother was in his Blazer. "I said things—"

"It happened." Mark was standing, not touching her, his breath warm on her cheek. "I'm sorry it did, but it happened."

Kim was miserable. "You have every right to blame me."

"I'm not blaming." Mark reached for the door handle but wound up touching Kim's hand instead. "You did what you thought was right. You had no way of knowing how she'd react."

She leaned into him, needing something, anything. "Thank you for bringing her here."

"Go home, Kim. I'll see you tomorrow."

IF ONLY KIM hadn't worn that soft sweater. If only her hair hadn't fallen over her forehead, begging for his fingers to brush it away.

Mark had been silent during most of the trip back to Grass Valley. Margaret had filled the silence with questions and recriminations. Once in Margaret's apartment, Mark had done his best to soothe his old friend's concerns. Now, instead of heading for his place, Mark was retracing his steps. He had no idea what he would say to Kim, or how he would attempt to explain his presence. All he knew was that he had to see her. Alone.

A light was on in the living room and the curtain was open. For the last time Mark paused, asking himself if he had taken leave of his senses. And then Kim moved into view, and she was the only thing in the world that mattered.

"She's all right," Mark said when Kim opened the door. Ignoring the questions in her eyes, he went on. "It was hard for her. Coming back here. The memories."

Kim stepped back and let him in. "I should have thought of that. I wish I could protect her. But—it's something she has to face."

"I know." Mark gently kicked the door closed behind him. The room still smelled faintly of the meal they'd shared. He was even more aware of the scent of roses. "We can love the people in our lives, but we can't protect them." Mark stopped himself. Loving and trying to protect had gotten him to the impossible situation he was in now.

He wasn't going to think about that tonight. "I didn't want you to worry about her. That's why I came back."

"I can't help it." Kim had wrapped her arms around her waist in the gesture that told him she was no more comfortable with what they were and weren't sharing than he was. "Do you know who her doctor is? Maybe I should talk to him."

Mark could have given her the name, but didn't. He'd stood, watching and not touching for as long as he could. He wanted to be a lawyer, only a lawyer. But if he was that and nothing else, he wouldn't have come back tonight. Gently Mark pulled Kim's hands off her body and placed them on his own shoulders. "I kept thinking about you," he whispered hoarsely. "I could have called, but that wouldn't have been enough."

"It wouldn't?"

Mark had no idea how he was going to guard himself against her. Or maybe the reality was that he didn't want to. He'd rather surrender to her power over him. "Did you think I might, come back that is?"

"No. After the way— Mark, the truth is, I didn't think I was going to see you again."

He was wrong. She was unaware of her power, and just as unsure as he was. "I'm not going to want to leave. You need to know that."

Kim's night had turned into morning when she opened the door and found Mark standing there. She'd taken him inside and found her way into his arms. She'd even found the composure necessary for speech. But now he was saying the only thing in the world she wanted to hear, and she didn't know what to say in return.

"It might be better," she whispered.

"Do you really mean that?"

"I don't know what I mean. Earlier, you were angry with me, weren't you?"

Mark nodded. The movement was almost her undoing. "I wanted to protect Margaret. I didn't want her upset."

"Neither do I, Mark. But she isn't a piece of china. She's strong. She can handle—I know. I should have picked a different time to tell her about the jewelry and the skeleton. I should have been more sensitive to her mood, to what she had to deal with, being back in this house. But it's too late for that now. And—'' Kim stopped talking when Mark drew her against him.

His body was hard and strong. Kim felt soft and feminine in a way she had never thought possible. This man could take over, guide her in ways she'd never dreamed possible, and she would be rich beyond measure for the experience.

"And what?"

"I don't know. Mark? Thank you for coming back. We need to talk."

"Talk?"

He was challenging her. Throwing caution aside, Kim rose on tiptoe, seeking Mark's mouth. It was a touch, a gentle feathering of lips against lips. Still, there was nothing gentle in what was happening to her heart. There was still a great deal she didn't understand about Mark. Maybe she never would know everything. But if she didn't at least try, Kim believed she would go through life knowing she'd turned her back on something that might become precious. Sitting across from him at the kitchen table and then watching him get into his car and drive away, had done things to her she never wanted to experience again.

She'd been given a second chance tonight. She would take whatever he offered and give everything that was in her to give. Tomorrow she would face the consequences of tonight's acts.

Kim was the first to part her lips, to seek with her tongue. The softening deep inside her was turning into something stronger. Something she'd never experienced before but had been waiting for for a long, long time. She fit against him. He was giving her warmth where a minute ago she'd been cold.

"Just before you came, the evening seemed like a bad dream. So much went wrong."

"I didn't know if I'd be welcome."

"I—" They were still standing in the living room with the curtains open and the moonlight washing over them. Needing to feel a little of the power she believed he possessed, Kim pulled at his shirt, freeing it from his waistband. She was touching his flesh, asking herself if she had the courage to go on, knowing she'd gone beyond that question.

"You want this? Kim, I have to know."

"I don't know what I want. No. That isn't true. Mark? I think you know what I want."

"I don't want either of us to regret this."

Kim took a deep breath. It didn't do enough to steady her. "There's no way either of us can be sure of that. But, Mark, you're important to me. So important. It happened so fast. I can't believe there's something wrong with the way I feel. What—I want."

"Are you saying—"

Kim didn't wait for Mark to say anything more. It had been terribly hard for her to speak. She believed that it was the same for him. But if they couldn't talk, maybe other things could take the place of words. Things like touching. And being touched. And letting go of restraint.

It was time to begin.

Mark helped with the undressing. When there was nothing between them, he stopped with his mouth on her throat. "There won't be any stopping tonight, Kim," he told her. "Do you understand that?"

"Yes." She was barely whispering.

A minute later they were in the bedroom. Maybe she should be frightened by what he was capable of doing to her; she wasn't. He explored slowly; Kim matched his pace, loving every inch of the journey. She put aside thoughts of tomorrow. They were together tonight. There was nothing else.

She hadn't known. She'd had no inkling it could be this strong. This wonderful. That she would want any man this much.

But she did.

"You're beautiful, Kim," Mark told her with one hand caressing her breast. "So soft."

Kim didn't feel soft. She was pulsing with life. Every nerve in her ached with the need for them to become one, and yet what small shred of sanity remained understood the wisdom of holding back from that point of no return. It had to be right. More than their bodies needed to come together. "When you came back, did you know—" she asked with her palms covering his nipples and her mouth inches from his chest. He was giving her access to all of him, a gift far richer than any she'd ever been given.

"Did I know we'd wind up doing this? No. Of course not. I still don't know what's going to happen."

Neither did Kim, but her need drove her on. Her hands and mouth became bolder, driving Mark onward just as she was being driven.

They became lovers with a sliver of moonlight slicing its way across Mark's back. Somewhere—Kim cared nothing for the passage of time—she opened her eyes to find the moon watching. To wonder at magic. Since moving into the house, Kim had slept with the curtains drawn against the shadows outside. She would never want to do that again. She couldn't imagine ever wanting to be anywhere but where she was now. Or with anyone except Mark.

SHE TASTED of salt.

Mark couldn't remember whether any other woman had tasted that way after lovemaking. What he did know was that he'd never been as lost as he'd been tonight.

They'd made love quickly, more quickly than he'd wanted. But she'd opened herself to him and cried out his name, and there'd been nothing left inside him but need.

The need had burned itself out. It would return; even now Mark was aware of what her body was capable of doing to his. The second time—there would be a second time tonight—he would pace himself and listen to her body's messages.

"Are you all right?"

Mark had never had a woman ask him that. "All right? I'm more right than I've ever been. You?"

Kim nodded. She was still breathing deeply and quickly. He lay on his side with one arm propping him up and the other resting on her rising and falling ribs. Beneath that silken flesh was her heart. For the first time, Mark asked himself how much of a woman's heart he'd reached. "You don't regret this?" he had to ask.

"No. Never."

He wondered if that was true.

Chapter Nine

Kim was alone. For close to two minutes the fact simply wouldn't register. Moonlight had been replaced by the early-morning sun. It should have been a glorious day, but without Mark beside her, she was unable to see the promise in dew and robins.

She didn't remember his leaving. Because she was a light sleeper, Kim knew he couldn't have left without her being aware unless he'd been very careful of his movements. She tried a half-dozen excuses but dismissed them as soon as they surfaced. No matter what his reasons, he should have told her.

Yesterday she'd been filled with enthusiasm for her job. Today work was nothing but a needed respite from lonely questions and an even lonelier body. She took a quick shower and pulled on clothes. She forced down a bowl of cereal and even drew in the fragrance of the roses she'd picked last night, but those acts were automatic. Today she decided to walk to the museum. She needed the physical exercise.

And she needed time alone with her thoughts and heart.

Kim had placed the small pocketknife on top of her dresser. She came across it while looking for her house keys. The knife's weight in the palm of her hand comforted her somehow. It had survived its owner and served as a link with the past. Although she had a full day of work ahead of her, Kim took the time to carry the knife into the kitchen and clean it with silver cleaner. Rust still obscured some of the design, but with the aid of a toothbrush, Kim was able to determine that some lettering had been carved into it. Unfortunately the etching was too faint for her to make out.

Kim dropped the knife into her purse, locked the door behind her and stepped out into the sunlight. There was something about the knife that fascinated her. She supposed she should have turned it over to the crime lab, but someone who'd died in the 1940s wasn't a priority with law enforcement. It would probably just be placed in storage somewhere and that would be the last anyone would see it. If she had time, she would try to research it by using the museum's resources.

Kim never made it to the museum. She'd gone around the cave-in and was heading toward the main part of town when Mark's now familiar Blazer pulled up beside her. He wasn't smiling as he called her over, but then neither was she.

"I was on my way to see you," he explained. "Something I need to pass on to you."

Mark was aware of Kim's withdrawal, but then he didn't expect anything different. With a beautiful, desirable woman sleeping next to him, Mark had slipped out of bed, tiptoed into the living room, dressed and then left like some kind of thief. Now circumstances were forcing them back together.

No, Mark amended, it wasn't circumstances. True, he had something to tell her but that could have been accomplished over the phone. He'd taken this early drive back to Camp Oro because leaving her last night had been the hardest thing he'd ever done and, somehow, without telling her enough, he had to make her understand it wasn't what he'd wanted to do.

He was traveling through uncharted territory this morning. He had no idea what he was doing, or what the outcome might be, and that disturbed the logical, practical lawyer part of him. Still, because his heart was involved, he had no choice. "You're walking." The words sounded stupid.

When she said nothing, he tried again. "Have you had breakfast?"

Kim nodded. Three bites of cereal counted as breakfast, didn't they?

"I haven't. Please join me."

"I have to get to work, Mark."

Anger, directed at himself, ruled him. Mark cut the vehicle's engine and pushed himself out of it. He was standing beside her before he spoke again. "We have to talk."

"We could have talked last night. Or this morning."

Damn. She was so right he could almost hate her for her wisdom. "That's not what I'm talking about," he told her, although that wasn't the truth.

"Are you telling me I don't deserve an explanation?" Her anger slapped him. "Forget I said that, Mark. You made your decision."

He couldn't leave things like that. Last night Kim had given him a precious gift and left him changed in ways he was just beginning to understand. If he let silence stand between them now, he would lose something precious. "Come with me. Please."

Kim did, not because it was the wise or safe thing to do, but because he was standing near, and she couldn't choose otherwise. Silently, he led her down the street to the Camp Oro Inn. Silently, they walked inside, and Mark chose a window seat where they could look out at the main street.

The Inn was almost empty this time of the morning. Before she had to ask herself how they were going to cut through the silence, the Inn's owner came by to visit. He stayed for at least ten minutes, comparing this year's tourist season with the last one and modestly accepting Mark's praise for some dinner the Inn had catered for members of the legal profession.

Finally Kim and Mark were alone. If he didn't say anything soon she'd leave. She wouldn't just sit here and watch him eat.

"I owe you an explanation." He was looking out the window, not at her.

"You don't owe me anything."

"You were sleeping so soundly. I didn't want to disturb you." Mark's whisper dropped a notch. "I was afraid that if I woke you, I'd never leave."

"You didn't have to leave."

"I think I did, Kim. No, please, let me explain. I'm a private person. Maybe it's a result of being in such a public profession. My clients dump everything on me. They spill their guts. It's my job to help them sort through their emotions."

Mark was rambling, or if not rambling, not getting to what Kim thought was essential. She couldn't let him do that. "What does that have to do with last night?" she broke in.

"What I'm saying, what I'm trying to say is— Kim, I've had years of listening to and dealing with other people's emotions. I think maybe I've learned to put my own feelings on hold."

"How convenient," Kim began and then stopped herself. This man, with his freshly shampooed hair and the smooth cheeks that had been covered in stubble last night, had made love to her twice. He had taken her out of herself and into him. She couldn't bear to attack him. "I'm not a client, Mark. I want to know what you're feeling. I believe I deserve at least that much."

"You do." For the first time since he had slipped out of bed last night, Mark touched Kim.

His fingers were gentle over hers. She could have pulled free easily. But because she couldn't release herself from him emotionally, Kim didn't draw away. Neither did she drop her defenses. He'd turned away from his study of the window. There was a new depth to his eyes this morning, a vulnerability she hadn't seen before.

"That's why I came back this morning."

"Is it?" Kim was surprised to find anger still in her voice. But maybe she shouldn't be. He'd hurt her by leaving, more than she'd been willing to admit until now. "Guilty conscience?"

"I guess that's as good a term as any. I didn't know it was going to mean as much as it did. Maybe—Kim, I think that's why I left. Does that make me sound like a coward? That's not it. I just . . . I needed time to think."

Kim accepted his explanation because the truth was she felt much the same way. They'd made love. But much more than that had taken place. The reality was overwhelming.

Although the waitress had arrived with Mark's breakfast, it still felt as if they were the only two people in the world. When they were alone again she told him, "I appreciate your honesty."

Mark could have started eating, but he was still holding Kim's hand and he didn't want to let go. "You've had an incredible effect on me. More than I knew possible."

"You're scaring me."

"Scaring?" Mark repeated. "I don't mean to."

"I know you don't. And it isn't anything you said or did. It's me." With her free hand, Kim tapped her chest. "We were talking about intensity. I'm thinking about—things I don't understand. Mark, your breakfast is getting cold."

"It doesn't matter. I'm sorry I left the way I did. You deserve better than that."

"Don't. It's all right. Now."

"Is it? Tell me the truth, Kim. That's what our being together this morning needs to be about."

"It is," Kim said gently. "Believe me. Please."

They shared the meal while watching the few people going about their business on Pioneer Street. Mark was into his second cup of coffee before he brought up the other reason he'd come to Camp Oro. "I got a call this morning. I was just getting up. I thought it might be you."

"Who was it?"

"Your boss. I guess I can call the museum board chairman your boss. Stephan wanted me to know that after a marathon session with Rogan last night, he and the director have finally seen eye to eye about something."

"About security? Why didn't they call me?"

"No. Not about security. Above the cave-in."

When Kim gave him a puzzled look, Mark continued. The essence of his conversation with Stephan Jarvis was that museum personnel and board members were going to be making a formal presentation to the town council advocating having the cave-in closed up and Rich Gulch Street reopened. To exploit an act of nature would turn the town into a freak show.

The ramifications for the town went deep. In order for Camp Oro to be listed on the national register of historic landmarks, the town had been placed under the administration of a federal agency. The agency was unwavering in its stand that because history evolved naturally, what was in existence today must be maintained in that same vein. It was one thing to restore an historic home to its original design. It was quite another to alter or exploit history with the intent of making money off it.

"Stephan can get pretty stuffy sometimes. I'm afraid I didn't follow everything he was telling me, just the high points. The upshot is, if the federal agency disapproves of the commercialization of the cave-in, which Stephan believes it will, the agency could go so far as to revoke Camp Oro's landmark status."

"And that would be bad?"

"Bad. As in capital letters bad. The historic buildings are on a tax freeze. Withdraw the status and taxes jump. You can imagine what kind of a stink those owners would raise if they had to pay taxes at current levels. Besides, without the historic draw, we'd lose a lot of tourist interest. Stephan is afraid the town would dry up. I'm inclined to believe he's right."

"So—" Kim was still having trouble making the adjustment from a personal conversation to one that had a direct bearing on the house she was living in. "He's going to make a presentation to the council?"

"Not Stephan. I guess Rogan's the one who came to Stephan. Rogan has considerable influence with the federal agency. I know he acts like a stuffy, slow-moving sloth sometimes, but he's a powerful man in certain circles. Anyway, he's already drafted a letter to the feds. As soon as he gets a response, he's going to add that to what he's planning to turn over to the council."

"Then that means the street will be repaired. Grandmother will be able to sell her house. I guess that's what she wants. I'm still not sure."

Mark held up a warning hand. "I wouldn't put up the For Sales sign yet, but that community pride bunch is going to have their work cut out for them trying to convince the council to turn the tunnel into their own Disneyland. It's going to be interesting watching the fur fly."

"I'm surprised," Kim admitted. "I really didn't think Rogan would get involved like this."

"Frankly, I am, too. So is Stephan. He thought he'd have his work cut out for him, to get Rogan off his duff, but Rogan had already begun the groundwork. My guess is, it has a lot to do with Rogan wanting to throw up roadblocks around Harden. Those two aren't exactly the best of friends. If you wind up with a usable street again, you're going to owe Rogan a thank-you."

If she'd been talking to anyone else, Kim would have kept her opinion to herself. But she could be honest with Mark and know he would keep her confidence. "There'll be a little eating of crow involved. Some of the things I've been thinking of that man are less than charitable. It's been impossible to light a fire under him."

"Like I said, a sloth."

Kim tried to tell herself not to get her hopes up too much, but it was impossible not to. She'd asked for a month's leave from her San Francisco job, which should have given her time to complete her assignment with the museum and, before the cave-in, have the house in the hands of a Realtor. Now, maybe, she would have to ask for more time. And she was particularly concerned that her grandmother be able to exchange the impersonal manor furniture for her own things. She mentioned that to Mark.

"I've been thinking about that myself," Mark told her. "In fact, I've lined up a moving company that's willing to haul some things out to the road and into their moving truck. I don't know when you're going to have time to supervise that."

"I'll make time," Kim reassured him. "I don't want to dictate what my grandmother does with her life, but I'd feel so much better knowing she at least has her own furniture. She's tried to tell me it doesn't matter, but I know it does."

Mark explained that he wanted to be on hand when the moving truck arrived so he could impress upon the movers not to park the truck near the cave-in.

By the time they'd finished breakfast, and Mark had convinced Kim to let him drive her to the museum, they'd tentatively set Tuesday of next week for the time to move most of Margaret's furnishings. Kim sat a few inches away from Mark in his car, marveling at how much brighter the day was without the weight on her heart.

"I don't know what the day's going to be like," Mark explained as she was getting out. "After I talk to the mayor,

I'll be in and out of meetings most of the day. There isn't a chance I'll be able to get away for lunch. Will you call me later?''

Kim couldn't say anything except yes. He was watching her with his incredibly deep eyes and she wanted to do or say something that they would both remember. ''Mark, the other day in the tunnel? I found something. I should probably have shown it to you before, but I guess I was being possessive.'' Kim reached into her purse and pulled out the knife. ''This was beside the skeleton.''

Mark took the knife from her. She watched as he ran his thumb over the newly exposed markings. When he looked at her again, his eyes were even deeper than they'd been a minute ago. He spoke in a flat tone she'd never heard before. ''What are you going to do with it?''

''I don't know. Nothing probably. I might look into its history.'' Mark was still looking at her, making her uneasy. ''You think I should have turned it over to the police, don't you?''

''No. No,'' Mark repeated absently. ''It's—Kim, don't tell your grandmother about this.''

''Do you really think it would bother her that much?''

''She doesn't need any more reminders of what you did. Last night, while I was taking her home, she kept talking about your going into the tunnel. She made me promise I wouldn't let you do that again.''

''I can't imagine ever wanting to. This—'' Kim indicated the knife. ''You don't think she'd be interested in it?''

''I think you'd be making a grave mistake to bring it up with her.''

''Isn't that a little strong?'' Kim began and then stopped herself. She'd ignored Mark's warning about the mourning pin last night and had to face her grandmother's reaction. ''All right. I don't know why it upset her so. Wait. Mark, Dow did some mining. I wonder—I'm sure it frightened her to think of him down in those mines.''

"She said something about that." Mark ran his hands over the steering wheel. "About being claustrophobic herself."

"She did? She never said anything about that to me."

Mark was still studying the steering wheel. "Pride, Kim. And maybe a little embarrassment. I just—I don't feel there's any reason to bring up the subject again by showing her the knife."

"All right." Kim dropped the knife back into her purse. "I still think it's interesting."

"Kim, don't do it, please."

Kim turned back toward Mark. "What—" she began but wasn't given the opportunity to complete her question. Charles Horne was walking toward Mark's Blazer. Mark rolled down the window.

"You're a hard woman to track down," Charles began. "You know, if I was going to have a business conversation with an attorney I wouldn't do it in his vehicle out in plain sight. But then maybe the conversation isn't all that business oriented."

Kim waited Charles out. From the way the corners of his mouth kept inching upward, she was pretty sure he was pleased to see her and Mark together. And she was sure that Charles's being at the museum wasn't a coincidence. The police chief had been looking for her.

"I just thought you should know. Some of the antiques that have been listed as missing? A couple of the pieces, a chair and a tea set, well, they were spotted in an antique shop in Oakland. There's a detective down there who's an antique buff. He's been scouting the antique places. According to the owner, his wife bought them a couple of weeks ago."

"Who'd she buy them from?" Mark asked.

"That's the problem." Charles shrugged his broad shoulders. "His wife is off on a buying trip back East. He doesn't expect to hear from her until the weekend. I thought, well, I'm thinking maybe we shouldn't give the museum staff this piece of information until we've talked to the wife. What do you think?''

Both Kim and Mark agreed. "It's a mess," Mark muttered. "I'd be willing to bet everything I've got that this is an inside job, but how do we prove it?"

"We will," Charles returned. "Sooner or later we will."

AT FIRST Kim didn't recognize what Rogan Coffers was handing her. She'd stood watching as Mark drove away. She'd been thinking, not about what was ahead of her or even what Charles had told them, but about the guarded, wary look he hadn't been able to hide from her when they were talking about the knife. Call me later, he'd asked her. There wasn't anything that would keep her from doing that.

"The blueprints." Kim acknowledged what was being placed in her hands. "You found them."

"Finally. I don't know what good they're going to do you, though."

A moment later Kim understood the museum director's comment. The blueprints weren't the originals but a poorly reproduced copy. Someone had tried to reduce them, which resulted in writing and measurements so small they could barely be made out. Rogan leaned over her as Kim spread the papers on his desk. "Maybe I can have them blown up a bit," she mused. "These are just about useless. Are you sure the originals aren't around?"

Rogan shook his head. "I've never seen the originals. Fortunately I've never had a reason to use them."

Kim stifled her disappointment. She would simply have to make do. She thanked Rogan for what he'd been able to accomplish, but before she could go off in search of a magnifying glass, Rogan stopped her.

It was the first time the director had touched her. She was surprised by the weight of his cool hand. "I'd like to talk to you for a minute."

Kim looked up from the blueprints. As deep as Mark's eyes had been a few minutes ago, Rogan's were even deeper. Part of the impact, Kim knew, came from the way his eyes were set so deeply into his prominent facial bones. But— maybe it was the unnatural coolness of Rogan's office, and his words to her the day they met, that reminded her of Mark's and Charles's warning not to trust any of the museum's employees.

"What about?" Kim forced herself to ask in a calm voice.

Rogan wanted to tell her about his efforts to involve the historic government agency in the cave-in issue. Kim broke in to tell him that she already knew.

"Mark Stockton? How—Stephan told him, didn't he?"

"Yes. Apparently Stephan believed Mark should have that information. I'm not sure what he's going to tell the town council." Kim thanked Rogan, explaining that because of her grandmother, she had a personal stake in getting the street restored to its former condition.

"That's exactly the way I feel, Ms. Revis. The fight isn't over," Rogan said. Then he went on to explain that apparently the head of the community pride group had already gotten wind of what Rogan was trying to accomplish. "I don't trust Harden Langford any farther than I can throw him. He's got considerable pull of his own. If he thinks this is going to be a power play between him and me, he's going to pull out all the stops."

"But what can he do if you have the federal government behind you?"

"You don't know Harden. The man hates me. This isn't about producing money that might or might not benefit Camp Oro. It's about Harden wanting me on my knees."

"Why? Why would he want to do that?"

"It's personal, Kim. Something between Harden and me."

Kim couldn't believe the tension coiling around Rogan. She'd felt his temper the morning they met, when he'd told her he considered her an intruder. But that was nothing like the cold fury glittering in his eyes now. Mark had called Rogan a sloth. No. This man was an animal backed into a corner and ready to come out fighting.

Kim fought to keep normalcy in her voice. "What do you think he's going to do?"

"If I knew, I'd know how to attack him. Listen, Ms. Revis, there's something you can do. Something you have to do."

Although the last thing she wanted to do was stay where Rogan could touch her, Kim stood her ground. Once again he placed his hand on her shoulder. Once again she felt his cool fingers and watched his glittering eyes. "You've got pull with Mark Stockton, but you can't use him because he works for the town. Get yourself a lawyer. Someone who goes for the jugular. Get him to threaten to sue the town for your and your grandmother's inconvenience. Make the council understand that if they side with Langford, they're in a hell of a lot of trouble."

Kim had considered retaining an attorney, not because she wanted to go for the jugular but because she felt a lawyer might be able to present her argument more clearly. Now when she nodded her head, it wasn't so much because she agreed with Rogan but because she wanted to get away from the man. "I'll think about it," Kim promised as she retreated.

With the aid of a magnifying glass, Kim was able to make a little more sense out of the blueprints. It was a struggle, but at least she now had a better idea of each room's dimension, the thickness of the walls and where the electrical system was routed. It was almost noon when Kim stood and stretched the kinks out of her neck. She'd gone into the staff meeting room so she could spread out. No one had come in while she was working. In fact, now that she'd thought about it, Kim realized that she'd heard nothing. There was a penetrating silence.

The thefts, most of them at least, had taken place during the day. How many people were in the museum now? Were the display rooms filled with visitors, or was the noon hour a quiet period? William, Garner, Rogan. One by one, the three men with the greatest access to the artifacts came to mind. William looked frail, but Kim wasn't sure whether she could best him in a struggle. She could probably outrun Rogan, but maybe she'd never have the chance to test that theory. She could still feel the cool strength of his hand on her shoulder and remembered the wild depth in his eyes. And then there was Garner, with his sculptured muscles. Kim wouldn't last a minute against the business manager.

Kim reached for the phone and dialed Mark's number. After two rings, his secretary came on the line. No. Mr. Stockton wasn't at his desk. The secretary wasn't sure where he'd gone only that he'd gotten a phone call and left a few minutes ago.

Kim didn't try to justify her quick exit from the meeting room. She couldn't deny that the shadows in the long hall frightened her, or that she had no defense against the unease pricking up and down her spine. She'd intended to spend the noon hour working up an electrical diagram, but now all she wanted was to feel the sunlight on her face.

When the front door closed behind her, Kim drew a deep breath of warm air. She could laugh at her fear now, but she knew she wouldn't be laughing if she went back inside.

Kim had no idea what she was going to do with her noon hour. She was hungry but too restless to sit down for a meal, and there really wasn't time to walk back to the house. Another double-decker ice-cream cone from the soda fountain relieved her hunger pains. Then she began walking aimlessly down the main street studying window displays and lingering in front of Norval's Antiques. There was an older woman manning the cash register and Kim saw no sign of Anthea. It was just as well. Kim was in no mood to talk to anyone.

Except Mark.

Charles wasn't in his office, but the door was unlocked and the office clerk barely glanced up when Kim mentioned that Charles was an old friend, and she simply wanted to use his phone.

Convinced that she was only wasting her time, and she'd get the secretary again, Kim was only half listening when Mark came on the line. "I didn't think you'd be there. I just called a few minutes ago and got your secretary," she explained.

"It was a quick trip. Now I'm holding down the fort so my secretary can get some lunch. Where are you, Kim? Are you all right?"

Was Mark telepathic? Was there some way he could know what had gone through her mind when she became aware of the museum's silence? "Of course," she said quickly.

"Good. You've been on my mind."

Kim took Mark's words into her heart. It was a moment before she remembered to tell him where she was. Kim relayed the essence of what she and Rogan had talked about this morning. "He's really upset," she finished. "I think he hates Harden. It's—maybe I'm reading more into it than there is, but it's as if there's this war between Rogan and Harden, and the town is caught in the middle."

"You're not wrong, Kim. Those two men have been at odds with each other for years. There are rumors, something about a personal disagreement. I try not to get involved in that sort of thing. As for your hiring a lawyer, I'm advising against it, at least for now. There's no reason for you to be out the money."

"I wish you could represent me."

"You know I can't, Kim. Not while I'm representing the town. Do you have to go back to the museum this afternoon?"

Kim explained that she had no choice if she was going to be able to present the two security firms with a workable set of plans. Then Kim asked the question that had been on her mind all morning. "Will I be seeing you tonight?"

Mark's silence lasted too long. Even before he spoke, she knew what his answer was going to be. "Something came up. An extension of why I was out of the office earlier. Kim, I'm sorry, but I'm going to have to see a client tonight."

Was he sorry, Kim wondered. A heartbeat later she shrugged off her unfair thought. He *was* a lawyer. There were bound to be times when work had to come first.

THE AFTERNOON dragged. It was colored by a return of Kim's earlier unease about being in the museum. Although she kept the door open and was aware of visitors trooping up and down the hall, she was also intensely aware of her isolation. Rogan dropped by twice to ask about her progress. Each time he seemed more interested in what she'd been able to make out from the faded blueprint than in what she would be submitting to the two firms later that day. He wasn't nearly as imposing in person as he'd been in her mind. He simply didn't seem to be a man with violence in him. Directors of museums didn't go around hitting people to prevent security systems from being installed.

Kim didn't bother with dinner that night. She ate half of a tuna sandwich, and then tried to distract herself by getting some of her grandmother's furniture ready to be moved. Vigorously waxing and polishing the sturdy old hardwood pieces relieved some of her pent-up tensions and allowed Kim to fall into bed physically weary. She'd listened for the phone all evening, hoping against all logic that Mark would at least be able to call her. But he didn't. Kim fell asleep with that grim thought on her mind.

BEFORE LEAVING the museum, Kim had arranged for a morning meeting with Rogan, Garner and Anthea Norval. If the security guard could make it, she wanted him there as well. When Kim pushed open the tall, heavy door, she made herself a vow. Today she would concentrate on work. She wouldn't think about Mark; she wouldn't call him.

Garner was already in the conference room. The business manager watched silently as Kim spread out the diagrams she would be using in her presentation. Finally he broke the silence. "The rumor mill is working."

Kim wanted to let the comment slide, but if she did Garner would know she was trying to ignore him. "What are the rumors?"

"That you and our illustrious town attorney are quite an item."

"We had breakfast at the Inn yesterday."

"And dinner together a few nights before. A rather tacky place according to Anthea, but then there isn't much that isn't tacky in her estimation. Are you sure seeing Mark Stockton is wise?"

A lot wiser than seeing you would be, Kim thought. "I don't understand why anyone would care," she said instead.

"Maybe I do, Kim."

Kim could no longer pretend she was interested in what her hands were doing. Tensing a little, Kim turned toward Garner. As was his custom, Garner was dressed to accentuate the mix of animal sensuality and dedicated businessman he liked to project. His black slacks strained across his flat belly. Kim wondered how long the seams would hold up. He was wearing a white, fitted shirt of a summer-weight fabric with no undershirt. He was, Kim could admit, a physically perfect man. But unlike Mark, she could look at Garner without wanting anything from him. "I don't know what you're getting at," she told him.

"Don't you." Garner rose to his feet, reminding Kim of a sleek, hunting cat. Hunger was in his eyes, but for what she didn't understand.

Before he could reach her, if that was what he had in mind, the door opened. Anthea Norval's cold laugh dissolved the tension in the room. "Bad timing. Would you like me to come back later?"

"No," Kim said too quickly. She took advantage of the situation by backing, casually she hoped, away from Garner. "You're right on time."

"You might ask Garner if he feels the same way. I hope this meeting is going to be productive. Ever since the media got wind of our little problem, I've been deluged with questions. Everyone wants to know what we're doing to plug the leak." Anthea slid gracefully into the chair next to the one Garner had vacated. She propped her elbows on the table and rested her chin lightly on her manicured hands.

Garner whistled. He turned from Kim and reached for Anthea's hand. "Nice rock, madam businesswoman. A present from the doting husband?"

Anthea was wearing a ring with a stone the size of a small boulder. Maybe that was an exaggeration, Kim admitted, but it was certainly the largest ruby she'd ever seen. Her first thought was that it was more than a little gaudy, but it wasn't her place to judge.

Kim commented on the ring. In return she got a smug smile from Anthea and a lengthy discourse on how she'd had to go to San Francisco to find a jeweler who understood her needs. "And to answer your question, Garner, my husband didn't give it to me. I decided I needed to reward myself. I work hard. I deserve it."

Kim might not agree with Anthea's taste in jewelry, but if she'd made the money, it was certainly her right to spend it however she saw fit. She was about to tell Anthea that when William joined them.

The man looked haggard. He seemed to have aged since the last time Kim had seen him. She was relieved when he folded his lanky body into the nearest chair. He didn't look at either Garner or Anthea. Instead he kept his dull eyes focused on Kim.

"Are you all right?" Kim asked. "Are you sure you should be here?"

"I was up all night."

Garner and Anthea had barely given William a glance, but Kim couldn't dismiss him that easily. "Problems?" she prompted.

"My brother. Sick again. I had to take him back to the hospital. The third time this month."

"Oh. I'm sorry," Kim muttered.

"Are you?" William's voice was as hard-edged as ever. "Sorry enough to help me pay the damn medical bills? How long is this going to take?"

Kim couldn't give William a definite answer. She'd just started to explain that they were waiting for the director to arrive when he came in. For once Rogan was wearing a suit that almost fit. Ignoring what it did to his jacket, Rogan slouched in his chair. Although not as exhausted as William, he, too, looked as if the night had been a long one.

Kim took a deep breath. If today's meeting was to accomplish something, she would have to anticipate potential disagreements and somehow keep these four people working together in the same room. She handed each of them a copy of the blueprint and was turning to the blowup she'd taped to the wall behind her when the door opened to reveal another figure.

It was Mark.

Chapter Ten

The room seemed to pulse. The long, empty night came back to haunt Kim. Surely the others in the room could sense her reaction, but Kim couldn't concern herself with that. She'd spent hours last night telling herself she didn't care. If Mark decided to put work before her, so be it. She could live with his decision.

Couldn't she?

Mark locked his gaze with each of them in turn, putting off facing Kim to the last. Her eyes glistened a little. He wanted nothing more than to take her in his arms and apologize for the hours of silence. But if he said anything, it would have to be a lie, and he couldn't do that to either of them.

"I have Anthea to thank for this," he explained. What he was about to say and what the wealthy businesswoman might say in return could back him into a corner. But in a perverse way, Mark was perhaps ready for that. "If I hadn't seen her last night, I wouldn't have known about this meeting."

"I'm surprised, Mark." Anthea laughed her careful, measured laugh. "You were so intent on your conversation with your client that I wasn't sure you heard anything I said. A word of advice," Anthea went on when Mark tried to interrupt. "If you want a private conversation, don't take your client to a public restaurant."

"I'll remember that, Anthea." Mark glanced at Kim. Yes, she was listening to every word. More than that, unless he was mistaken, Kim was trying to read what was going on inside him. In an attempt to prevent that, Mark hurried through his explanation that he was here on behalf of Camp Oro. "The town is more than casually interested in the problems the museum is having. I've been contacted by the mayor and council. They would like me to keep them abreast of developments. I hope—" Mark turned toward Rogan. "I trust this meets with your approval."

"We have nothing to hide," Rogan muttered.

"I'm glad to hear that." It was then that Mark moved forward to find a seat. He deliberately chose a spot as far from Kim as he could. When Garner looked at him with a questioning half smile, Mark chose to ignore the business manager.

Anthea was talking. "That's right, Mark. Take over. That's what you've always done, isn't it." She waved her hand with the new ring at Mark. "Far be it from you to wait for a formal invitation. You should run for mayor, you know. You hold the position in everything but name as it is."

"Is this a formal objection to my presence?" Mark countered.

"Of course not." Anthea's laugh was cold. "I certainly wouldn't do that."

The meeting lasted the better part of an hour. Kim wound up strongly, telling those assembled that she had drawn up what she believed to be the most effective security system for the money. Yes, it called for certain security measures that would be obvious to the public, but she would stick by her proposal. "It's going to cost money, more money than any of us would like. But I don't believe we can get away with anything less."

Garner waved the figures Kim had given him in the air. "All I can say is, I hope those firms' estimates come in under what you've projected. This is going to damn near bankrupt us, Ms. Revis."

"I doubt that," Kim countered. She wasn't going to look at Mark or think about him. For as long as she was in this room, she was nothing but a professional hired to do a job. "Yes, it's going to tax the museum's budget, but I think you have to agree that we really have no alternative. Not if we're going to have any artifacts left under this roof."

Anthea snatched the figures from Garner. Her ring flashed. "This is going to cut into my projects. We can't have this. We can't."

"We can't let people walk away with everything that's valuable," Mark said.

Kim had expected questions, but for a moment she didn't fully understand the force of what was being thrown at her. Then, beyond all reason and wisdom, her eyes met Mark's. There were other messages in his gaze, questions she couldn't begin to answer. But foremost was the warning she'd almost forgotten. Neither of them had any doubt that the person responsible for the museum's losses was in this room.

Anthea, with her expensive tastes? Garner, with his arrogance and his empty life? William, with a sick brother draining his finances? Even Rogan, who hadn't wanted her here in the first place?

Kim stilled the wish to take a calming breath. She wasn't going to show any sign of anxiety or weakness. "There won't be a Comstock Museum much longer if it remains vulnerable. I don't believe we have any choice in the matter. I also believe that the board is going to back me."

The grumbling continued. Rogan took particular exception to the money earmarked to provide a security guard with formal police academy training. As he'd done earlier,

William said nothing. But his fingers were knotted together and his knuckles white. Kim could hear him breathing.

No formal endorsement of Kim's proposal was forthcoming from the employees, but that wasn't what she had been after. The truth was, she was under no obligation to inform them of her proposal before presenting it to the museum board. However, she believed they had a right to be kept informed.

"You're looking a little rocky," Mark whispered as the meeting was breaking up. Rogan had already left. Garner was still teasing Anthea about her taste in jewelry. William hadn't made a move to get to his feet.

"Rocky?" Kim repeated. She tried to concentrate on the business of returning her material to its folder, but there was no way she could ignore Mark's presence or her body's re- action to it. They could have been together last night. And if they couldn't, he could at least have told her why not. "I'll survive."

"I'm sure you will." Mark took her elbow firmly and pulled her away from the table. He leaned close to her and continued. "What you did took guts."

"I'll take that as a compliment," Kim said, expelling her breath slowly. She wished Mark hadn't touched her. She was finding it almost impossible to think. "What are you going to tell the council?"

"That you have guts. That the museum board spent its money wisely when they hired you. What are you going to do now?"

"Get in touch with Stephan and the rest of the board members. I'm just about ready to make my presentation to them."

"That's not what I mean." Mark's voice was low and rumbling, the way it had been the night they made love. "When you leave here, where are you going?"

Kim wasn't given the chance to answer. Anthea's laugh effectively shattered the quiet conversation. "Consorting with the enemy, are you Mark? A piece of advice, if I were you, I'd be more discreet. Another piece of advice. Getting to the granddaughter through the grandmother should be beneath you.''

Mark tensed but said nothing. Instead he helped Kim with her papers until even William had struggled to his feet, leaving them alone. He'd done it. Backed himself into a corner. Now all he could do was wait.

''What was that about?'' Kim asked.

''Anthea? Let's just say she isn't my biggest fan.''

''I rather suspected that.'' Mark was standing close but not touching her. It was safer that way. Safer and lonelier. ''Why?''

It had happened almost four years ago, but obviously Anthea Norval had a long memory. One of Anthea's customers had bought several pieces of furniture from Anthea, relying on her contention that the pieces were originals. When the customer had learned that they were in fact copies, he'd sued Anthea. Mark had been the customer's lawyer. Although Anthea maintained that if the pieces had been copies, she hadn't been aware of it, Mark had won the case. He'd worded his complaint so that Anthea was held accountable whether the misrepresentation was done willfully or through ignorance. Not only did Anthea have to return the purchase price, but she'd also wound up having to pay all legal fees.

Kim whistled when Mark finished telling the story. ''You're talking thousands of dollars, aren't you?''

''Thousands that Anthea has never forgiven me for. She won't say anything when we're in social settings. Anthea is much too civilized for that. But, in private, she never fails to get her digs in.''

''Being successful means a great deal to her, doesn't it?''

''More than most people realize. If there's one word that sums up Anthea Norval, it's ruthless.''

''Ruthless?''

"Don't dismiss her," Mark warned. "Don't dismiss any of them. And Kim?" His hand on her forearm was light; still, Kim was a million miles from being able to dismiss her response. "Don't turn your back on any of them."

Kim could have told Mark that he was overreacting, but she didn't. She had faced an unreasoning, unthinking fear in this very room yesterday. "I won't," she told him.

Mark turned and picked up Kim's folder. "Let's get out of here."

Neither of them spoke until they were outside and Mark had stowed the files in Kim's car. He glanced at his watch and groaned. "I wish I had more time.'

"I wish you did, too. Will I see you tonight?"

They might be seen; it didn't matter. No matter how many tongues might wag, Mark couldn't make it through the day without holding Kim in his arms. He sensed her surprised reaction to being pulled against him, and then her quick surrender.

He'd been cruel to her last night. He should have given her more of an explanation. If nothing else he should have called after he got home. But if he'd gone that far, he would have told her everything.

And because Mark tried to be the best damn lawyer he knew how to be, he knew he couldn't do that. "Kim?" He almost decided to tell her that he was falling in love with her, but he wasn't free to. "Tonight? I can't see you tonight, either."

"Oh."

She wasn't asking questions, as she had last night. She was accepting what little he gave her. Because he was afraid it didn't matter as much to her as it did to him, this time Mark explained everything. He was due in court tomorrow morning. Because of conflicts in schedules, his client hadn't been able to meet with him before tonight. Unless Mark was lucky, and he knew he wouldn't be, the meeting would last half the night.

"I'm sorry. Not because I'm going to have to walk into court with two hours of sleep under my belt, but because— we need time together, Kim. At least I think we do."

"We do," Kim muttered from the cradle of his arms. "We do."

THE NEXT DAY Kim made her presentation to the museum board and after receiving their approval to move ahead, she invited representatives of the two security firms to the museum for extensive tours. It was late afternoon, and Kim still hadn't been able to reach Mark at his office when she collected her material and stepped out of the museum into the sunshine. She was almost to her car when Charles Horne pulled up in the police car. He gave her a brief nod, and then turned his attention to the museum. "I didn't expect you to be here."

"Are you disappointed?"

"Not disappointed. Just surprised. Do you mind if we take a walk?"

"A walk?" Kim indicated her armload. "I brought my car. I wanted to get rid of this stuff."

"I can wait."

A minute later Kim had deposited her files in her car and rejoined the police chief. Charles had been studying the solid building. "Not many windows in that place, are there? I've been sitting all day. Occupational hazard, I guess. You don't mind helping me get a little exercise, do you?" He touched Kim's arm to indicate they should cross the street. He didn't ask if this was what she wanted to do.

"You certainly are causing a stir," Charles said, once they were heading down a side street away from the museum. "I haven't seen this much excitement in town in years."

"What do I have to do with things?"

"Everything. You come back to town and everything blows up. If I'd known that was going to happen, I wouldn't have rolled out the welcome mat."

"Don't lay that on me." Kim threw a good-natured punch at Charles. It felt so good to be with someone she didn't have to weigh every word around. "The thefts were a fact long before I came on the scene, and you certainly can't blame me for the cave-in. Between you and me, I can hardly wait for Monday night."

Charles frowned and then gave Kim a quick if not easy grin. "The council meeting. Yeah, I imagine you are eager to have things resolved."

Kim told him she didn't understand why things were taking so long. "I don't know why the council didn't set another meeting for this week. Or maybe I do," she amended. "I think they're hoping things will resolve themselves without the council having to make a decision."

"Fat chance. Both Rogan and Harden are big guns. They're going to come to that meeting blazing away at each other. Between you and me, I wouldn't miss that meeting for the world."

"I wish I could."

"Don't let it get to you, Kim," Charles soothed. "Mark'll be there. He knows how to keep things in hand. One thing you can always be sure of with Mark. He'll be square with everyone."

Is he being square with me? Kim wondered.

"Speaking of Mark," the police chief went on. "I was talking to him, what was it, this morning I guess." Charles glanced behind him and then started walking again. "He'd run into town on some business and we got to talking. Something— It's not the most pleasant thing to think about Kim, but it's reality."

Kim waited for the chief to go on. In truth, she was unable to keep up her end of the conversation. Mark had been in Camp Oro this morning? He hadn't tried to get in touch with her. Distance—once again distance was coming between them.

"Let's say you get this security system in place in a couple of weeks. The thefts stop. Everyone pats you on the back for a job well-done. It sounds good as far as it goes. But— maybe we'll never know who's responsible. Maybe that Oakland dealer's wife will come back and won't be able to tell us anything about who she bought the merchandise from. If there's a go-between—"

Kim's focus had been on safeguarding the museum's valuables. Naturally Charles was concerned with bringing a criminal to justice. "I'm sorry." She shook her head. "I almost asked what you were going to do about that, but there isn't anything more you can do, is there?"

"It doesn't look like it." For the second time, Charles glanced behind him. "Unless we get incredibly lucky between now and the time the system is in place, there isn't much chance we'll ever get any more of those, what do you call them, artifacts back."

"I know. That bothers me."

"Don't. That's my problem. You're doing a good job. A damn good job."

Kim and Charles walked and talked for another couple of minutes. Charles was planning on taking the family fishing Saturday morning. Kim remembered going on fishing trips on the Yuba River with her father. She envied Charles and Sandy and the boys. She didn't want Charles to leave. She didn't want to return to her car. As long as he was with her, she could think about sunburning her nose while sitting on a rock overlooking a river. She didn't have to ask herself why Mark hadn't gotten in touch with her this morning.

"Do you do this much?" Kim asked as their seemingly aimless walk brought them to the museum parking lot. "Walk around town, I mean."

"Not as much as I'd like to." Charles's voice lost the casual tone it'd had when they were talking about fishing. "Kim, you take care of yourself, you hear."

"I will. Charles, are you all right?"

"All right? 'Course I am. Well, almost all right. I've got to see Anthea later today. You're the lucky one. You get to spend the evening with Mark. You are seeing him tonight, aren't you?"

"Anthea?" Kim sidestepped the question. "What do you have to see her about?"

"Who knows." Charles was looking up at a second-story window with its heavy curtain. "Something about needing the alley behind her place blocked off while some delivery truck's there."

Anthea. Kim was almost to her car when what the woman said yesterday hit her full force. Anthea had accused Mark of trying to get to Kim through her grandmother. Margaret Revis was Mark's client, and he had spent the other evening with a client. A client he hadn't wanted to talk to her about.

Had it been her grandmother?

Numbly Kim reached for the door handle. There was one way of finding the answer. She would go to Mark's place tonight and ask him.

Above Kim, a second-story curtain was pulled back. The person watching had seen the police chief and Kim Revis walk away from the museum grounds together. The person had ticked off every second that they were gone, mind going a thousand miles a second, asking questions, speculating, sweating. Now the chief had come into the building and Kim was heading toward her car.

What had the two talked about? Was it the beginning of the end? And, most important, was there any way of hiding the evidence?

KIM WASN'T GOING to take a chance on calling Mark and being put off. She had no plan beyond being at his house when he got home. How and when she would ask if he'd spent the evening after they became lovers with her grandmother, she had no idea. What Kim did know was that it wasn't a fool's question and that the answer, if he was honest with her, would explain a great deal.

It never occurred to her that the truth might shatter her.

Mark wasn't home, but Kim was patient. She sat on the front steps reading the evening paper until she heard his Blazer pull into the driveway behind her car.

She put down the paper, leaned forward and waited. For an unguarded minute, Mark's features came alive with an emotion that touched her deeply. Then caution and wariness settled in, and Kim steeled herself to accept that change.

Kim waited until Mark was on the steps. Then she held up her hand so he could help her to her feet. She brought her body close to his, waiting for his reaction. First came an embrace so freely given that she almost wept with relief. Then, just as she was close to believing that all was well between them, he pushed her away and held her inches from him.

"What are you doing here?"

"I need to see you."

"What—are you all right?"

"Of course I'm all right," Kim told him although that wasn't the truth. "I heard you were in Camp Oro this morning. I—I guess you didn't have time to get in touch with me. I wanted to see you."

"Oh, Kim. I'm so glad you did."

Mark was scaring her. This was a man everyone said was in control. But he was holding her so tight; the emotions flowing through him were so raw.

They were inside before Kim was aware of what had happened. "Mark? Why didn't I hear from you this morning?" He opened his mouth, but she waved off whatever he might say. "I shouldn't have asked that. We ... how long have we known each other? Only days." Mark was looking down at her with his fingers laced through hers. She should know where she stood with him. If he were any other man, she either would, or it wouldn't matter so terribly.

But this was Mark.

"I probably shouldn't be here," she went on. Kim had no idea what she was going to say. She'd planned a million witty things while she was waiting for him, but now he was here. "You're busy. You have so much on your mind."

"Stop it, Kim. Nothing's more important than you."

"Do you mean that?"

"I should have dropped by the museum to see you. I was going to. And then...Kim, Charles said something I couldn't shrug off."

Kim waited. She could wait the rest of the night for the right words from Mark. Please, make them the right words.

"He said something about danger."

"Danger? We've talked about that before."

"Maybe not enough."

"Mark," Kim said impatiently. "What does this have to do with seeing me?"

"Maybe nothing. Maybe everything." Mark propelled Kim into the living room and sat them both down on the couch. "Kim, what if you came across something? Something the thief didn't want found out?"

"Nothing's going to happen to me."

"You don't know that. We have no idea how desperate this person might be. That's what Charles and I were talking about. If either he or I were seen spending too much time with you, well, it could give whoever is responsible more ammunition, more of a push to do something. Something rash. I'm not a policeman, but I do represent authority and the law."

"Mark—" Kim was going to tell Mark that that didn't make sense, but she couldn't get the words out. If that possibility had made an impact on Mark, she couldn't dismiss it. "That's why you didn't come see me today?" she asked instead.

"Kim, we're dealing with someone we know nothing about. You've been working with the thief for days now. If the thief hasn't done anything yet, maybe it's because he or she hasn't been pushed far enough yet. But what you're doing represents the end to what that person had been free to do. If you and I are seen together, who knows what that might trigger? I wasn't going to risk your safety Kim, either by seeing you or calling you at work."

Kim loved Mark for his concern. She loved him for a great deal more than that, but for this moment it was his protective instinct that won her heart. She wanted to lean into him, to let him carry her weight and let the other night repeat itself. But first . . . "Mark, Charles and I bumped into each other this afternoon. He wanted to go for a walk. He kept looking back at the museum. I never thought—"

"Did he say anything?"

Kim shook her head. "Maybe he didn't want to worry me. Mark, I don't want to be treated that way. Anything you and Charles are thinking, I have a right to know."

Mark had spent the afternoon in court. Although he and his client had come out on the winning end of a relatively simple civil trial, Mark was feeling the effect of three hours of questioning and cross-examinations. He'd wanted to go home, change clothes and then call Kim. Now Kim was in his house. In twelve years of being a member of the legal system, Mark had never let anything come before his commitment to that system.

But that was before Kim had come into his life. She'd said something to him; he should be responding to that. But she was looking at him with her incredible honest eyes. He saw the hurt and desire in them. Hurt because he hadn't been there for her enough, and desire because, thank God, she hadn't given up on him.

It had taken a great deal of courage for Kim to come here tonight. He hadn't let her know enough, and he hadn't given her as much as she needed, and yet she was still here.

She was offering so much. Her eyes left nothing hidden and exposed her greatest needs. Her greatest fears. She wasn't sure of him. He'd made her doubt what he felt for her.

Damn! With everything in him, Mark didn't want it to be like that for her. Unlike most of the people he dealt with, Kim was without secrets or deception. She could give him one thing he hadn't had enough of in his life—honesty. If she was to stay with him, if things were ever going to be right between them, he had to give her the same.

But that couldn't be; he couldn't give her everything.

But maybe, for tonight, he could give her more than he'd ever given another woman. "I promise," he whispered. "From now on, Charles and I will tell you everything we come up with."

"I believe you." Was it happening? Were the hours of doubt and fear going to be swept aside? Tomorrow Kim would ask herself that question again, but not now. Now Mark was drawing her against him, and she was feeling his strength.

"I didn't know if I should come," she told him from the shelter he offered. "I wasn't sure you wanted to see me."

"Oh, Kim. I've hurt you, haven't I?"

Kim didn't want to tell him yes. But if they were to be more than shadows passing through each other's lives, she had to be honest. "I understand your job. At least I'm trying to. But I wanted to be more important than anything else you had to do."

"You are, Kim. You are. I should have explained. Called you."

"That's all right. We're together now." Then, although it was the last thing she wanted to do, Kim asked her necessary question. "It is all right that I'm here, isn't it?"

Mark couldn't handle her fear, her uncertainty. He might not have the words to make things up to her, but perhaps what was in his heart didn't need words.

He pressed his palms to her temples and felt her pulse. He buried his face in her hair and breathed in her essence. Mark wanted only to let her understand how important she'd become to him.

Mark's bedroom was almost twice the size of the one Kim had been sleeping in since coming to Camp Oro. For a moment it bothered her that this was the first time she'd seen it, but she cast the thought away. Mark had brought her in here, and now he was holding her, and she felt full. Too much still hadn't been said; there was still too much distance between the two of them. But Kim would take what was being offered in this darkened room with its masculine smells, and in the taking, gain a great deal.

Kim wanted to undress him. She wanted to slowly reveal him to herself, to tease her senses as much as she hoped she was teasing him. He'd taken off his jacket and tie when he left the office, but she could free him of his shirt, slowly pull the belt off his waist, reach for his zipper.

Kim's fingers hesitated there. They'd been lovers before; there was no reason for her to feel this unsure. But... A deep breath restored Kim's courage. She took Mark's scent deep inside her. His hands were on her shoulders, slowly sliding fabric over her sensitive flesh. What she needed to believe was in his eyes; he was ready for her to continue.

"I like being undressed by you," he told her when she was done.

"I'm shaking. I don't know why, but I am."

It was his turn. With his mouth soft and parted and his nostrils flared, Mark lifted Kim's soft sweater higher and higher, pausing at her breasts while his thumbs gave her a taste of what was to come. Then the air was on her shoulders, and Mark's fingers were reaching beneath her bra for her waiting flesh. Kim wanted to go on looking at him. She needed to know what he was feeling.

There were no doubts now. His eyes and hands and breath told her that. Kim felt the same wanting, but it was more than that for her. Deep inside, so deep that until tonight she hadn't known it existed in her, she felt a fullness, a sense of having come home.

As Mark lifted her in his arms and placed her on the bed, a thought slid through her and took over her heart. She was in love. Not just for tonight. Not just for as long as she and Mark made love. Forever.

With that terrible and wonderful knowledge ruling her, Kim reached for Mark and pulled him down to her.

"I wanted it to be slow for you," Mark said, moving his fingers on her thigh slowly closer to the core of her femininity. "I wanted to make this take forever. But I don't think I can."

How honest he was. How vulnerable and honest.

"We have the night. We do, don't we?"

"Oh, yes, Kim. We have the night."

Yes! This was right. This was wonderful. Mark was moving, slowly at first, and then with more power. Kim clung to him with her spine arched toward him and her tongue taking in his taste.

She was losing herself. She'd wanted to cling to the world, to savor the sweetness of his giving of himself to her. But his surrender became hers and they went together.

"YOU'RE CRYING?"

"I am?"

"Tears. I can taste your tears."

Inch by inch Kim pulled herself back from where Mark had taken her. He was lying beside her now, with a leg still over her and an arm resting on her breasts. He was weight and substance, and power. Again he touched his tongue to her lashes.

"I don't feel like crying," she told him.

"I hope not." There was no need for him to whisper, and yet he was. "I don't ever want to make you cry, Kim."

That might not be possible. It was a world of action and emotion. Maybe that explained her tears. But her tears were tears of joy. "You haven't had dinner," she remembered. "I—we didn't take time for that."

"As long as we had time for the important thing." Mark shifted position, not to leave her, but to catch a nipple between his teeth and draw it into his mouth. Kim's spine arched. With that touch she wanted him again.

"Don't do that if you want to get out of this bed."

"I don't care. Maybe we'll stay here forever."

They didn't eat until midnight. Wearing the shirt Mark had worn to work that day, Kim carried two Mexican dinners from the microwave to the table. She was aware of Mark's eyes on her legs, but there was no modesty left in her. For hours Mark had explored her, come to know every inch of her. She'd done the same with him. This might not be the first night they'd spent together, but the exploration had been new. Now she could look at him and know there was no doubt.

She was in love.

"Is this what you eat when you're alone?" she asked.

Mark picked at the beans and melting cheese. "Sometimes. But never this late. We might regret this."

"We might." Kim picked up a forkful of enchilada and swallowed. She was starved. "I'll take the risk," she finished.

Mark ate more slowly, watching her. "Is that what making love does to you? You should have fixed yourself more."

"Maybe I will. Aren't you hungry?"

Mark nodded, but not because he was aware of what his stomach was trying to tell him. By the kitchen clock, it was now 12:13 a.m. There were memories, wonderful memories of playing with Kim's body until play would no longer suffice and his need took him into her. He still tasted the salt of her tears. His fingers remembered the feel of her soft flesh over bone and muscle. His heart carried the memory of her murmured cries.

His heart. There was a great deal more in his heart than a memory. He was awakening, coming out of a slumber he hadn't known had claimed him. He, Mark Stockton, was a man in love.

"Kim? Why did you come here tonight?"

"Isn't that obvious?"

Mark smiled easily. She wanted him. Incredible as it was, she honestly wanted him. He would say what had to be said and risk losing that to be worthy of it. "That wasn't the only reason."

The shadow was there. Where it had come from and why the transformation had to be so complete, Mark would never fully understand.

"No," she was telling him. "No. The other night, when we couldn't be together, you said you were with a client. Was it my grandmother?"

He didn't want to answer. With all his heart, Mark didn't want to take that risk. But his alternative was to lie, and he couldn't do that. "Yes."

"Oh." She barely got the word out. "Why didn't you tell me?"

"I couldn't, Kim. Lawyer/client confidentiality."

"But I'm her granddaughter."

That's precisely why I couldn't tell you. "She asked me not to."

"That's all you're going to tell me, isn't it?"

Mark took Kim's hand, waited until she dropped the fork and then lifted her fingers to his lips. Across the table their eyes met. "I'm sorry. I can't tell you anything more."

"Can't or won't?"

"Can't. Kim, your grandmother's easily upset these days. She trusts me. There are certain things I'm trying to do to calm her."

"Wait," Kim interrupted. "What is she upset about? Money. It's money, isn't it?"

Mark shook his head but kept the eye contact. "Don't, Kim. Don't ask me questions I can't answer."

Because the conversation was about a woman she loved, Kim couldn't honor his request. "She should be confiding in me. We could always talk."

"It'll happen again. Just give her time."

"Time?" Kim repeated. "For what?"

Mark just shook his head. That was one thing he couldn't tell her.

Chapter Eleven

"I don't want you back in that place."

Kim continued working on her hair with Mark's comb. She understood his concern, however, she was unable to comply with his request. While Mark shaved, she explained that one of the two security firms wanted more information than they'd gotten during their first tour of the museum. "What if I make sure there's always someone around me. I could get one of the gray-haired volunteers to ride shotgun."

"It isn't funny, Kim."

Mark was right; it wasn't funny. Neither did she believe the situation as serious as Mark and Charles did. "I just don't see violence in any of those people," she told him as she was getting ready to leave. "Greed, maybe. All right. Definitely greed. But someone who has a taste for fine antiques isn't going to hit anyone over the head."

"You don't know that." Mark stopped Kim from opening the door. "Tonight?" he asked. "I'm free. No meetings. Time for us to be together. Maybe we could go to a movie and out to dinner."

Kim wanted that more than she was able to tell Mark. She reached up for his kiss and wound up clinging to him with a desperation she barely understood. She wanted to trust this man; she felt the same need in him.

But something stood between them, and unless the barrier was knocked down, Kim was afraid of the consequences. She suggested a comedy she'd heard about and dropped a hint about Chinese food. Using that conversation as an excuse, Kim managed to remain in Mark's arms a few more minutes, but then it was time for her to leave.

Kim turned her thoughts to what had been good about the night. They'd made love with a freedom and closeness that hadn't been possible when they were new with each other.

And then she'd asked a question he couldn't fully answer and that closeness had been compromised.

Before going to the museum, Kim wanted to run home for a change of clothes and to call her grandmother. She parked her rental car near the cave-in and got out. Before she'd taken more than a couple of steps, a truck bearing a load of gravel rumbled toward her. Kim held up a hand to stop them. When the driver rolled down his window, she explained that they would have to go around and use California Street.

"That's not what we were told," the driver informed her. "We're supposed to deposit this at 431 Rich Gulch. Something about the owners having to put in a new driveway because of this hole you've got here."

They were talking about the only other residents on Rich Gulch Street. Kim explained that the new driveway, if one was actually going to be constructed, would exit on California Street. "I don't know who told you to try to get around the cave-in, but it isn't going to work. There's no way you can safely do that. That's what the barriers are for."

"It looks to me as if there's room." The driver pointed at what was left of the street and shoulder. "Look, this way we've got a straight shot. California Street, it's on a hill. We're going to have a devil of a time dumping the load."

"I'm sorry," Kim stood firm. "An engineer and the city attorney have been down there. They don't want any more weight than necessary on the street."

"That's not what I was told."

"By who?"

"By the guy who owns the house, I guess. Look, I know how to be careful. I've had this business for fifteen years."

"I really don't think it's safe. The police have let a few vehicles past the barriers, but nothing as heavy as what you're driving."

The driver stared at the cave-in for the better part of a minute. Finally he muttered something about making a phone call and wandered away. Kim shook her head in exasperation. Technically speaking, the dump truck probably could get around the cave-in, but only a fool would take the risk. She hadn't talked to the only other residents of Rich Gulch Street, but it surprised her that they were going ahead with rerouting their driveway already. There was a good chance that next week's council meeting would decide in their favor and resolve the whole issue.

At least the confrontation with the truck driver gave Kim something else to think about. She quickly changed clothes and then called her grandmother. "I was out late. I thought you might have tried to call me."

"I did, once. You're all right, aren't you, honey?"

"Yes, Grandmother, I'm all right." This wasn't like her grandmother. Margaret Revis had been the next thing to a permissive parent, believing that children, and grandchildren, learned by making their own mistakes. "You never used to be such a worrywart."

"I know." Margaret's laugh sounded hollow. "It's just that so many things these days are out of my control."

"You don't have to take responsibility for everything, Grandmother," Kim said. "That's what we have a police chief and town council and lawyers for."

"I know that." Margaret sighed. "I just—oh, honey, I worry about you."

"Don't." Kim sank deeper into her chair and closed her eyes. For the first time in her life she felt as if she was the adult and her grandmother the child. The love she felt was just as fierce as it had always been. Only now it was tempered with a sense of responsibility that hadn't been there before. "Grandmother, I know you don't like the idea of me doing what I'm doing at the museum, but believe me, I'm being well taken care of. Both Mark and Charles have given me lectures about keeping my eyes open. Things are fine."

Margaret sighed again; this time there was a quiet sob in the sound. "That's not all—I wish you wouldn't feel so responsible for the house. I can get someone else to take care of it."

"You'll do no such thing," Kim managed around the knot of concern growing inside her. "I feel like a dog guarding a bone. I'm not about to let anyone pull a fast one on me. Grandmother, you would have been proud of me. Some fool truck driver was going to try to drive around the cave-in. Can you believe that?"

"That damn cave-in. Kim?"

Kim didn't breathe. "What?"

"Nothing. I don't know what I was going to say. When will I see you again?"

Kim promised to come by later in the day and then found a way to say goodbye. She got to her feet and walked outside, her head pounding. Not enough had been said; too much was still hidden.

Her grandmother was scared. Kim had no idea why.

Margaret Revis had sworn. Kim had never heard an oath from her before.

The cave-in. Kim stopped.

She could go to the museum a little later, after she'd answered some questions. The tunnel had held a skeleton and a rusted pocketknife. When Kim had mentioned the skeleton, Mark and her grandmother had exchanged looks she couldn't begin to understand. Margaret had turned white at the mention of something she should have been able to shrug off.

Mark hadn't wanted her to go down there. He hadn't wanted her to tell her grandmother about the knife she found; he'd been adamant about that.

One branch of the tunnel went onto Revis property.

Lawyer/client confidentiality, Mark had called it. It didn't make sense; none of this did.

Mark had to honor his client's request, but Kim didn't. She stepped to the edge of the tunnel and dropped to her knees. Some gut instinct told her that the answer, if there was one, was in the tunnel. She'd been through her grandmother's house and found nothing that she didn't already know about. She'd seen her grandmother's will. She knew about the savings accounts, the old bonds in a safety-deposit box. There was nothing for Mark to keep from her.

Or was there?

One branch of the tunnel went through Revis property.

Kim rose, walked to her car, pulled the flashlight out of the glove compartment and returned to the ragged asphalt. For the second time she dropped to her knees. Then she slid around and lowered herself into the hole.

The floor of the cave-in felt a little warmer than it had the first time Kim had gone down there, but maybe that was because she was concentrating on her destination and not the narrow corridor's impact. Her shoes weren't the best for crawling, but Kim didn't intend to spend much time down there. Her plan, if it could be called that, was to go beyond the "room" where they'd found the skeleton. What she expected to find, Kim had no idea.

Kim was at the "room" in a matter of minutes. The total silence had already made its impact on her nerves, but she swallowed down whatever was trying to crawl up her throat and continued onward. The opening narrowed, forcing Kim to propel herself forward with toes and elbows. She was breathing heavily, a little giddy because the air was stale. At every bend in the tunnel, Kim told herself this would be the last one. She was no longer sure where she was and even less sure of how she was going to turn around.

She kept herself sane by thinking about the man who'd dug the tunnel. Had he been someone Margaret and Dow knew? Had—the question grew—had Dow been that long-ago miner?

Dow Revis wasn't a wealthy man, not like the father of his wife's children. Had he been one of those men who clawed their way through the earth for the gold that would feed those dependent on them?

Was that it? Dow Revis had dug this tunnel and neither he nor his wife had told the children and now Margaret Revis was afraid the secret could no longer be kept?

Oh, Grandmother. It doesn't matter. He was a good man. He did the only thing he could.

Finally the tunnel became so narrow that Kim was in danger of becoming stuck. From what she could see, it ended a few feet farther on. Breathing deeply in an attempt to hold her growing claustrophobia at bay, she started to back up. Dow Revis was down here with her. In spirit anyway. He would keep her safe. And when she reached the surface, Kim would go to her grandmother and gently ask for the truth.

The reverse journey went slower and left Kim with too much time to think about the insanity of what she'd just done. She'd lost all sense of time. With nothing but night around, she was no longer sure whether she'd slipped back through the years or not. How long had she been down here?

Kim breathed a little easier when she was able to turn around. Her thoughts were on getting a shower, doing what little she needed to at the museum today, talking to her grandmother.

Telling Mark—telling Mark what?

Kim was past the "room" now. In no more than three minutes, she would be piling up the broken asphalt until she had enough of a step to reach for the pavement. A quick hoist and she would be in the sunlight.

Kim never saw the sun. One moment there was the silence that had found its way into her veins. The next, her world began to rumble and shake. Dirt exploded into dust; she drew the dust into her lungs. Kim screamed and spun away.

The roar overhead drowned out her scream.

MARK TENSED. Had the phone rung? Had his secretary come into the room? He heard nothing except the faint sound of a typewriter in the next room and the smooth hum of air conditioning.

"Peggy?" Mark asked over the intercom. "Did you page me?"

"No, I didn't. It's quiet this morning. Maybe you're not used to it."

Mark tried to go back to work, but his mind wasn't on it. A moment later he was calling the museum and, despite his agreement with Charles, trying to leave a message to have Kim call him.

"Ms. Revis hasn't come in yet, Mr. Stockton," he was informed. "But I believe she said she was going to do some work here today. I'm sure she'll show up any minute."

Once again Mark signaled his secretary. When was his next meeting? he wanted to know. When he was told, he asked Peggy to reschedule it. He would be in Camp Oro.

"Insane, insane, insane," Mark repeated constantly during the fifteen minutes it took to drive to Camp Oro. He would find Kim already at the museum and have to stammer through a ridiculous sounding explanation about a feeling that had no basis in fact. He would have to tell her why he'd come to see her in the middle of the day when he'd just told her it wasn't safe for them to be seen together.

Kim's car wasn't parked in front of the museum. Mark didn't bother going in. He headed toward Rich Gulch Street. It was there that he found the car—and a gravel truck dumping its load a few yards beyond the cave-in.

Mark vaulted out of his Blazer.

"What are you doing?" he yelled over the sound of hydraulic machinery. "How'd you get here?"

The driver shrugged twice before Mark managed to make himself understood. Not to worry, he was informed. There was no need to go around the long way after all. It was a tight squeeze, but the truck had made it around the hole with no trouble. He might have knocked a few pieces of asphalt loose, but they'd have had to be removed anyway.

"Why the hell didn't you go around?" Mark didn't care whether this man thought him crazy or not. "Didn't you see the barriers?"

"That's what the lady tried to tell me, but I've got my orders. I called. I was told it was all right."

Mark didn't care who have given the insane orders. He knew who the lady was.

Mark ran all the way to Margaret's house praying he'd find Kim there, but the locked door told him otherwise. Less than a minute later, Mark had dropped into the hole and was staring in sick horror at a mound of freshly disturbed dirt where the tunnel opening had been.

"Kim! Kim!"

No answer. Surely she hadn't gone back into the tunnel. She'd promised not to. Hadn't she?

Maybe she hadn't.

Mark was already clawing at the dirt and yelling at the truck driver to get the city work crew over here. His heart beat a terrified tattoo. The man with the logical mind and immaculate suit who'd been sitting behind his desk a few minutes before no longer existed.

If Kim was beyond the dirt—or under it—

"Mark! What the hell are you doing?"

It was Charles, and close behind him, the members of the work crew. "Don't ask," Mark gasped. "Dig!"

Mark paused long enough to shove his hands into a pair of work gloves and grab a shovel. The claylike dirt came away in large clumps to be thrown behind the diggers. Between gasps and grunts, Mark spelled out his worst fears.

There was no time to ask what Kim might be doing down there.

There was only time to dig for the woman he loved.

A foot. He'd found a foot.

Mark turned stricken eyes toward Charles. "Don't think," Charles warned him. "Let's get her the hell out of here."

It took another couple of minutes before they were able to clear all the dirt off Kim's legs. At least—thank God—the debris hadn't completely covered her. Dust had settled over her hair and face, but Mark kept himself sane by believing she'd been able to breathe.

If she was breathing.

Mark tried to catch that blessed sound, but his own ragged breaths pounded through him, making him almost deaf. His hand rested on her throat in an agony of waiting. Then—

"She's alive, Mark," Charles whispered. "I'm getting a pulse. Someone make sure the ambulance is on its way."

Mark waited beside Kim with his hands on her throat and chest, breathing with her, until a stretcher was lowered into the tunnel and he had to make way for the ambulance attendants. He was vaguely aware of hands helping him to the surface and a ring of spectators, but nothing mattered except the dirt-caked figure lying too still on the stretcher.

He didn't ask permission. Before anyone could say anything, Mark climbed into the ambulance behind Kim. He nodded when Charles told him he'd be following in Mark's vehicle.

"Is she going to be all right?" he asked the two men leaning over her.

"Hard to tell. Her pulse is strong and her breathing's okay. You say her legs got the worst of it?"

"I think so."

Mark couldn't bring himself to speak again until they were in the emergency room and a nurse had cut away Kim's clothing. He was grateful when someone cleaned her face.

With a doctor and two nurses looking on, Mark bent over and kissed her. "Can you hear me?" he whispered. The words tore at his throat. "Oh, Kim. Do you have any idea how precious you are to me?"

Was she trying to open her eyes? Mark couldn't be sure. Still, that didn't stop him. "Hang in there, sweetheart. Please."

Yes. This time he was sure he saw a movement. For the first time since he'd guessed what had happened to her, Mark was able to think rationally. What his heart told him was that there was only one thing that needed to be said. "I love you, Kim. Remember that, I love you."

Someone came in with an X-ray machine and Mark was relegated to the waiting room where he found a tense police chief waiting for him. "I talked to the fool who drove that truck around the cave-in," Charles told him. "You aren't going to believe where that man got the go-ahead to use Rich Gulch Street. Or maybe you are."

"Tell me."

"Someone at the museum. That damn driver's too upset to remember the name. Either that or he has orders not to say anything."

"Charles, that doesn't make any sense."

"Sense or not, it's the truth. According to the driver, they were told the museum was going to pick up the tab for the driveway. Apparently Kim questioned what he was doing. After that, the man called the museum and got confirmation. In fact—if that driver is to be believed—whoever placed the order was adamant that Rich Gulch Street be used."

Mark was a breath away from smashing his fist through the nearest window. If it weren't for the haggard-looking young woman with the two preschoolers sitting across from them, he would have filled the room with words no three-year-old should hear.

"I wasn't going to tell you," Charles explained with his big hand over Mark's fist. "I knew this would be your reaction. Believe me, we're going to find out what the hell this is all about."

"You better believe it."

"And you're not going to go off half cocked."

"She was almost killed, Charles."

"I was down there. Remember. First, we find out how she is. Then we act."

Mark couldn't be content with Charles's slow pace. He stalked to the reception desk where he called Margaret Revis to let her know where her granddaughter was. If he'd been thinking calmly, he wouldn't have given his client that kind of news over the phone, but there was nothing calm about Mark today.

"I can't come after you, Margaret," he said with none of the warmth he usually had for his client and friend. "You'll have to find a way here. No. I haven't talked to the doctor. Yeah." The word came out hard-edged. "I have a damn good idea why she was down there. Margaret, she's trying to put the pieces together. And I don't blame her."

He'd just gotten off the phone when one of the nurses attending to Kim touched him on the shoulder. "I thought you should know. She's started to come around."

"Is she going to be all right?"

"We don't know everything yet, but she's responsive. That says a lot."

Mark sagged against a wall. He didn't care who saw his naked relief. A moment later he didn't care who might feel his anger.

Mark stalked back into the waiting room. "We're getting to the bottom of this. Today," he told the police chief.

Charles was on his feet. "We will," he said, his tone matching Mark's. "Believe me, we will."

"Someone's got a lot of answering to do. And that someone is going to have to confront me."

"There's only one problem, Mark. We don't know who that someone is."

"Maybe. Maybe not. Charles, someone at that museum almost got Kim killed today. If he or she has to look at Kim, face her—I don't see how whoever it was can keep what he's feeling inside."

"Yeah. Maybe." Charles nodded. "Get back on the phone, Mark. Get them all over here."

KIM WAS AWARE that she was being asked questions. She tried to answer and tried to concentrate when she was told to move her legs, but all she really wanted to do was stay in that safe, vague place her mind had retreated to. Some small part of her was aware of pain and dirt. If she left her retreat, she would have to deal with those realities.

"Oh, Mark. I had no idea."

What was her grandmother doing here? With a groan, Kim released her grip on the soft cocoon and returned to the world. Her legs felt as if someone had been pounding on them. When she swallowed, she tasted dirt. But she was no longer in the dark tunnel.

And Mark was holding her hand.

He wasn't alone. There was a man she took to be a doctor nearby, and a nurse beside the bed adjusting the blanket over her shoulders. She wanted to concentrate on Mark, but before she could speak, her grandmother stepped up and brushed her hair from her face. Kim saw her tears.

"I'm all right," Kim managed. "Don't cry."

"I—I can't help it. Oh, Kim. Why did you go down there?"

For a moment Kim didn't know what her grandmother was talking about. Then she remembered, everything. "Don't ask. It was stupid. So stupid."

Margaret wiped at a tear. Her face was so white and that worried Kim more than her own condition did. The older woman tried to speak. Her mouth trembled and she had to try again. "If only you hadn't . . . anything but that."

Suddenly Kim was angry. Angry at herself, and at the dirt in her mouth, and the nurse fussing with her blanket, and

Mark. But most of all she was angry at the dear woman who'd raised her.

"I didn't believe I had a choice," Kim said tightly. "You've been keeping something from me. Something that's tearing you apart. Something that's come between us."

"You're wrong. Oh, honey, you're wrong."

Kim wanted to believe. The child in her needed to believe that her grandmother was the woman she'd always known her to be. But the adult she'd become was facing a side of her grandmother she'd never seen before. "I don't think so," she said. "You're afraid of something. I'm a part of it. I can't turn my back on that."

"What—what were you looking for down there?"

"Answers." It still hurt to talk, but Kim pressed on. "I didn't know where else to look." She turned toward Mark. He was still holding her hand, but he was looking at Margaret. "No one will be honest with me."

"That isn't—" Margaret took a shaky breath. Her face was still ashen. "Oh, honey, none of this—"

"Don't." It was Mark.

Kim turned from her grandmother to the man she'd fallen in love with and still loved. His eyes, hard and compassionate at the same time, were still on the older woman. "Don't lie anymore, Margaret. For God's sake, give it up."

"Mark," Margaret moaned.

"I mean it. Tell her, or it'll never be right between the two of you. Between any of us."

AN HOUR LATER Kim had been cleaned up and was decked out in the finest of hospital gowns. She still felt as if she'd been run over by a steamroller, but with the dirt brushed out of her hair and the doctor's word that there was nothing worse than bruises wrong with her legs, she felt much more like a human being. True, her head was pounding, but aspirin would take care of that. Mark and her grandmother had left for a while, but now they were back again. Margaret was clinging to Kim's hand, her eyes red rimmed.

Because she couldn't face her grandmother, Kim focused on Mark. She'd been told of Mark's frantic attempt to free her and his insistence on riding with her in the ambulance. She wasn't sure. She could only hope that she hadn't imagined his words of love in the emergency room.

Mark was telling her that the loaded dump truck had been responsible for the cave-in that had trapped her. He spoke in clipped, angry sentences, but she had no idea whether he was angry with her or the truck driver. It didn't matter.

Right now all she wanted was to watch the sunlight from the window behind him play in his hair and make a lie of his hard expression. He could be gentle. She remembered that gentleness. She couldn't forget the words he'd said to her grandmother or Margaret's stricken look, but she'd face all that in a few minutes, when she felt stronger.

His gaze was on her. Relief was an emotion he had too little control over.

"I was going to spend some time at the museum," Kim whispered. "I can't remember. Some more information I needed..."

Mark left the windowsill he'd been sitting on. "That should be the least of your concerns. I told a few key people what happened. They should be here soon."

"What? Mark, I don't want to see anyone."

"Probably not." Mark drew out the word. "But—let me run this show, will you?"

Kim had no idea what Mark was talking about. She'd been given something to counteract shock, and although she could keep up with what was being said to her, her mind seemed to be operating in low gear. She wanted to pull her too-quiet grandmother close to her and ask Mark what the earlier exchange had been about. But that would have to wait until she was clearheaded.

Mark had again taken up his station by the windowsill and was dividing his attention between Kim and Margaret when the door opened.

"You look like something the cat dragged in," Garner Dillon told her after a silence that went on long enough to become uncomfortable. The handsome business manager waved a single rosebud in front of Kim. "When I heard—I'm glad it turned out all right."

"Are you?"

Kim started at Mark's harsh question. Despite the fog surrounding her, some small voice of wisdom warned her to remain silent. She might be the one who'd been injured, but she didn't want or need to be the center of attention.

"What are you talking about?" Garner let the rose dangle from his fingers. His voice was deep and more unsettled than Kim had ever heard it. "You make it sound as if I'm sorry Kim isn't still down in that hole."

"Is that what it sounds like? I have reason to doubt someone's concern. I just need to know whose."

Garner grunted and looked around uneasily before finding a place to sit.

"Actually," Mark went on, "I'm surprised you're the first one here."

"You are? Why?"

"You were at the museum? All day?"

"Yes, all day. Look, the receptionist came running into my office saying Kim had been in an accident. Of course I dropped everything to get here. I sure as hell didn't expect this ... reception."

"Didn't you?"

"Spit it out, Stockton. What are you getting at?"

"Plenty. You didn't happen to see Anthea did you?"

"Anthea?" Garner rubbed his free hand over his thigh; his knuckles whitened. "You know how seldom that socialite blesses the museum with her presence. She's too busy trying to make a buck."

"She wasn't there today?"

Again Garner rubbed his thigh. "For a while. Not long I don't think."

"What about the others? Rogan and William?"

"What am I, their social secretary?" Garner glanced at Kim and lowered his voice. "Our illustrious director was there when we got the news about Kim's accident. I thought he was on his way over here."

"And William?"

Margaret Revis supplied the answer to that. She'd been in the hall a few minutes ago when she spotted the museum guard sitting in a small waiting room. "His brother had surgery today. He's waiting for him to come out of recovery."

"Did he say how long he'd been there?"

"No. Mark, what is this all about?"

When Mark didn't answer, silence settled over the room. Kim tried to concentrate on Mark, her grandmother, Garner. Even in her slowed state, she knew something was out of place. They were all waiting. But Kim had no idea what they were waiting for.

When Rogan and his wife came in, Kim could swear she smelled Charmaine Coffers's perfume from the doorway. The elegantly dressed woman slid close and patted Kim on the forehead. "When Rogan called and told me what had happened to you—my dear, I'm shaking just thinking about it. Whatever possessed you to do something like that?"

Kim couldn't say anything without giving away too much. She tried a shaky smile. "That's what I've been asking myself. When I think of what almost happened—"

Fortunately that was all the encouragement Charmaine needed. With her husband standing as far from Kim as he could, Charmaine launched into a series of stories about her health adventures over the years. Kim was wondering if it would be impolite to ask for another aspirin when Charmaine finally wound down. "I'm just so glad it wasn't me trapped down in that terrible place. Rogan is no good in an emergency. I'm sure he wouldn't have known what to do."

"You'd never get in the dirt anyway, my dear." Rogan spoke for the first time. "So it's a moot point, don't you think?"

Charmaine brushed off her husband's comment. "You should have seen him when his parents were in an automobile accident. I practically had to carry him into the hospital. I'm surprised he isn't waiting outside right now."

Rogan had been holding his pipe since he came in the room. Now he clamped it, cold, between his teeth. He glanced at Mark but didn't acknowledge the attorney. "I don't like hospitals, dear. I don't know why you need to belabor the point."

"I know you don't, my dear. It just seems so silly." Charmaine turned back toward Kim. She waved her hand expansively. "A grown man with a phobia about hospitals."

Kim didn't hear another word Charmaine said. The ring on her middle finger first caught her attention and then held her riveted. It looked— Ignoring the complaint from her beaten body, Kim sat up straighter. Charmaine was about to move away. She couldn't let her do that yet. "Will you be honest with me?" she blurted out. "Do I have a lot of bruises?"

Charmaine came closer, subjecting Kim to even more of her perfume. The older woman touched Kim gently under her right eye. "I've seen worse. Not that I've done it, of course, but I've seen women who've had plastic surgery. Now that really is bruising."

Kim hadn't imagined it. The black stone perched on Charmaine's finger—

"I THOUGHT they would never leave," Margaret breathed ten minutes later. "That perfume of Charmaine's is enough to give anyone a headache."

Kim wasn't interested in Charmaine's perfume. She didn't know whether to be relieved that Rogan and his wife had decided to leave when Garner did. What she did know was that what she was about to say didn't make enough sense.

"Mark? Did you see Charmaine's ring?"

Kim thought she heard her grandmother suck in her breath, but much as she wanted to spare Margaret pain, she couldn't do that. "I swear, the stone's the one that was in Grandmother's pin."

"You're sure?"

The sedative was starting to wear off. Either that or the harshness of Mark's question was enough to cut through anything. "It was jet. I'm sure of it. And—there was that white slash through it. I don't understand. I'm sure I'm not mistaken."

Margaret Revis's face was bloodless. Her eyes flickered to Mark and then back to Kim. She looked trapped and frightened and utterly vulnerable. Kim missed none of it.

"It *was* your stone, wasn't it?" Kim asked gently. She was shaking. But it had nothing to do with the accident. "Why does Charmaine have it? Why isn't it in a pin anymore?"

"I don't know," Margaret whispered. "I—"

"Tell her, Margaret."

"Don't," Kim warned Mark, but Margaret brushed her off. Margaret still looked so shaken that Kim was afraid her grandmother was going to faint.

"I don't understand," Margaret whispered. "It was, the last time I saw it, it was in the museum."

"What?"

Margaret opened her mouth but nothing came out. She sagged into a chair, her body seemed to shrink.

Kim tried to reach her, but her body refused to move. She felt sick. Sick and wise.

Margaret had entrusted the pin to the museum. Whatever her reason, the decision had been difficult.

"You don't have to explain," Kim told her grandmother gently. "I'm sorry. I asked before I thought. But Charmaine?"

Margaret wasn't looking at Kim. She'd turned toward Mark, her face half hidden. "I don't know."

"Tell her, Margaret. Before it's too late, tell her."

"I can't! Mark, please, I can't."

Mark turned and stalked out of the room, and Margaret followed him.

KIM WAS UNDER ORDERS to rest. The directive came from the nursing staff, her grandmother and Mark. Her aching body wanted nothing more than to obey orders. Unfortunately her brain couldn't do that.

Even with everyone out of the room, Kim still felt as if she could reach out and draw in the tension.

She wanted to understand her grandmother's mood. She tried to tell herself that being reminded of what she'd once had was what had prompted Margaret to turn the pin over to the museum. Every time her grandmother looked at what reminded her of her first husband, the memories must have been painful. Finally the pain had become too much.

But Margaret Revis wasn't a woman who lived in the past. Yes, she'd tragically lost the father of her children. But her life had gone on from there and become full once again.

It didn't make sense. Margaret could have told her granddaughter that she'd turned the pin over to the museum because she wanted to share its history with others. Kim would have understood. Margaret hadn't had to lie.

But she had done so. And—and this was the part that hurt— Mark had known.

Chapter Twelve

Kim would have gladly given up a year's salary to remain where she was, but the need for answers overruled her body. Mark and the police chief were going to the museum. They wouldn't tell her why.

She was already out of bed when William slipped, silently, into the room. For a moment Kim froze. She might have been strong enough to open a closet door to look for something to wear. She certainly was in no shape to fend off the lean security guard.

"What are you doing here?" Kim asked.

"I heard. You've been hurt."

"An accident," Kim explained, although accident might not be the operative word. "You didn't have to come."

"Yeah, I did." William closed the door behind him. He took in Kim's inadequate attire. "Where are you going?"

"I'm—" Kim took a deep breath. She'd had the courage to face her fears in a mine tunnel. Surely she could face this man. "I want to get out of here."

"I don't blame you." William folded his hands across his chest. Now that she was getting used to the reality of him being in her room, she noted the signs of exhaustion in him. He cleared his throat and continued. "A hospital's no place for anyone."

"That's why I'm leaving. I need to call a taxi."

"Taxis cost money. Are you going home?"

Kim avoided the question. Instead she stared down at the bruises already showing on her bare legs. If her face looked anything like that... "My grandmother said she saw you in the waiting room. Have you been here long?"

"Too long. It isn't the first time, Ms. Revis. It never ends. That's the hell of it, it never ends." William's voice ground down. He took a step forward.

If she cried out, help would be in the room before he could do her any harm. Forcing a smile, Kim pointed at her gown. "I can't walk out dressed like this. Could you get a nurse—"

"I've got something you can use."

Kim blinked. "You what?"

"I brought a robe for my brother. For when he wakes up. He hates what they give him. Would you like that?"

Kim nodded. Her throat felt tight, not from the dirt she'd inhaled but from compassion for William. "Your brother. Is he going to be all right?"

"This time he is. I don't know about next time." William shifted his weight, bringing him closer to the sunlight coming in the window. Kim saw his pain.

"That's all we have, isn't it? Today." She wasn't sure she was saying enough.

"Today? Yeah. That's all we have. I'll take you. I can't do nothin' for my brother now. And I gotta get out of here, too."

"I don't want to put you out," Kim said, although caution and not a concern for inconveniencing the man was what forced the words.

"You're not putting me out. Look, you don't trust me. But I'm not going to hurt you. I've never hurt anyone in my life. I mean it, miss. If you want out of this place, I'll help you."

"You don't know where I'm going."

"It doesn't matter. Let's get out of here."

There might be a thousand things Kim didn't understand about William Lynch, but she could sense his exhaustion and his need to get out of the place that claimed his brother and was in danger of claiming him as well. The only question that remained was whether she could trust William enough to let him help her escape. "I didn't think you liked me."

"I didn't. I'm still not sure I do."

The man was honest. Kim needed to be the same with him. "I'm not sure I can trust you, William."

"I've pretty well figured that out. The way I acted...Miss, have you ever loved someone and had to sit there watching him go through hell? I—" William raked a bony hand through what there was of his hair. "I can't hate my brother. And it does no good hating what's happening to him or the doctors or this damn hospital. But I can hate my job. Maybe that's the only thing I *can* feel that way about."

Sympathy welled up in Kim and propelled her away from the bed. She didn't embrace William. Neither of them was ready for that. But she could take his hand and give him her warmth. "Not me?"

"No, not you. I tried. Does that sound crazy? I tried." William squeezed back. "But it isn't your fault."

"No. It isn't." Kim was, once again, close to tears. She didn't know how much more she could handle. "I don't blame you for hating your job and the people you associate with it. But, William, it can be better. You and I, together, we can make it into a job you can be proud of."

Neither of them said anything more until William brought her a threadbare robe to wear, they'd slipped past the nurses' station and Kim had forced her aching body into William's ancient pickup. Then she began talking to distract herself from what the old shocks were doing to her bruises. By the time they'd reached Camp Oro, Kim knew that William's brother had been sick for three years, and, although this latest operation would improve the quality of his life, there wasn't a long-term solution. William told her that he'd held on to the security job because taking care of his brother hadn't left him with the energy to think about anything else.

He'd never told anyone because no one had ever been interested, but he had figured out a way to remodel the museum so it would have access for the disabled. If it was his to run, he would build an annex and equip it so children could experience firsthand what it was like to be a logger before power tools came on the scene, to bake their own bread, to sit in an old-fashioned classroom with an inkwell at the front of their desks.

"You like that man, don't you?" William asked. "He drives you crazy, but you like him."

Kim didn't have to ask who William was talking about. "What makes you think he drives me crazy?"

"That's the way it is when you're in love. Hell of a mess, isn't it?"

Kim could laugh. She squeezed William's arm in affection and understanding and let him see the tears that went with her laughter. "I want to trust him," she said softly. "I want that more than anything. But—"

"If it's meant to be for you two, that'll come. If it isn't . . . you'll get through it. You don't have any choice."

Just like William didn't have any choice but to stand by his brother, Kim thought as William walked with her to the house so she could change into something presentable. He waited patiently while she dressed and then offered to take her to the museum. "You're probably going to fall on your face before today's over," William observed. "But there's no way you're going to be able to just sit quietly at home asking yourself questions."

Kim and William weren't the only ones getting out of a vehicle in front of the museum. Two parking spots behind them, the town police car came to a rest. Although Charles got out immediately, Mark didn't move. He'd left Kim resting in the hospital. She shouldn't be here.

"Kim?" Her name was like a leaf in the wind. He got out of the car and walked toward her. "What are you doing here?"

Clearly Kim hadn't been ready to see him again. She turned too quickly, almost losing her balance. But the wary, wounded look in her eyes prevented him from reaching out for her. "I'm looking for answers," was all she could say.

"You should be in bed."

"Not now. I was almost killed today. Strange as it may seem, I need to know why."

"That's why we're here." Mark indicated the sheriff. "Trust us, Kim."

"Trust you? To do what? Keep things from me?"

They weren't talking about solving a series of robberies or learning who had ordered that truck to test the cave-in's strength; Mark knew that. "We'll talk," was the best he could give her. "We'll explain later, Kim. Later."

"Is that a promise?" She shifted her weight, winced, but didn't ask for help. "And when we do, are you going to tell me everything?"

"I don't know. It isn't up to me."

"Why? Never mind." Kim waved an angry hand in his direction. "Maybe I'm not interested after all. Maybe it isn't worth it."

"You don't believe that. Your grandmother—"

"Not just my grandmother," Kim interrupted. "You, too."

"I took her home. I've never seen her so upset."

"I'll call her later." Kim struggled against an urge to cry. "What am I going to say? I can't ask her any questions because she won't give me any answers. Just like you. No one is interested in answers."

"That's why we're here, Kim."

Kim had forgotten that she and Mark weren't alone. She took refuge in the distraction the sheriff was providing. "What are you going to do?"

Charles held up a piece of paper. "A search warrant. I figured we'd better have that."

Kim still didn't understand, but, if they would let her come along, she could be patient. She allowed Mark to take her elbow for the walk into the museum, but once they were inside, she drew away from him. A family was going into one of the exhibits at the far end of the hall, but the volunteer receptionist wasn't at her usual station. "No one knows we're coming," Mark whispered. "Or maybe I should say they don't know when we might show up. My guess is, someone will be working overtime, trying to cover his or her tracks."

"Where are you going first?" Kim asked in a whisper.

"Where do you think?"

Rogan Coffers was on the telephone when the four walked unannounced into his office. The director started but quickly composed himself. He muttered a quick goodbye to the person he was talking to and hung up the phone. "Kim. You shouldn't be here."

"So I've been told."

Rogan glanced at the others and then rose to his feet. He indicated that Kim should sit in his comfortable chair. Grateful, she sank into it—and waited.

"What are you doing here?" Rogan asked after perching himself on the edge of his desk. For a man who'd gone pale a moment ago, he now looked more composed than Kim had ever seen him. "William, if you're here you should be on duty."

"Later," the guard said, shortly.

Rogan shrugged. "I was talking to someone from one of the security firms. You were supposed to meet with him, Kim. They waited around here for an hour this morning and then left. I felt it my responsibility to tell them about your accident. You can reschedule whenever you feel up to it." Rogan glanced at Charles and Mark before turning his attention back to the woman sitting behind his desk. "Kim, I apologize for the display between my wife and me. It doesn't take much to upset Charmaine. When she gets that way, she tends to take things out on me. I'm afraid I didn't handle that as well as I usually do. By the way, she considers you incredibly brave for going into that tunnel, although your reason for doing it escapes both of us."

Kim could have taken the easy way out and not looked at Mark, but she didn't. "I'm not surprised," she said, without emotion. "I don't think anyone understands. Anyone but me, that is."

Charles cleared his throat. "Rogan, we're not here to talk about what happened to Kim."

Rogan reached for his pipe and clamped it between his teeth. "No? I'm afraid you're going to have to spell out your reasons."

Kim divided her attention between Charles and the museum director. If she was the one being confronted by a law-enforcement officer, she would have been uneasy, even if she didn't have anything to hide. Rogan, however, seemed utterly composed. He smiled and nodded at Kim before focusing on the police chief.

"You were at the museum when Mark called to tell everyone about Kim's 'accident'. Could you tell me what you were doing?"

Rogan frowned. "Is it important? I'm afraid . . . wait . . . Stephan had called. We'd talked about the best way to get an official stand on the cave-in issue from the federal historic preservation agency." Rogan smiled at Kim. "This is one arm of the bureaucracy that acts quickly. We should have a formal statement shortly."

Kim started to nod; Mark spoke.

"That's quite a ring your wife was wearing this morning."

Rogan blinked. "Her ring?"

Mark spoke. "Kim is convinced that the stone once belonged to her grandmother and that Margaret Revis entrusted the stone, in its original setting, to this museum. And now it's on your wife's hand. You might say we're curious."

"Oh." Rogan shifted his weight and looked down at his hands. When he looked up, he was able to meet Kim's stare. "Oh, Kim, I'm so sorry."

"Sorry?"

"I didn't think. I was so worried about you that it never occurred to me. Charmaine should have removed it before coming to see you today."

"Then you did want to keep something from Kim," Mark prompted.

"I'm afraid so." Rogan reached behind him for the pouch holding his pipe tobacco. "Believe me, I would have done anything to save Margaret from this embarrassment."

Kim wanted to concentrate fully on what the director was saying, but her aching body made that incredibly difficult. She shifted position and shivered. Why was she so cold? Was she still in shock? "Why would my grandmother be embarrassed?"

"Because... I'm afraid it's too late to try to pretend this hasn't happened, isn't it? I just hope there's some way we can keep this from her. You didn't say anything to her about it, did you?"

Kim didn't answer.

"Kim, your grandmother is a proud woman. I want you to understand that."

"I do." Kim glanced at Mark, took her cue from his nod, and went on. "What does that have to do with the stone?"

"A great deal, I'm afraid. I hope—I trust this won't go any further than this room." Rogan opened his pouch and took out a pinch of tobacco. "Mrs. Revis would like the community to believe she's comfortable financially. I can understand that. To have people know that her husband was unable to provide for her old age... Well, you can imagine how difficult that would be for her."

"I've talked to my grandmother about finances. She assures me—"

"I'm sure she does, Kim. In a moment of weakness, Mrs. Revis confided in me that no one, not even her attorney, knows exactly what she has to operate on. Pride. Your grandmother has a great deal of pride.''

''What does this have to do with you?'' Kim asked.

''A great deal. A simple explanation for why my wife has the stone from Margaret's pin in her ring. Kim, the truth is, Margaret was forced to sell it to me. She set great store by it. She had, shall I say, an inflated idea of its value. It had sentimental value to her, but in the original setting, its monetary value was limited. I had the stone turned into a ring for my wife. I didn't tell your grandmother that. I suppose I should have, but I think you can understand why I didn't. Even Charmaine doesn't know the stone's origin.''

''No!'' Kim took a deep breath.

''I'm afraid so. Kim, I understand your reluctance to believe me. I'd like to tell you to discuss this with your grandmother, but I promised when I bought the pin that I'd keep Margaret's confidence.''

''You really expect us to believe this garbage?''

Kim was shaken by the anger in Mark. She almost said something herself, but in the end decided to remain silent. Her grandmother wasn't in the room. She couldn't be hurt.

''Call it what you will, Mr. Stockton,'' Rogan informed him. With his eyes trained on Mark, Rogan continued loading his pipe. ''I'm aware of the deep affection you have for your client, but even you must know she doesn't tell you everything. She has needs most women her age don't. She's seen out in public a great deal. She can't get by with the same wardrobe year after year. She had a need and a commodity she could sell to meet that need.''

''My grandmother would never have sold that pin. It meant too much to her.''

Sadly, Rogan shook his head. ''Margaret didn't get into the specifics of the stone's origin. That wasn't my concern. The only thing I was interested in was helping a dear woman out of a financial bind and being able to give my wife a unique gift. I apologize if this has caused you consternation, Kim. I would have given anything to spare both you and your grandmother this." Rogan turned toward Charles. "I'm surprised that the police have somehow found it necessary to involve themselves."

Charles shrugged. "We had certain suspicions."

"Which I hope you'll feel free to tell me about." Rogan paused and then went on. "I hope this has answered your questions. Certainly it was never my intention to be anything but honest. Considering what has been going on here lately, I can understand your suspicions that the stone came into my hands by a less than, shall we say, ethical route. Believe me, nothing is farther from the truth."

Mark muttered something under his breath that Kim couldn't catch. She'd been warm enough when she came into the room, but she was so cold now that it was almost impossible to concentrate.

Rogan was still speaking. "I suppose you could go to Mrs. Revis for confirmation, but I'm strongly advising against it. Strongly. Kim, your grandmother was greatly pained to have to sell the jewelry. To question her about it, to bring up the whole issue again, couldn't we just let things rest?"

Kim opened her mouth to agree, but she wasn't given the chance.

"You'd like that, wouldn't you?" Mark challenged. "Sweep everything under the rug and send us all on our way with promises that we won't say anything to Margaret. Sorry, Rogan, it isn't going to wash."

"What are you going to do?" Kim turned her chilled, aching body toward Mark. "If you're thinking of questioning my grandmother—Mark, I can't do that to her. I don't care— No matter what, I can't let that happen to her."

"Kim? You're shaking."

"Of course I'm shaking," Kim managed. "I won't have you put her through hell."

"Do you really think I'd do that to her?"

"I haven't forgotten what you said to her in the hospital."

Mark rose to his feet. He didn't stop until he was standing toe-to-toe with the museum director. "Later, Kim. We'll talk about it later. Charles and I made a brief stop before we came here, Rogan. A little something we thought we might need. I believe it's called a search warrant."

"A what?" The pipe almost fell from Rogan's lips. He grabbed it and held it between his fingers. "For what?"

Mark's chuckle was without warmth. He'd been steeling himself to feel nothing, but it wasn't working. He knew Rogan was lying, just as he knew that a great gulf stood between him and Kim. "That's what a search warrant's about, Rogan. To find things."

"You can't. You don't have any proof."

"What kind of proof are you talking about?"

"I'm not. Mr. Stockton, I've never in my life been treated this way. Do you honestly believe I'd have anything to do with something illegal?"

"You. Or someone else who works here. Two points, Rogan. One, the thefts are an inside job. Who's responsible, we aren't sure, but that's what this is all about. Two." Mark held up two fingers. "We know that certain orders came from someone at the museum today. Orders that came very close to killing Kim."

Rogan didn't immediately respond. Instead he took his suit coat from the rack in the corner of the room. Only when he'd put it on and buttoned the buttons did he turn back toward Mark. "What are you intending to do?"

"Search. Search every inch of this damn place if that's what it takes."

"Be careful, Stockton. If anything's damaged—"

"Trust me."

"Trust?" Rogan's laugh sent a shock wave through Kim's trembling body. "You come in here with rash statements about an inside job and cryptic comments about some phone call I can't pretend to understand and then you ask me to trust you?"

Mark folded his arms and rocked back on his heels. He wasn't enjoying this. But he hadn't enjoyed keeping the truth from Kim, either. Sometimes things had to be done. "Rogan, only a fool would think these robberies were anything but an inside job. The casual visitor isn't going to walk out the door with a rocking chair. Not without one of the employees seeing."

"Unless that employee was the thief. An underpaid man with a sick brother draining him." Rogan turned toward William. "Why don't you start your search with him?"

"Because we're starting it with this room. Let's just say I'm a long way from buying that story about Margaret's jewelry."

"That's a damn poor excuse for defaming a man's character."

"I haven't defamed anything, Rogan. You're not the only one who works here."

Rogan was no longer interested in his appearance. "I was about to point that out. What about Garner? He didn't believe we should be spending money on a security system. And he's been anything but cooperative about discussing finances with Kim."

"I've got no quarrel with that."

"What about Anthea if we're looking to point fingers." Rogan was calm. If it hadn't been for the tension in the room, Kim would have thought the conversation was about ordering a meal. "What's the word, fence? Who but she has a better outlet for fencing stolen goods? Anthea has been talking to my wife. I don't suppose it's a secret. Anthea is filing for divorce. There goes the benefit of being married to a wealthy man. If I were you, I'd be taking that search warrant to her shop."

"Maybe we will. But since we're already here, why don't we start with you?"

"And why don't I call my lawyer?"

"A lawyer?" Kim got out. This wasn't real. None of this possibly could be.

"Let him," Mark told her. "He has every right."

Kim sat, shaking and numb, while Mark and Charles went through everything in Rogan's office. Rogan left to place his call, but returned almost immediately. He stood in a far corner, his face impassive. A couple of times he warned the searchers not to disrupt the order of some files. Once he even assisted the men in opening a drawer. Other than that, he said nothing. And his gaze made Kim feel even more chilled than she had before.

Finally Kim could no longer stand the tension. She pushed herself to her feet and slipped out of Rogan's office. She knew Mark was watching her exit, but she didn't feel up to meeting his eyes. Her intention had been to go into the conference room for a cup of coffee. However, she was stopped by a curious volunteer. Kim spent less than a minute telling the volunteer that she wasn't at liberty to tell him anything, but in that minute, Kim realized she'd stopped shaking.

It wasn't just being out of that tension-filled room. The rest of the museum was several degrees warmer than Rogan's office.

Kim stepped back inside. Rogan hadn't moved. He looked calm, and confident. For a moment she believed his body language; his innocence would be upheld, and Mark and Charles would owe him an apology.

William touched her elbow. "Are you all right?"

"I'll live. William, is it just me, or are you cold?"

William frowned. "I haven't thought about it, but, yeah, I never did like coming in here. Rogan keeps the heat turned down too low."

Kim might have believed that to be the explanation, but this was summer. The museum didn't have air conditioning and depended on several fans to keep the temperature down. It made no sense for Rogan's office to be cooler than the rest of the building unless—

Unless.

"Did you find the blueprints?" Kim asked. She felt calm and excited and a little frightened.

Mark straightened. He'd seen Kim leave. He hadn't expected to see her back again. He wasn't prepared for his own relief at seeing her here. "Blueprints?"

"I've been asking for them since the first day. I was given something that passed as a poor copy, but I never did get the originals."

"What are you getting at, Kim?" Charles asked.

"I'm not sure. Maybe nothing. But I did some work at a small museum in the wine country last summer. They didn't have air conditioning, either, and yet the old building was always cool. They—" Kim deliberately drew out what she was going to say. Rogan remained impassive. "The building had a full basement. That's what kept it cool."

"This place doesn't have a basement," William offered.

"Maybe not a full one, but what about a partial?" Kim risked a glance at Rogan. He was no longer leaning against the wall.

"You think so, Kim?"

Kim nodded at Mark. She wouldn't think about anything except what she needed to say. "It's what, at least ten degrees cooler here than the rest of the building."

Kim would never forget the smile that Mark let unfold slowly. For the first time today, she sensed something of what they'd shared before. "It would be convenient, wouldn't it?"

"There's no basement." Rogan was speaking around his pipe. "I would know if there was."

"How? There aren't any blueprints. At least none you want to share with anyone."

Rogan's office had a hardwood floor. With Mark's help, Charles started moving furniture. William was standing close to Rogan; his eyes never left the director's face. Rogan watched the action, his teeth digging into the stem of his pipe. "I don't believe this, Ms. Revis. After what I did for your grandmother..."

This was an insane dream. In a minute Kim would wake up to discover she'd been watching TV. But the dream didn't end. Instead Kim watched as heavy shelves and bookcases were shoved first one way and then the other. Rogan's angry muttering continued. Maybe she was the crazy one. Just because Rogan couldn't find the original blueprints... Even if they found a basement . . .

"Bingo."

The trap door was under the protective mat that kept Rogan's chair from scarring the hardwood. Kim made her way to the middle of the room and stood staring down at the short length of rope that served as the trap door's hinge. Her eyes met Mark's in disbelief. "I wasn't wrong," she said in awe.

Rogan left the room. He was followed closely by the security guard. Kim didn't have time to think about that. She watched as Charles yanked on the rope. The trapdoor opened easily. Cold, musty air wafted into the room.

A slender but sturdy ladder led into the dark. With a fascination borne from her earlier plunge into the earth, Kim stood by and watched Mark descend. Light from the lamp Charles was holding made it possible for Mark to see. A few seconds later Mark was standing on ancient cement.

"It's pretty big. And cold. Just as cold as the tunnel. I need better light."

Charles explained that he had a flashlight in the police car. He hurried out for it. "Either we're on to something, or we're going to come out of this looking like fools," Charles observed when he returned.

Mark had uncovered a hundred-year-old cellar. And answers. With Charles and Kim squatting over the opening, Mark described everything he found. There was a pile of the packing blankets like those used by moving companies. In one corner of the room, he came across a neatly wrapped box and inside the box, a collection of depression glass. "A rubber mallet, too," Mark explained. "With a couple of pieces of glass embedded in it. Interesting, wouldn't you say? I'd imagine someone could take a mallet to a glass case,

and it wouldn't make nearly as much noise as a hammer
would. Wait—"

"What?" Kim asked when Mark didn't finish.

"Where's Rogan?"

"I don't know. William's with him. Give me a minute."
Once again the police chief slipped out of the room. When
he returned a minute later, both Rogan and William were
with him. By that time Mark had emerged from the basement. Although Rogan was offering no resistance, William
kept his fingers locked around the man's waist.

Mark stood, handed Charles the flashlight and bent over
to wipe his pant legs. Only then did Charles step toward
Rogan and read him his rights. Mark just stared at Rogan.
"I'm not saying a word to you, Rogan. And I don't want
you saying anything, either. Let's get your attorney in here
first so there's no question we did this by the book."

Kim had started to tremble again. It wasn't the cold that
affected her so much this time, as the look on Mark's face.
Slowly he turned from Rogan toward her. Slowly he closed
the distance separating them. He took her cold hands and
wrapped them in his. "There's more than an underground
room down there, Kim. There's a tunnel."

"A tunnel?"

"I don't think I'm wrong about this. If you think about
it, it's a pretty straight shot from Rich Gulch Street to the
museum. Digging underground, I'm betting it's no more
than five or six hundred yards."

Kim's legs ached, but what she was hearing made it possible for her to dismiss her body. "The tunnel I went into,
there was a fork."

"Yeah. One fork went toward your grandmother's house.
That's the one we found the skeleton in. But the other, I'll
bet anything it ends up here."

"And Rogan?" Kim closed her eyes. With Mark looking
at her, it was almost impossible for her to think; and it was
essential that she think. "Rogan was using the tunnel to
carry out artifacts."

"Exactly. What about it, Rogan? Are we getting close? Never mind. Get your attorney here first. Because, if Charles agrees with me, I think we have a case for attempted murder."

"Murder!" The sharply spoken word forced Kim to open her eyes. The director had lost his calm demeanor. His pipe dangled forgotten from his fingers. He seemed oblivious to William's restraining hand. "I didn't . . . I never . . ."

"You didn't order that gravel truck to try to go around the cave-in instead of taking the safe route on California Street?"

Rogan clamped his mouth shut. When Kim brought her searching gaze back to Mark, he was ready for her. "I'm not psychic, Kim. I would have never put it together if I hadn't gotten in touch with the people living in the house where the gravel was being delivered. The truck driver wouldn't say anything. I figured he had his reasons. Those people, they rented. They'd tried to talk to the property management company they paid their rent to, but the company wasn't about to authorize a new driveway without consulting the owner. The management company was busy, they said. They'd get back to me. I didn't wait. I called the title company and got the owner's name."

"Rogan?" Kim barely got the word out. She was grateful for Mark's supporting hand. Her knees suddenly felt like water. "He's the owner?"

"You aren't going to deny that, are you, Rogan?" Mark questioned.

"You don't know what you're talking about, Stockton."

"Don't I?" Mark shifted so he could place his arm around Kim and pull her against him. "You paid the driver a little extra to make sure he did as he was ordered. That order just happened to include taking a loaded gravel truck around a cave-in, over asphalt that was already undermined. Your driver wasn't too sure when Kim called him on it, but he called you and you made it worth his while. You almost got away with it."

"Why did you want me dead?"

Kim's hard question rocked Mark. Still, although he would have given anything to spare her having to ask it, he admired her courage.

"I didn't. God help me, I didn't!"

Mark held Kim tightly, accepting that right now even the strength of his love couldn't stop her from shaking. "I don't believe you."

"Do." Rogan's confidence was gone. The man's face had gone deathly white. "You have to. I didn't know she was down there. Do you think I would have..."

"I don't think you've done any thinking since this damn thing started," Garner interrupted.

"I can guarantee you the man hasn't done any thinking for years," Anthea added.

Neither Kim nor Mark were prepared to have Garner and Anthea come into the room. Garner was concentrating on the shifted furniture, the open trap door. Anthea, however, was more concerned with the conversation she'd interrupted. Once she had Kim's and Mark's undivided attention, she explained that she'd just left Charmaine Coffers. "You upset your wife," Anthea told Rogan. "She isn't used to threatening phone calls from her husband. I'd have thought you'd know better. Charmaine isn't a woman you can do that to."

Rogan pulled out of William's grip. He made no effort to leave the room, but collapsed in his chair. He leaned forward, his eyes trained on the trap door.

Anthea was still talking. She explained that as soon as the visit to the hospital was over, Charmaine had called her and Anthea had gone to the Coffers house. They'd been talking about Kim's accident when Rogan called. "I didn't get the whole gist of the conversation until after Rogan hung up. According to Charmaine, her husband was jumping all over her because she was wearing some ring he didn't want her to. Charmaine sets a lot of store in that ring. Of course she sets a lot of store in anything she can flash and impress people with. That's what you bought it for, isn't it? So your wife could flaunt it, and people might believe you've still got what it takes to hold on to her.''

Kim had no idea what Anthea was talking about. But before she could open her mouth, Anthea started talking again. It didn't surprise Anthea at all that Rogan had finally crossed over the line. Desperation, or pride, could do that to a person. Anthea didn't want to speak evil of a woman she saw socially, but the operative word was ''gold digger.'' Charmaine would never have married Rogan if he hadn't been rich. Not rich in his own right, Anthea explained, but his parents had been wealthy and that money had held Charmaine's loyalty until she'd finally gone through it like she had her own inheritance. Anthea had wondered when the time would come when Charmaine would demand more than Rogan was able to provide.

''You want motive,'' Mark said to Charles. ''Maybe that's it.''

''Maybe. I've been thinking. That woman who has that antique place in Oakland? Somehow it wouldn't surprise me if she fingered Rogan as the man who sold her those items.'' Charles tapped Rogan on the shoulder. The man didn't seem to notice. ''Come on. I don't want to put cuffs on you, and I don't think you want it, either.''

''Wait.'' Kim tore free from Mark's grip. She faced Rogan, wondering which of them looked the more haggard. ''I—I know you don't have to answer this, but… What you said earlier about my grandmother selling the pin to you. It wasn't the truth, was it?''

''What does it matter?''

Kim could almost feel sorry for Rogan. Almost. ''I think you know the answer to that. Which was it? Please. Did you steal it from the museum, or did Grandmother sell it to you.''

''Don't, Kim,'' Mark warned. ''Wait until he's talked to his lawyer.''

The civilized woman who'd come to Camp Oro and fallen in love no longer existed. Kim had been torn apart both mentally and physically today. There was nothing left of her except gut reaction. "People have been lying to me for days. People I thought I could trust."

Mark backed away. He could have reached out to touch her; he was still close enough for that. But he didn't.

For too long Kim could think of nothing except the pain she'd inflicted on him. And the pain he'd inflicted on her. She barely noticed when Rogan began to speak.

"Your grandmother doesn't need the money, Kim."

Those words had been important a minute ago, but they no longer were. Now there was only Charles and Rogan leaving the room, Anthea and Garner and William looking into the hole, and Mark watching her.

"Charmaine? He did it for Charmaine?"

It was Garner speaking. The handsome man no longer seemed handsome. His emotions were making inroads on his features. "He risked everything, stole from the museum he'd spent years building up, because of his wife?"

"Does that surprise you?" Anthea asked in a gentle tone she'd never used before around the business manager.

"Yeah. It does. She isn't worth it."

Anthea was still being gentle. "You really believe that?"

"I think you know the answer to that. Put it together," Garner went on. He slumped against a wall. "I chase skirts. Any skirt. At least I used to. Charmaine and I..."

Kim roused herself from the quicksand of her thoughts long enough to whisper her question. "You and Charmaine were—?"

"Yeah," Garner interrupted. "Were is the operative word. I've been playing the swinging single for years. The game's getting old, Kim. So old. I'm tired of it. I just don't know how to stop. Yeah, she's older than me, but the woman's a looker, and she knows how to make a man feel like a man." Garner focused on Kim. He was still powerful, but today she sensed she was the stronger one. "I'm sorry, Kim, for what I put you through."

"It doesn't matter." Kim wasn't sure anything mattered.

"I'm still sorry. I wanted you to know that. Charmaine? She's exactly what Anthea called her, a gold digger. She dumped me damn fast when she found out I didn't have the kind of money she was looking for. The last I heard, she'd set her sights on Harden Langford. I saw the two of them together one night. She didn't give a damn who saw them, including her husband."

The only time Kim had ever seen Harden Langford was at the town council meeting when the president of the community pride group had been presenting his plan to develop the cave-in. That night Charmaine had been with her husband.

Kim thought she shouldn't feel sorry for Rogan, after all his lies and the attempt to collapse the tunnel, which had almost resulted in her death, but she did. Rogan, had wanted his wife's love and loyalty. He hadn't gotten either. And, right or wrong, in desperation he'd stolen from the museum to try to keep her with him.

Kim could never imagine resorting to breaking the law to keep someone she loved with her. But she knew what Rogan had gone through. She'd fallen in love with a man. She'd placed her heart in his hands.

And he hadn't accepted her gift. He hadn't given her the truth.

Chapter Thirteen

"Kim? It's for you."

Kim stared at the telephone Garner was holding out to her, as if she'd never seen such an instrument before. She felt like a boxer left too long in the ring, not yet on the canvas but in no condition to continue the fight. "I don't want to talk to anyone," she managed.

"It's your grandmother."

Kim reached for the phone, hating the fact that there was no opportunity for a private conversation. Five minutes ago Charles had led Rogan Coffers out of what had been his office. The others: Anthea, Garner, William and Mark, were still here with her. Kim had been listening to Garner's explanation of Charmaine Coffer's expensive tastes in both money and men. Her thoughts had been on Mark.

"How did you know I'd be here?" Kim asked after Margaret's strained greeting. She sank into Rogan's chair and closed her eyes. For a few minutes, she needed to hold, and be held, and she longed for things to go back to what they'd been before. "Are you all right?"

"I'm the one who should be asking you that." Margaret's voice was thick with concern. "I tried to reach you at the hospital. They said you'd left without being released. You weren't at the house. I didn't know where else to try. What's happening, Kim? You should be in bed."

Kim wasn't going to dispute that. However, it would be a long time before her mind would allow her the luxury of relaxation. Briefly, and as gently as possible, she told her grandmother about Rogan's arrest. "I've always thought of him as almost without emotion. But I guess he loved Charmaine."

"Love? What those two had wasn't love. Kim? How are you?"

"I'll survive. Don't worry about me."

"But I do. I can't help it. Kim, can you come here? Please?"

Mark couldn't hear what the woman on the other end of the line was saying, but he was achingly aware of the impact it was having on the battered woman sitting across the room from him. Kim's mouth twitched and her eyes became enormous. For too long she stared at nothing. When she fastened her gaze on him, he wasn't sure he could handle that, either. "Are you sure?" Kim was asking. "It's been a hard day for both of us. All right. No. I don't know."

Kim hung up. "She wants you to take me to her."

Ignoring the others, Mark took Kim's icy hands. "Did she say why?"

"She wanted to talk."

Talk. What a simple word for what was going to happen. Mark wasn't a man given to fears. Even when he entered a courtroom knowing the odds were stacked against him, he accepted that reality as a challenge. He might not win his case, but he would do his best to give his client competent representation.

Mark felt different today. He had no ammunition for this fight. Nothing to contribute. He would be a silent bystander. And either Kim could accept his role in what had been kept from her, or she couldn't.

"Are you coming?" Kim asked in a tone void of emotion.

Mark nodded, not because he wanted to do this thing, but because it was unthinkable for him to refuse. He loved the woman staring up at him with searching eyes. He would hurt for her today, and no matter what her reaction was to what she was to learn, he would never stop loving her.

He drew her to her feet. "Take care of her, Mark," Garner Dillon said as they passed the business manager.

"Kim?" Anthea called after them. "I'll get in touch with you tonight."

William Lynch was the last to say goodbye. The museum guard said nothing, but his fingers reaching out to trail over Kim's shoulder and down her arm said it for him.

"They're shaken, all of them," Mark said to fill the silence once he had Kim settled in his car. "This has really knocked them out of the complacency, made them take a hard look at their lives."

"They aren't the only ones."

Mark nodded but said nothing. Kim didn't want to look at him. She wanted to stare out the window and take comfort from the crystal-clear summer afternoon. But that was impossible. She'd almost been killed today. She'd watched a man be arrested. The hardest fight was still ahead of her. And this man was going with her. He already knew what her grandmother was going to say. Still, he wasn't telling her anything. He wasn't trying to prepare her.

Lawyer/client confidentiality. Was that what it all boiled down to? Was it as simple and complicated as that? He's with you, Kim reminded herself. Don't forget that, he's with you.

But that wasn't enough. Mark was concentrating on driving, his mouth frozen in a strong, distant line. He'd touched her in Rogan's office, but he wasn't touching her now. Maybe he didn't want to. Maybe, like her, he didn't know how.

They'd been so close, closer than she'd ever been with another human being. Kim wanted, needed that closeness back. But it wasn't to be. Not now, and maybe not ever again.

Neither of them spoke during the rest of the drive to Grass Valley. Kim tried to concentrate on her surroundings, to make sense of everything that had happened in Rogan's office, to divert herself.

Those tactics didn't work. She was scared. More scared than she had been in the tunnel.

Margaret Revis was waiting for them in the manor lobby. "Do you mind if we go outside?" she asked, after hugging Kim. "I've been pacing around my place ever since Mark brought me home. If I have to stay in there any longer, I'm afraid I'm going to start screaming."

"Are you sure you're up to this? We can wait."

"No. We can't."

Kim took her grandmother's hand and let her lead the way to the secluded courtyard set with a half-dozen outdoor tables and accompanying chairs. Margaret chose a table with a white-and-yellow umbrella in the middle and sank into one of the rattan chairs. She watched closely as Kim slowly lowered her aching body into another and Mark took a seat next to Kim.

"What happened?" Margaret was staring at her hands as if fascinated by the state of her fingernails. "Why did you go to the museum today?"

Kim had been able to keep her emotions under control until it was time to tell her grandmother why she'd begun to suspect Rogan. "You were there when I told Mark about the ring Charmaine was wearing. You didn't want to talk about it. I'm sorry, but I couldn't accept that."

"I didn't think you could."

Margaret Revis's voice was low, but there was strength in it. Kim took courage from that strength. "You were frightened. Grandmother, why?"

"Frightened?" The word hung in the air, a formless sound. "Such a simple word. It doesn't say nearly enough."

"No. It doesn't." Kim could be patient. Her grandmother had invited her and Mark here because there was something she needed to say. It might not be easy. It might not come quickly. But it *would* come. And then Kim would understand.

"You were right, Kim. It was the stone from the pin your grandfather gave me."

"Why didn't you want to talk about that before?" When her grandmother remained silent, staring at her nails, Kim went on. "Rogan stole it from the museum. He had it made into a ring for his wife, a bauble to keep her with him. What I don't understand is what it was doing there."

"I know you don't." Margaret leaned forward and then pushed herself back. She gave up her study of her nails and focused, not on her granddaughter, but on her attorney. "Mark said I had to tell you. When I first learned you were going to be working at the Comstock Museum, he told me I would make myself sick if I didn't say something."

"Grandmother. You *are* making yourself sick."

"I know." Margaret sighed and closed her eyes. "Don't interrupt me, dear. Please. I gave the pin to the museum."

Kim waited. Her grandmother looked frail and vulnerable even with the sunlight on her face. Kim turned toward Mark to find him carefully watching his client and friend. The sun was playing with Mark's features as well, sanding them down, somehow, and giving her no insight into what was going on beneath the surface.

Margaret began talking again. "I was so afraid you'd see the pin while you were at the museum. That's why I said those crazy things about hoping you wouldn't have to spend much time there. I knew you'd recognize it if you saw it. And you'd ask me questions I didn't want to answer."

"I don't understand," Kim whispered. She couldn't remain silent. She had to, somehow, help her grandmother. "You could have told me you'd donated the pin. I would have understood that."

"Would you? I suppose, if that's all I told you. But, Kim, I didn't donate it. One day...one day I walked into the museum with the pin in my pocket and left it there. I turned around and walked out without telling anyone what I had done.''

''What? Why?'' If only her grandmother would look at her Kim thought she might understand. But because Margaret refused to meet her gaze, Kim had only words with which to try to reach her.

''Why?'' Margaret repeated. ''A thousand reasons. No reason. None that can possibly make sense. Kim, you'd just graduated from college. My first grandchild was out in the world on her own. I was so proud of you. So proud. You had accomplished something I never had. You didn't need a man to support you.''

''Grandmother!''

Margaret's eyes remained closed. ''It's crazy, isn't it, what triggers a person to do something? I'd hung on to that damned pin for years. Thinking I had to have it to remind me. But I'd just come back from your graduation, and when I looked at it, the only thing I knew was that I didn't want any more reminders of the past. Your future was opening up for you. I—I wanted the same for myself.''

Her grandmother had sworn again. Kim was on her feet but only for a moment. She dropped to her knees before Margaret Revis, barely stifling a moan as she forced her bruised legs to do it. ''You could have told me that.''

''No.'' Margaret opened her eyes. ''No.'' She tore her eyes off Kim and forced herself to face Mark's unwavering stare. ''I couldn't tell you a partial truth. Oh, Lord, do you hear what I said? I couldn't tell you everything so I told you a lie. Mark?''

Kim turned. Mark hadn't moved, but he didn't have to. Kim felt his energy touching her, supporting her. Compassion and understanding and a relentless commitment all battled for control in him. With his unspoken energy, he was pressuring her grandmother to continue. Kim could tell him to stop and save them all pain. She could tell her grandmother that she would accept the partial truth she knew now and not ask for anything more.

But if she did that, there would always be something between her and her grandmother. And something between her and Mark.

And because she didn't want that, she didn't try to stop Mark.

"I can't help you, Margaret," Mark was saying. "Not anymore."

Kim didn't expect her grandmother to smile, but although the older woman's eyes still looked trapped, the corners of her mouth turned up. "You're an honest man, Mark. Cruel and honest."

"It's time for both things."

Kim had no idea what Mark was getting at, but she sensed that if she continued to hold her grandmother's hands and wait, she would soon know. "Grandmother, I said something to Rogan today. I demanded the truth from him. I told him I'd been lied to too much."

"You have. Kim, please sit down. You're going to hurt yourself."

Kim did as she was told. She continued to lean forward in her chair, her emotions straining to reach out to both her grandmother and Mark.

"Kim?" Her name came out at the end of a deep sigh. "I kept that damn pin, not because I needed a loving reminder of the father of my children, but because—because I didn't want to ever forget."

"Forget what?" Kim asked. Mark was getting to his feet. He came to stand behind Kim. His hands rested lightly on her shoulders. He didn't say anything. "What didn't you want to forget?" Kim repeated.

Margaret was shaking her head. Her lips moved, but for a moment nothing came out. "Kim, the skeleton you found..."

"Yes."

"It was your grandfather."

Now it was Kim's turn to find herself without words. Denial screamed through her. Her grandfather had been killed in a logging accident in the woods. He'd been brought home and buried in the Camp Oro cemetery. "No," she managed. "No."

"Yes. Yes, my dear. Why do you think I reacted the way I did when I learned you'd found it?"

"No," Kim repeated. She started to get to her feet, but Mark stopped her. His breath was on the back of her neck, his strength holding her still, supporting her. "That's not—"

"I know. That's not what I told you. But I told you a lie. One of too many lies."

Kim couldn't demand that her grandmother stop. They'd gone too far now for anything but the truth. "No more lies," she whispered. "Please, no more lies."

"No. Oh, Kim, you might hate me when I'm done. I—I don't blame you if you do. That's why I've never told anyone. I—I should have rehearsed this. Maybe it would have been easier."

With Mark supporting her, Kim found the strength to help her grandmother. "Does anyone else know what you're going to tell me?"

"Only Mark. And Dow. But Dow's dead, isn't he?"

Kim didn't understand what this had to do with Margaret's second husband, but she sensed that she soon would. "What did Dow know? And Mark. Why Mark?"

"Because. . . ." Margaret smiled up at the man standing behind her granddaughter. "I had to tell someone. Mark was the only one I could trust. Kim, I said that skeleton was your grandfather. I know that because I put him in there. Dow and I did."

Kim was getting light-headed. She might have slumped to the ground if it weren't for Mark. But if her grandmother could say the words, Kim could listen. Mark would give her the strength.

It was an ugly story, years of shame and fear and sudden explosions. Jeromiah Jacobs wasn't the man Kim had believed him to be. Yes, at the time he'd married a seventeen-year-old girl, he'd been the wealthiest man in Camp Oro. On the outside he was successful, powerful. He'd showered wealth on his wife and paraded his three babies around for all to see.

But there was the dark side to him as well. The half of Jeromiah Jacobs that no one but his wife ever saw. "He beat me, Kim," Margaret said with emotion blocking her throat and altering her voice. "The first time, before your father was born. He never apologized. Never regretted. I told him I was going to go home to my parents, but I didn't."

"Why not?" Kim got out.

"Pride. Shame. No," Margaret amended. "It wasn't that simple. Honey, the man terrified me. He said he'd come after me if I tried to leave him. He'd hurt me again. And he said he'd hurt the children. I believed him. I believed my husband. My parents had moved north and I didn't have anyone nearby who I could trust. They...I'm sure they thought they'd left me in good hands. After all, I lived in the biggest house in town. I didn't have any skills or any way of supporting myself and my children without him. I didn't know what to do. For years, I just didn't know what to do."

The afternoon was warm. Still Kim shivered and when she did, Mark drew her back against him. She wouldn't cry. She wouldn't say anything. This was her grandmother's time, and Kim could be patient.

The physical and emotional abuse never let up. With each baby she'd felt more trapped. She dreamed of fleeing in the middle of the night. Twice she had tried, but Jeromiah was careful not to keep any money in the house. It had been easy for him to track down his wayward wife. Others might have guessed what was going on within those freshly painted walls in the big house on the hill, but because Jeromiah Jacobs practically owned Camp Oro, no one had come forth to defend Margaret.

No one, that is, except Dow Revis. "We weren't lovers. Please believe me, Kim. Dow worked for your grandfather.

He was his woods foreman. Sometimes he came to the house for meetings. He was always so good to my children. He gave them something they never got from their own father. And I...maybe I fell in love with him then. But, Kim, I was so afraid of my husband that there wasn't enough of me left over to know what else was going on in the world."

One night Jeromiah had come home drunk. He'd been having trouble at the mill. He couldn't take his frustrations out on his employees or the machinery, but he could take them out on his wife. "He went crazy that night," Margaret said in her too-controlled voice. "He said he was going to kill me. And our children. Your aunt was just a baby. Still sleeping in a crib. Jeromiah picked her up and held her over his head."

The silence stretched for a long time through the peaceful garden setting—too long. Kim's shoulders, under Mark's heavy hands, felt numb. Finally she did what she could to help her grandmother along. "Had he ever hurt the children before?"

"No. He had threatened. That's how he kept me in line. But I knew, that night, it was in him to kill my baby. I—" For the second time since bringing Kim and Mark out here, Margaret shut her eyes. For almost a minute she remained in the darkness she'd created. "Kim, I killed him. He was drunk. I picked up a poker from the fireplace. I told him to stop. I was screaming. Crying. He put down the baby. Then he started after me."

Kim had known that was coming. As the story unfolded, she'd felt her hands turn into fists. Her nails were digging into her flesh. Her scream of outrage could barely be contained. If it had been her, she would have done the same thing. Kim might be a civilized woman. Her grandmother might be the most gentle, loving woman she'd ever known. But the man who had held her in slavery was threatening to kill her baby, and that night there hadn't been anything civilized left of Margaret.

"What did you do then?" Kim asked in a calm voice.

Margaret opened her eyes. "You understand?"

"Oh, yes. Believe me, I understand."

"You don't hate me?"

"Hate? Oh, Grandmother, I could never hate you. You're a mother. Someone you hated and feared was threatening your children. You didn't have any choice."

Dow had agreed. When Margaret, terrified and crying, had shown up on Dow's doorstep with her three babies, the foreman had taken them in. They had stayed up all night talking, putting the children to bed, getting Margaret to the point of being able to think. Before dawn they made their plans. Dow knew about the tunnels running under the town. One of them went through his property. He would open up the tunnel and place Jeromiah's body in it. Then he would tell everyone that he and Jeromiah Jacobs had gone into the woods and Jeromiah had been killed by a falling tree. He'd say the body had been badly crushed and he'd wanted to spare Jeromiah's widow the shock of seeing him, so he'd built a wooden casket in the woods and brought the body down on a buckboard.

The funeral was closed casket. Rocks, not Jeromiah Jacobs, were buried in the Camp Oro cemetery.

"I thought your father might remember." Margaret's voice, laced with emotion during the telling, was now exhausted. "He was three. But he didn't. And Dow, Dow kept me sane. Everyone thought I was a rich widow, but Jeromiah had made sure I wouldn't get a dime if something happened to him. I didn't want to be dependent on another man, not after what I'd been through. But the children fell in love with Dow. And so did I."

"And you kept that inside you all those years. No one but you and Dow knew." Kim rose and again stepped over to her grandmother. She reached out her hands and drew Margaret Revis to her. Kim cradled her grandmother against her, marveling at the incredible strength and courage that lay beneath the frail surface. A woman without skills or a family to turn to, a woman entrusted with the safety of three small children, a woman bullied and terrorized by the most powerful man in town....

"The first day I came to see you here," Kim started slowly, "I talked about how fortunate you'd been to have had two loving husbands. I didn't help, did I? I just made it harder."

"No, dear." Margaret didn't try to pull free. She stood with Kim's arms around her. "That wasn't your fault. I'd set myself up for that years ago. Talking about my wonderful first marriage. I don't know why I did that."

Kim believed she did. Margaret Revis had spent years in hell. And it had all ended in a nightmare. Kim didn't blame her grandmother for spinning a fantasy to take the place of that nightmare, for wanting her children to believe that their father had been a loving man and not an animal.

"Now three of us know," Kim whispered. "Only three."

"Can you understand?"

Kim held her grandmother at arm's length and waited for the older woman to meet her tear-misted gaze. "Yes, I understand. I love you. Nothing will ever change that."

Except for the faint murmur of the wind slipping through the pines on the Revis property, there was nothing to distract Kim from the man sitting across from her in the dark. Margaret had insisted on taking Mark and Kim out to dinner. Their dinner conversation had been light, a welcome relief from the intensity of the courtyard. Margaret had done most of the talking as she talked about the years of contending with three growing children in a small community where the only curfew was that they be home by dark. Mark had been quiet. Kim had concentrated on her grandmother. What they had to say to each other would have to come later.

By the time they returned to the manor, Margaret was obviously tired. Although she invited Kim and Mark to come inside for coffee, they begged off. Kim wanted to get home so she could rest. She promised she would call in the morning.

Now only Mark stood between Kim and her finally coming to terms with the day. He hadn't had to walk her up to the house, but he had done so. She hadn't had to invite him in, but she had done so. She'd gone into the bedroom to change into a loose lounge robe. She'd thought Mark might turn on the lights while she was gone, but he hadn't. Now he was sitting in an overstuffed chair on the opposite side of the couch where Kim was stretched out.

"What's going to happen now?" Kim wondered aloud. "The Comstock Museum is going to need a new director. I don't know if the board's going to want to go ahead with the installation of the security system until the other matter is taken care of."

"You could call Stephan."

"Tomorrow. Everything can wait until tomorrow."

"Almost everything."

"What can't wait until tomorrow?"

"I think you know the answer to that."

Kim did. What needed to be dealt with was the man who'd put duty before the woman in his life, who'd risked losing her because he believed in a code of honor. Either Kim could accept that or she couldn't. At the moment, sagging with exhaustion, Kim didn't know the answer to that question. "I didn't ask her, Mark. Somehow, after everything she told me, it didn't seem that important. But why did she tell you about my grandfather?"

Mark shifted his position. Kim could hear the chair's tired protest. For a long time he didn't speak. When he did, he sounded as weary as she felt. "I think it was because she trusted me. And because, after Dow died, she didn't have anyone she could talk to."

"She couldn't trust anyone in her family," Kim said with finality.

"She'd told too many lies, Kim. It had all started when she'd thought she had to keep the terrible realities of her marriage from her parents. It snowballed when she couldn't bear to tell her children what their father had really been like. And, Kim, she and Dow were building a good life for themselves. She'd gotten out of the nightmare. She didn't want to be sucked back into it."

"And so she kept quiet. Until Dow died."

"Until a year after Dow died." Again Mark shifted.

Kim focused on his shadow, but she had no idea what he was thinking. Or feeling.

"I remember—do you want to hear this?"

"Yes."

"I remember the day she came into my office. We'd been working on her will. There were changes that had to be dealt with after Dow's death. I hadn't pressed her about it. I'd waited until she was ready. We were talking about the way Dow had provided for his stepchildren. I asked something about why wasn't there something from her first husband. That's all it took. I think I was just in the right place at the right time."

Kim didn't believe that. Yes, maybe losing Dow had forced her grandmother to deal with the past again. But if Mark hadn't been compassionate and understanding, Margaret Revis would have never told him what she had.

"She was afraid I would find out certain things. Why? Because I would be going through the house?"

"No. There's nothing here. But she knew you would be working at the museum."

"Where she thought the mourning pin was. She thought I might find it."

"She called me the day you came to town. She was so afraid. I tried to tell her that if you did come across the pin, she could just tell you that she'd donated it to the museum. But of course the museum would have no record of who had made the donation. She was afraid you might discover that and start asking questions."

"Such a little thing." Kim wanted to curl up on the couch and let sleep divorce her from her aching body. But Mark still hadn't touched her, and she hadn't touched him. Until she'd come to grips with the question of what to do about that, she couldn't sleep. "You were willing to help her with the lie, weren't you?"

"I didn't know you then."

"We got to know each other after that. And you still kept something from me."

"I'd made a promise to your grandmother."

"A promise." Kim ran the word through her mind, trying to make sense of it.

"What do you want me to say, Kim? That I can look into the future? When I fell in love with you...I think I know how trapped your grandmother felt."

"When I fell in love with you." The words were precious to her. "You felt trapped?"

"Yes." Kim watched Mark's shadow close the distance between them. He was standing over her with his hands hanging at his side. She could take them, but if she did, he might not finish what he had to say. "Trapped. I wanted to be honest with you. Honesty can be a selective thing with an attorney. Feed it out an inch at a time in the courtroom. Be totally up-front with a client. And sometimes you can work it to your advantage. Only, with you, I couldn't do any of those things."

"And that bothered you?"

"More than you'll ever know."

Mark was all too aware that Kim still wasn't moving. He had told her he loved her, opened himself up and made himself vulnerable as he'd never done before. And still she was sitting there in the dark, not reaching out for him. He'd said everything there was to say. It seemed it wasn't going to be enough.

"I think Stephan and the board members will want to go ahead with the security system," he made himself say. He didn't give a damn about the subject, but he had to say something. "You'll be free in a few days."

"Free?"

"To go back to San Francisco."

"Oh. Yes."

He couldn't stay here any longer. Kim's silence was the greatest truth he'd ever heard. "Go to bed, Kim," he told her with his back to her. He could find his way out without having to turn the light on; he didn't want her to see his face. "You're exhausted."

"Mark? Where are you going?"

"Home."

"Home. I don't want to sell this place. I don't think I can do it."

"Your grandmother—"

"I know. Maybe she'll sell it to me."

Mark didn't know what Kim was saying. What he did know was that she was speaking to him, and he couldn't leave. "What would you do with it? Rent it out?"

"Live in it."

"What about San Francisco?"

What about San Francisco, Kim thought. That cool, foggy place was a million miles from where her heart was. Where her heart would always be. "I don't want to go back."

"Why?" Mark asked her.

It was both the hardest and easiest question she'd ever been asked. "You know why."

The distance was gone again. She was no longer staring at the strong shadow of his back and wondering how she would survive his leaving. She could feel him wanting to stay. "Because..." She stopped. She could say nothing as her grandmother had done for years, or she could take the greatest risk of her life. "Because I love you. Because I don't want to leave you. I want to talk to Stephan about working for the museum. It has promise. It can become something good."

"You would make Camp Oro your home again?"

"Yes. If you want—"

"I want. Believe me, Kim. I want."

KIM WASN'T AS EXHAUSTED as she thought she was. Either that or Mark had magic in his hands. They lay together on her grandmother's bed with the wind touching them lightly and the pines humming with the breeze. They had the rest of their lives to make love, he'd told her. Tonight he wanted nothing more than to soothe her aching muscles. To hold her.

Tonight there was touching, and whispers, and falling even more in love with a strong, gentle man.

Tonight there was forgiving and being forgiven. And after that there were words. Plans. A future being mapped.

And just before dawn, together, they fell asleep.

HARLEQUIN
American Romance®

COMING NEXT MONTH

#333 SIGHT UNSEEN by Kathy Clark

It wasn't a whimsical flight of fancy that stable owner Nicki Chandler reported to detective Jake Kelly. Nicki had been visited by a series of waking dreams—dreams she was convinced mirrored a real-life tragedy. Jake never expected that Nicki's dreams held danger—and a direct challenge to a new and fragile love.

Don't miss the second book in the ROCKY MOUNTAIN MAGIC series.

#334 MEANT TO BE by Cathy Gillen Thacker

He was a man with everything—everything but a family. Tom Harrigan, the eldest son in the prominent Harrigan clan, had always won his heart's desire. But now, the surrogate mother of his baby son threatened to destroy his dreams. Cynthia Whittiker, the attractive court-appointed guardian, showed him that love was never a game of lose or win.

#335 NIGHTSHADE by Ginger Chambers

Christian Townsend was rich, handsome, self-assured and smart, and museum employee Sonya Douglas didn't know how she was going to manage him. When Christian probed the unsolved theft of priceless artifacts, he brought the museum close to scandal. But when Sonya finally succeeded in dividing his interest—which then focused on her—the situation got totally out of control.

#336 TALL COTTON by Lori Copeland

Kelly Smith had always planned to follow in her father's footsteps on the horse-racing circuit, but now it seemed those footsteps led to betrayal. Could she prove her father had been innocent of the charges against him? She'd been forced to deceive Tanner McCrey, the man behind the accusations, to find out whether he was ally or enemy. Now would she ever be able to win his love?

THE STANLEY HOTEL—
A HISTORY

Upon moving to Colorado, F. O. Stanley fell in love with Estes Park, a town nestled in an alpine mountain bowl at 7,500 feet, the Colorado Rockies towering around it.

With an initial investment of $500,000, Stanley designed and began construction of The Stanley Hotel in 1906. Materials and supplies were transported 22 miles by horse teams on roads constructed solely for this purpose. The grand opening took place in 1909 and guests were transported to The Stanley Hotel in steam-powered, 12-passenger "mountain wagons" that were also designed and built by Stanley.

On May 26, 1977, The Stanley Hotel was entered in the National Register of Historic Places and is still considered by many as one of the significant factors contributing to the growth of Colorado as a tourist destination.

We hope you enjoy visiting The Stanley Hotel in our "Rocky Mountain Magic" series in American Romance.

RMH-1